Divine Torment

Veraine had never experienced a mouth as muscular and capacious and clever as Jilaya's. It was a vampire's mouth, draining the world dry of its reality until there was nothing under the sun but that rapacious orifice.

He felt himself grow deaf and blind to everything else, and he did not care. In a moment of pause he caught up handfuls of her hair and spread the glowing locks over his thighs. Her head rose and fell. His fantasy was solidifying about him. He tried to imagine it was the Malia Shai's face he glimpsed sucking and nuzzling, her full lips swollen and dark around the pillar of his flesh. The superimposition was surprisingly easy; perhaps only because Jilaya had the same skin tone, perhaps because of some angle of her brows or flash of her eyes that brought to mind the goddess he wanted. Veraine could picture that cool, passionless avatar flushed and straining as she nursed upon his cock. His balls were filled to bursting. He fell back upon the bed, white lightning building from his loins up his spine.

Other books by the author:

Cruel Enchantment – Erotic Fairy Stories

Divine Torment
Janine Ashbless

BLACK LACE

Black Lace books contain sexual fantasies.
In real life, always practise safe sex.

First published in 2002 by
Black Lace
Thames Wharf Studios
Rainville Road
London W6 9HA

Copyright © Janine Ashbless 2002

The right of Janine Ashbless to be identified as the Author of
the Work has been asserted in accordance with the Copyright,
Designs and Patents Act 1988.

Design by Smith & Gilmour, London
Printed and bound by Mackays of Chatham PLC

ISBN 0 352 33719 2

Contents

1   *The City in the Desert*   1

2   *The Malia Shai*   22

3   *Foreign Gods*   49

4   *Jilaya*   76

5   *The Slave*   108

6   *The Devouring Earth*   137

7   *I Saw Smoke and Gold*   166

8   *Spoils of War*   184

9   *Desecration*   215

10   *The Mask*   234

Textual Note:
Two passages in this novel are quotes from
ancient Sanskrit sources. They are:

     in chapter 2 the paragraph beginning,
     'Everything rests on me as pearls . . .'
and
     in chapter 6 the paragraph beginning, 'Come,
     come in haste . . .'

To Jules,
who came to my rescue.

1 **The City in the Desert**

On the second day after the river crossing the army reached the pass through the barren hills beyond. And shortly after noon General Veraine, Beloved of the Eternal Empire, son of the Glorious General Morin – may his star look down upon us – and Champion of the Irolian People ordered his chariot to be stopped at the very highest point of the road so that he could relieve his bladder.

Having performed this office, Veraine took the opportunity to walk about and stretch his legs. Standing upright in a chariot as it is driven over unpaved tracks is harder work than it looks, and his throat felt furred with the dust raised by the two horses. He thought, not for the first time, that he would far rather have ridden for the last fortnight. But a general was considered too dignified to ride, at least on imperial business, and his recent promotion had forced him from the saddle and onto the footboards.

Around him his officers and aides were allowing their mounts to draw to a halt, the horses blowing and snorting from the long and tedious climb through the hills. Veraine looked back to the east. On the track below him the main body of his army, composed of foot soldiers who had inevitably lagged behind the horses on this terrain, was snaking up towards them on the twisted road. The fierce sunlight flashed on their bronze armour and long spearheads. Veraine was pleased to see that they were holding formation well.

Behind the rearguard, so far in the distance it was almost swallowed by dust, the silver gleam of the huge Amal Bhad river could be glimpsed. The Eternal Empire had no officially defined boundary on this, the western frontier, but there was no arguing with the Amal Bhad. Once you had crossed it you were beyond civilisation. On that side lay cities and roads and cultivated fields. On this were deserts, a half-savage people and their ancient gods of blood and stone. Veraine pushed his hands back over his hair and mentally bid farewell to the bright river. He turned again to his officers.

'Let them rest when they reach the top,' he told his second-in-command, a rugged professional soldier named Loy. 'It won't be for long. They're to keep their armour on, but they may drink.'

Loy, who had been waiting impassively on horseback, nodded without speaking and dismounted. Veraine strode back to his chariot, where Arioc, his driver, was wetting the horses' muzzles from a leather waterbag. He took his own wineskin from its hook inside the chariot and walked forward, past the scattering of men and beasts, until he could see down the western slope of the hills into the open land beyond. That way lay their destination. That way lay the sacred Yamani city of Mulhanabin.

Veraine's gaze searched the terrain below him. Dust and movement on the coils of the road betrayed the position of the army's advance guard, scouts mounted on sturdy, fast ponies who would, at the first sign of danger, race back towards the Eighth Host with their warning. Not that trouble was expected here on the pilgrim road; even this barren fringe of the Empire rested at peace under the Irolian yoke. Yet it would not have done for Veraine to be complacent, nor to be seen to be so – not on this, the General's first command. And, he was aware, it would be a bloody, terrible place to get caught in an ambush. His soldierly instincts leered and bristled at the narrowness of the road, worn out of the close-crowding hills by the feet of pilgrims over ages that no scholar could even begin to count. He wanted to be out in the open where he could see what was coming towards him.

His eyes still ranging over the landscape below, he took a sip from the wineskin, but the tepid liquid tasted more of goat than of grape. Beyond the hills lay a great flat plain which, from this height, looked silver with heat haze and featureless, the sparse stippling of desert vegetation invisible. In the middle of that shimmer, barely visible to the eye at this distance, was a tawnier smudge which Veraine knew denoted a bank of hills. Clinging to those hills, chiselled from the living rock, was the temple-city of Mulhanabin, home of the Malia Shai. His future as a soldier and a shaper of the Empire would be decided there, carved out among the sandstones and the scree. Despite the wine his mouth felt dry.

Beyond Mulhanabin there was nothing but desert lands for hundreds of miles. And somewhere out there were the Horse-eaters. They were getting closer with every passing day.

Veraine sat down on a rock in the shade of a boulder and idly weighed the soggy wineskin in his hands, his imagination racing forward to the task ahead and backward into memory. He was peripherally aware of the officers behind him talking and moving about, and anyone watching him would have seen the new general sunk in the sombre contemplation that was already becoming his hallmark. He might have risen to this rank because of his paternal connection, but he did not take his command lightly.

He was young, though, for a man in command of an

army. Still young enough that the hard lines had only just begun to etch his face. Yet though the stubble that shaded his jaw was dark, as dark as his eyes, his hair was so streaked with grey that the original blackness of it was half lost. Like every Irolian warrior he wore it long and tied back, but it looked strange, that old man's hair on a young man's head. He knew that one of his nicknames among the soldiers – all officers had nicknames, though some were obscene and never voiced in front of them – was 'Greyhead'. It had been his father's name years before. He did not know yet whether this was an honour or a burden.

Dressed in the knee-length, short-sleeved Irolian tunic of bleached linen and high, many-strapped sandals, his bare arms and calves hard with muscle, his skin browned by the sun, Veraine looked every inch the combat-hardened warrior of the Eternal Empire planning the tactics of battle. No one could have guessed the direction in which his thoughts drifted.

A month ago, Veraine had entered the house of the Glorious General Slaithe and been ushered into a room on the upper floor by a slave who had bowed and retreated, leaving him to look around him and wonder what whim of fate had brought him here. He had no idea what the Glorious General's intentions were and had never met the man personally but, nevertheless, orders bearing Slaithe's seal had been brought to him at the Imperial Barracks. He had abandoned the drilling of his cohort and hurried across the city to this immense house on the Procession Way without even stopping to change his tunic or wash the dust of the parade ground from his face. It would not do to keep the Glorious General waiting.

Now he stood in a cool room in the strange and

uneasy silence that falls on hot afternoons. Even the sounds of the city of Antoth, capital of the Eternal Empire, were muted in this place.

Unable to keep still, Veraine walked slowly around the room, taking in his surroundings. Through the carved wooden trellis that covered the window he could see the ziggurat of Shuga, the sun god, at the end of the Procession Way, towering above every other building in the city. It was faced in marble and shone blindingly white in the summer glare. Even a moment looking at it left a blue imprint on the inside of his eyes and meant that they had to grow accustomed to the shade of the interior before he could see again. He blinked to clear the dancing spots and stared at the floor, which he then realised was laid out as a mosaic map of the Eternal Empire. Chips of semi-precious stones delineated the rivers, cities and roads of the vast territory. Seen like this, the totality of Irolian conquest, the result of bloody invasion and tyrannical control, was a beautiful and intricately crafted whole.

Two of the walls were painted with figures and he looked idly at them to pass the time. They depicted the gods at rest amidst vineyards and orchards, handmaidens waiting upon their every whim. The walls which were not painted were draped in hangings of patterned silk, the stirring of which betrayed the presence of doors or archways beyond. There was one low table flanked by two couches. It was a pleasant, informal room. Veraine wondered why the Glorious General had chosen to meet him here.

One of the curtains lifted and two slave girls came into the room, bowing as they saw him. Both smiled shyly, though their eyes did not meet his. Veraine watched them as they carried wine glasses and bowls to the table, feeling the same uneasy admiration for them as he had done for the rest of the palatial house and its furnishings. They were an extraordinarily lovely pair, and quite unlike any woman of the Empire that he had ever seen. One was small and slight, with almond-shaped eyes, a tiny snub nose and the sheerest black hair, glossy as oil, that fell so far it brushed the back of her calves as she walked. The taller woman was even stranger, with pale skin and thick locks the colour of wheat-straw. They must have originated in far distant lands, countries he could hardly guess about. They both moved deftly and silently in their work, casting each other little glances as they moved about as if speech were too gross a medium for communication. Veraine found himself unable to look away. They wore simple shifts of the thinnest cotton and narrow leather collars, stitched with silver beads, about their necks.

He could feel the dried sweat itching on his scalp. Their presence made him feel even filthier and more unprepared than before. It was also very arousing. Lust like a serpent began to uncoil slowly within him. Those white dresses sheathed and yet somehow hinted at every hidden curve, making it impossible not to imagine how the warm flesh would feel through the gauzy fabric.

The yellow-haired slave must have felt the intensity of his stare, because she turned, caught his eye quickly and then looked away, biting her lower lip. She put both hands on her companion's waist from behind, an intimate gesture that made Veraine's pulse jump, then leaned in to breathe a whisper in the darker girl's ear. Pink lips brushed golden skin. Both girls, still clinging delicately together, turned to face him.

At that moment a man pushed open the door and strode into the room. Veraine swung round instantly, his attention snapping onto the newcomer with a soldier's discipline.

The Glorious General Slaithe, thickset and balding from the front, his tunic edged in scarlet, opened his hands in greeting. 'Veraine!'

Veraine raised his palms to his forehead and bowed a short military salute, replying, 'General Slaithe.'

With the barest hint of sound the slave girls withdrew.

'Commander Veraine.' The jowled and grizzled officer surveyed him enthusiastically. 'You couldn't be anyone other than your father's son! Ha – look at you!' He slapped the younger man on both shoulders. 'Sun's blood, my boy, but you're the spitting image of him, you know?'

'I did not, sir. But thank you.'

The General stared into his eyes from less than an arm's length away. 'We were the greatest of friends, myself and Morin,' he said. 'Your father – may his star look down upon us – and I met in the barracks on our first day of training. We shared salt and beer and blood over the years; and I tell you, I never met a greater man.'

'I am honoured to hear it, sir,' Veraine said.

Slaithe released him. 'And if you're cast from the same mould as Morin, my boy, it's my honour to meet you,' he growled. 'Come over here and take a drink.' He led the way to the table and with his own hands poured wine for both of them into the fragile blue glasses waiting.

Veraine took a mouthful of the wine, feeling like a lion standing on the edge of a pit-trap. He trusted flattery like he trusted a snake. 'You summoned me with all urgency, sir,' he enquired obliquely.

The General's eyes flashed. 'Yes. I've been following your career, Commander Veraine. People say good things about you.' He smiled a cold, hard smile; a soldier's smile. 'You fight well. You ride well. Your men respect you. You were loyal during the army unrest last year. You've acquitted yourself on the Northern Rises with courage.'

Veraine nodded very slightly, but felt it better to say nothing.

'But you stand in a long shadow, Commander. If you are going to prove yourself a worthy successor to your father then you'll need the opportunity to demonstrate your ability to lead men in battle. I've been watching for this moment. Now it's my pleasure to offer you that opportunity.'

The younger man felt the hair on his arms rise, but he made sure he betrayed no sign of emotion. He bit back his impatience and merely said, 'Sir?' as attentively as he could.

'Come over here.' The Glorious General motioned him over into the centre of the room, so that they were both standing on the mosaic map. 'We've had news from our spies in the west. The Horse-eater horde has failed to invade the Empire of the Blue Bull. King Darsid met them in battle on his north-eastern frontier and threw them back. The barbarians have turned aside and are heading this way.'

'We anticipated that, sir,' Veraine said. 'We're ready for them. The army is mobilised.'

'Yes.' The old soldier looked at him keenly. 'If you were attacking the Eternal Empire, where would you take your armies?'

'The Northern Rises,' Veraine said without hesitation. The northern border straddled an area of hills that were notoriously difficult to defend, especially from fast mounted troops like the Horse-eaters. The army for years had been pressing for further expansion of the Eternal Empire in order to establish a securer frontier, but His Radiance the Emperor had refused to take their advice.

'Right. But the Horse-eaters are taking the more direct

route, it seems. They are coming up the Western Spice Road through the Twenty Kingdoms. Apparently they have sacked a number of cities already. It is slowing them down, but they'll hit us from the west.'

Veraine raised his eyebrows. This was better news than anyone had hoped for. He was aware that the two slave girls had re-entered the room and were discreetly placing dishes of food on the low table. He could smell hot bean sauce. 'That's no problem, sir,' he said guardedly. 'We can hold them on the western border far more easily.'

'Hmm,' Slaithe grunted. He looked down between them at the map. 'Where?'

Veraine moved one foot to better reveal a line of lapis-lazuli tiles. 'The Amal Bhad,' he said. 'They'll never be able to cross the river once we drop the pontoon bridges. They're not boat-builders, and there is nothing to sustain an army of that size in the hills beyond. They are barbarians. Once they lose their impetus they will break up.'

'Good,' said Slaithe, in a voice that implied anything but. 'We have a small problem though.' He pointed with the toe of one foot at a stud of inset red coral, across the Amal Bhad. 'There. The city of Mulhanabin.'

'It's a Yamani city,' said Veraine flatly, searching his memory for what he knew of the place. 'It has no strategic value and no resources. The land is nearly desert anyway.'

'So?'

'So let it fall.'

Slaithe shook his head. 'Mulhanabin has no value to us,' he said, 'but to the Yamani it is sacred. In fact it is one of their oldest, greatest temples. They believe that one of their gods is physically incarnated in the high priestess there; the Malia Shai.'

9

Veraine considered. 'We have time to move her,' he suggested.

Slaithe smiled wearily. 'It wouldn't do, Commander. The temple at Mulhanabin marks the place where, in their ignorance, the Yamani believe that the first humans were created by the gods. It is sacred earth. If it fell into the hands of the Horse-eaters, then the horror and fury among the Yamani would be immeasurable. We could be facing insurrection on a wide scale. We cannot afford that when there is an enemy outside the door too.'

Veraine realised where this was leading. 'I see,' he said, not sure whether to be elated or appalled.

'We as rulers have a duty,' Slaithe said with a twisted smile, 'to protect our subjects. To protect even their foolish superstitions.'

'You want me to go to Mulhanabin, sir?'

'I need you to take an army there and hold the city from all attack. It needn't be a great force – I understand the city is quite defensible. In fact you cannot afford an excess of soldiers because food and water will be limited. The men will have to go on foot, with the minimum of baggage. They won't like that, but the desert can't sustain horses for long. That is our strength. The Horse-eaters won't be able to put up a long siege. They'll waste their efforts on Mulhanabin and break for ever on the banks of the Amal Bhad.'

'Yes, I see, sir.'

'You accept the commission, Commander Veraine?'

'Of course, sir.' He saluted. 'It will be an honour.'

Slaithe's jowls tightened as he drew himself up. 'Then it's in my power to appoint you to the rank of general, and give you the command of the Eighth Host. Congratulations, General Veraine.'

The newly promoted officer kneeled before his benefactor and clenched his hands over his heart. 'I swear by the Seven and by my own star that I will serve the Eternal Empire faithfully to the last drop of my blood,' he said, renewing the oath he had made when he first became a soldier. Silently he also vowed, *And I swear that I will live through this mission, and I will walk in the sunlight with all the other nobles of the Irolian people.*

He let Slaithe raise him to his feet.

'Well done, son,' said the older man, gripping his shoulders tightly. 'I hope we'll be as proud of you as we are of your father, may his star look down upon us. Now come and eat. You'll need it, I should think.'

In fact Veraine had never felt less interest in eating. What he felt like doing was running the two miles through the baking streets of Antoth to the barracks and there smashing his old general against the wall, to laugh in his face. Or perhaps marching into the Hall of the Imperial Concubines and fucking every one of its three hundred inhabitants in full, horrified view of their radiant master. But he let himself be led over to one of the couches and sat upon it, facing Slaithe over the full table.

'Eat,' said the Glorious General, reclining to one side and sipping from his glass.

Veraine stared down at the food. It looked wonderful; tiny roast fish, burnished grapes, the fattest olives he had ever seen. There were cream and fruit confections fit for a lady's fancy and roast pigeons steaming in rich sauces. He had no appetite. The dark slave bent before him to fill his goblet and the sweet perfume of her flesh did tickle his senses, but he was very careful not to glance at her.

'Do you speak Yamani?' Slaithe asked.

'Yes, sir,' he said, picking up a tiny golden fruit with a papery calyx. It seemed safest to eat something.

'Well?' Slaithe's voice was sharp.

'Very well, sir.' Veraine felt no need to explain his language skills.

'Good. You'll need to in Mulhanabin – the locals won't speak anything else.'

The two slave girls, having poured the drinks, went and kneeled, knees just touching, slightly behind Slaithe's couch. This put them out of their master's casual view but directly in Veraine's line of sight and he found it extremely distracting. The fair girl had large breasts that pushed up against her dress. The bleached cotton was strained between them and he could see her hard nipples forming little shadows where they defied the tautness of the cloth. He tried to concentrate on what his superior officer was saying.

'We'll be sending an adviser with you. His name is Rumayn. Not army, not even a good family really, but he knows more about Mulhanabin and the Yamani religion than anyone else I could lay my finger on.'

The slave with the smooth, dark hair and the narrow eyes leaned in to her companion and kissed her throat softly. At the same time her hand stole up to pinch the nearer of those impudent nipples. The wheat-haired girl shuddered under that touch, arching her back. Her eyes half-closed in pleasure.

'Sir?' said Veraine suddenly, realising that he had missed a sentence completely.

'I said, you'll need him in dealing with the priests. They have a lot of power in places like that. Are you all right, General?'

'Very much so,' said Veraine. His mouth was dry and he grabbed hurriedly for another fruit. The two girls had started to kiss, their wet pink tongues intertwining very visibly.

'The Eighth Host is currently under my own wing. I can vouch for them. The senior commander is a man called Loy. A sound man to have at your side. Twenty years a soldier.'

'Good.' Veraine managed to nod. The girls were taking it in turns to bite the other's lips, their hips rolling softly to the same internal rhythm. He was aware that under the linen tunic he was hard and getting harder. I'm a general now, he thought wryly; I shouldn't be getting the horn in public.

'I will send word back to the Imperial Barracks at once. You'll have new quarters from tonight and I shall send round a chariot for your own use in the morning.'

'Thank you, sir.' Veraine had lost any struggle to keep his eyes off the sight of the foreplay between the two women. He was aware that Slaithe was still talking, trying to give advice and instruction, but the lion's share of his attention was fixed on the sight of the erotic games being played in total silence within yards of where he sat. The fair girl had now kneeled up so that the shorter one could fasten a wet and pliant mouth around her nipples. The damp patches on the dress grew translucent under this attack, the dusky buds showing clearly through the cloth when she moved her mouth away. The victim of this assault retaliated by winding her assailant's long hair into a silken rope in her fist and forcing her dark head from nipple to nipple as the whim took her.

'Well, I can see you need some time to sit and think this out,' said Slaithe, rising to his feet. With a physical effort Veraine wrenched his gaze around to meet the other's eyes. It occurred to him in an appalling moment that there was no way he could stand up too without flaunting his erection, but Slaithe seemed not to need a formal departure. 'Stay, stay,' he insisted, waving him back into his seat as he tried to gather himself. 'You finish your meal. I have work to do. Meilin and Hilde here will fetch you anything that you want. Just instruct them. What's the point of being a senior officer unless you enjoy the privileges of your rank?'

The two slaves in question stood demurely as their master left the room, no flicker of expression on their faces betraying their suddenly curtailed activities. As soon as the curtain had fallen on Slaithe's exit they turned to face the young General.

'Come here,' he said hoarsely.

They obeyed, squeezing in between the couch and table to kneel one at either side of him. Soft and wicked smiles were on their lips. Veraine ran his thumbs across both mouths simultaneously, finding the lips slightly swollen, and wondered which to start with. He tasted first Meilin – languorous and yielding – and then the wheat-haired Hilde, who mewed breathily under his exploring mouth. He was shocked to find when he gazed into her eyes that they were blue, but the novelty was exotic rather than unpleasant. He pulled their faces closer to his, so that all three were joined in a trinity of touch and vision.

'Now what in hell is General Slaithe playing at?' he whispered, his hands tightening ever so slightly on their necks.

'I don't know, lord,' Hilde protested.

'He wants us to please you, lord, in any way you wish,' Meilin said. Her almond eyes were dark and knowing. Behind her the curtains on the walls swayed in the breezes from the hidden spaces beyond.

'I think he wants to renew the memory of an old, very close friendship, don't you?' he suggested.

Hilde moaned under his grip, the vibration in her throat stirring in his fingers. Meilin shaped a silent, suggestive circle with her lips and suddenly Veraine realised that he did not care what Slaithe's motivation was. There were plenty of intense relationships formed in the barracks and if the old man wanted a show to remind him of times long gone then he was going to get a good one.

With a shrug Veraine leaned back and released both women. 'Fine. His hospitality can't be faulted. You can carry on.' Both women moved with no hint of reluctance to caress his legs but he interjected, 'Undress first.'

The simple robes were delightfully easy to remove, needing only the release of a single bow at each shoulder. The two women peeled each other free of clothing like delectable fruit, wriggling the dresses over their hips and tossing them under the couch. Veraine was enchanted. Meilin's slender figure was as smooth and golden as a bolt of imperial silk, the cushion of her pubis shaved free of hair so that it felt like hot satin under his fingers. He stroked a spiral on that mound and felt her quiver. Hilde, on his right, ran her hand up his bare inner thigh, demanding his attention in turn. She was extraordinarily pale – so pale that he could see the blue veins in her upper arms – and her big, puckered nipples were the pink of rose-candy.

'What shall we do first, lord?' she asked winningly, her hand cupping the hard curve of his imprisoned cock. It thumped impatiently against her hand, but its owner had more protracted plans.

'I was thinking we shouldn't waste all this food,' he murmured, appreciating her firm touch nonetheless. He reached forward between them, took a cup of syllabub from the table and emptied the creamy confection over Hilde's large, firm breasts. It oozed slowly over the curve of those warm globes, and they quivered as she flinched from the coldness of the cream. Her nipples hardened even further. 'You can carry on from where you stopped before.'

'Lord?' said Hilde, jiggling her cream-splattered breasts.

'Suck her,' he told Meilin.

Meilin leaned forward eagerly and began to lap the thick sweet cream from Hilde's white body, sucking it from the swollen nipples with undisguised appetite and causing the pale woman to moan and whimper over the little slurping noises of the suckling. Hilde arched backwards to push her breasts up into Meilin's face and finally abandoned Veraine's crotch altogether, taking both her breasts in her cupped hands and lifting them up, pressing them together so that both nipples could be snatched in the other woman's greedy mouth. Veraine could feel the pulse hammering in his groin but he restrained himself for as long as he could, until Meilin had devoured most of the fruit-pulp and cream. When he was at the apex of frustration he snatched Hilde up in his arms and pulled her up and over him so that his face was buried in her wet and slippery cleavage, with the smell of berries in his nostrils and her slick and yielding flesh under his lips and between his teeth. She wriggled against him and squealed as he sucked clean the last traces of confection, rasping her with his unshaven skin. Then he became aware that Meilin had sent deft hands questing up under his tunic, had found the knot that held up the loincloth beneath, was tugging at it and – as he stopped moving, almost stopped breathing – had at last released the painfully hard shaft of his cock from its confinement. It felt as if it were red hot, but when she took it in the wet grip of her mouth it did nothing to soothe the heat; instead his whole groin seemed to incandesce in a rush of flames.

Veraine gave a thick groan and released Hilde. She slid down to her knees and the two women between them managed to force his tunic up over his hips. He stared down helplessly at his braced and splayed thighs, the pathetic rag of his discarded loincloth pushed to one side, the dark fuzz of his crotch hair dimmed by the shining blackness of Meilin's head, as it rose and fell over the length of his cock. The things she was doing with her tongue seemed to strip every thought from his mind. And Hilde was crouching even lower, right down between his thighs so that she could nuzzle and lick his balls.

'Ah,' was all Veraine was able to say as the flaxen-haired slave pressed his knees even further apart and ran her tongue all the way from his bulging scrotum to his arsehole and back, pausing at one end of her journey to gently engulf each bollock in turn in her mouth, and at the other to tease and probe mercilessly with the pointed tip of her tongue. Meilin was taking what seemed an impossible length of his cock down her wicked throat, her tongue tangling with Hilde's when they met on the soft skin of his balls. Their breath, coming in hot gusts, caressed the sensitive pubic hairs. Veraine lay back, braced himself on his elbows and surrendered to their expertise, not even trying to resist as the pressure built in him to a white wave of pleasure. He bucked and gasped and filled Meilin's mouth until she nearly choked on his ejaculation.

When the room stopped spinning Veraine stared down the length of his body at the two slave girls with a certain degree of self-satisfaction. His cock, still bloated with lust, stood upright, dark and glossy, framed between their two faces. The women both kissed it softly, slightly wistfully he thought, their full lips pressing its bone-stiff column. He decided it would be a shame not to make use of its hard length while it lasted and, sitting up, he took the pouting Hilde around the waist and lifted her into his lap. She settled over his cock with the perfect tightness of a sheath on a sword, surprise flashing in her eyes. She smiled too and planted a hot and open kiss on his lips.

'You're very hard, lord,' she said simply.

'You can keep it that way,' he murmured. 'Oh gods. Probably till I die.' He squeezed her breasts until they overflowed his hands. She tightened her thighs and moved upon him, rising and sinking a little, her inner muscles clenching about him. He let slip a little grunt of appreciation. Meilin, still kneeling on the floor and almost hidden from view, gently raked the skin of his inner thighs with sharp fingernails. His scrotum tightened in anticipation.

'May I, lord?' Hilde asked, teasing out the knot of his belt. He let her wriggle the close-fitting military tunic over his shoulders and throw it on the floor, leaving him naked to her gaze and touch. Pleasure bloomed in her face. His torso was tight and well-muscled from years of military service – a commander was not exempt from daily combat practice – and she ran her hands over it covetously, tracing paths from his dark flat nipples through the scattering of chest hair down to the hard ridges across his belly.

'I like this,' she said, fingering a white scar that crossed his left ribs.

'Good,' he said. 'What I like is when you rock your hips. Oh gods yes. Like that.' For a moment purpose failed him, then he managed to lie back and swivel round until he was lengthways on the couch, Hilde still straddling his hips.

Meilin, deprived of his balls to play with, leaned over and took his right nipple in her teeth, tightening her grip until shudders ran through him like waves. Veraine stared up past her dark hair at Hilde gyrating slowly on his crotch and thought, I hope Slaithe is appreciating the show.

'Get up,' he told Meilin. 'Across my face.'

She mounted the couch in a single fluid motion, facing Hilde, her thighs spread wide across the width of his shoulders. Veraine was presented with the finest view of a shaven pussy he had ever witnessed, inches from his face. He was vaguely aware that the two women were fondling each other over his prone torso, but Meilin's cleft filled his vision and his consciousness to the exclusion of almost everything else in the world. Her arse was thrust out well and the globes of her buttocks filled his horizon like golden moons. He could see everything from the amber starburst of her arsehole to the tiny gold ring protruding from between her labia at the apex of their meeting. He parted those soft folds with his fingers, finding her golden on the outside and pink and juicy within, like some extraordinary ripe fruit. Very juicy indeed; his fingers were instantly slick with her moisture. He was gratified beyond words. He gently teased the pierced hood of her clitoris and was rewarded by a visible welling of further moisture from her cunt. His head swam with the scent of her musk. He loved that smell. She writhed on his tickling, stroking fingers.

With his free hand he pulled her down on his face. She made a noise like a kitten. He ran his tongue up the entire length of her cleft, from ring to arse, probing for the points of greatest pleasure. His tongue sank deep into the wet depth of her hole. When he licked her bejewelled clitoris she danced and twisted, pressing herself down on him, so he covered her with his mouth, both sucking and licking. Her moist flesh was all over his face, juices running over his nose and clotting in the lashes of his closed eyes. He could see nothing and could barely breathe, his nose buried in the wet grip. He could feel Hilde sliding up and down faster and harder on his pumping cock. He could feel the blood pounding in his temples. He was not getting enough air, blue lights were flashing behind his eyelids, but he pulled Meilin closer, smothering himself in her engulfing slit as she wriggled and jerked. He could hear Hilde crying out wildly, the sound muffled by the grip of the thighs around his head. But when Meilin's climax took her he did not hear it so much as feel it, the shuddering of her tortured body going through him like an earthquake. The blackness behind his eyes yawned like a pit and he swung help-lessly above it, the pulse pounding in his head, lungs screaming for air – but all he could breathe was the musky sex juice that was flooding his face and running down his throat and burning in his nostrils.

A heartbeat from unconsciousness, Veraine hit orgasm and convulsed beneath the two women, tearing Meilin from his face as he did so. His gasp sounded like pure agony, but that could not have been further from the truth. The three collapsed together in a shaking, sweat-ing heap, and even when they rolled apart they could do nothing but stare wordlessly at each other for many moments. Meilin at last pushed her hair back behind her and stooped to plant a soft kiss on the tip of his penis.

Veraine looked down at himself with something like amazement. Numb with overstimulation, nevertheless, his cock still stood hugely erect. Feeling as insatiable as any hero, he seized the opportunity.

'Lie down,' he told Hilde. 'Get your legs open.'

She obeyed. He bent over her and ran his finger through the sodden ringlets of her thatch. She smelled strongly of his come, the stink of a sweet chestnut tree in flower, and as he watched little rivulets of jism began to leak from her open slit.

'Get your face in there,' he ordered Meilin. 'I want you to ream her with that wicked tongue of yours.' Wide-eyed, she hastened to do his bidding, sinking her glossy head between Hilde's thighs. Veraine hefted her arse from behind, lifting it high so he could ease his cock into the wet hole she presented. Standing at the end of the couch he was at just the right height to enter between her spread arse-cheeks, and slowly, with great deliberation, he filled her to the brim with his shaft.

This third movement of the piece was different to the others, wrought less of uncontrolled lust than of a desire to create a sexual monument. He could see Hilde, spread-eagled, her face flushed and contorted with sensation as Meilin lapped and suckled at her muff. Of Meilin, all that he could make out was the wild tumble of her hair and the golden slope of her back rising up to the arse under his hands. Her buttocks slapped off his crotch with every stroke. He felt like a god with the entire world spread beneath him. He felt as if each thrust of his was passing right through Meilin into the woman beyond her so that he was fucking them both simultaneously. His cock was tight in its scabbard and he could take his time, utterly absorbed, a divine artist at work. He wanted to remember this moment for ever.

As before, Hilde climaxed first, then Meilin, followed at an unhurried pace by Veraine. This time he was content to rest after his labours, drained and entirely satisfied. When they had both recovered their strength the two slave girls led him to a perfumed bath, where the sweet stains of their exertions could be washed from them.

Lying in the tepid water, watching his companions lazily playing with each other's slippery bodies, it seemed to Veraine that if these were the rewards of a general's life, then he could very quickly come to accept his new status.

2 The Malia Shai

'The Irolian army is on its way,' said Rasa Belit. 'Pilgrims report that it has already crossed the Amal Bhad.'

'I know,' she said. She was looking out of the window, down over the jumbled roofs of the city. The panorama shuddered with heat haze and behind it the stone was a featureless blur of ochre, its shadows all fled into hiding from the midday sun. She had been dancing the daily adulation of that merciless blaze and her dress was stuck to her back and thighs. She hardly noticed the discomfort.

'You knew?'

'I dreamed it last night.' She laid her hands on the carved window sill in front of her, looking down at the slender fingers. The heat that lashed up at her palms from the sun-baked stone was enough to make any other person flinch away in pain, but she ignored it.

'Hmm. What did you see?' the priest asked, moving up and standing close behind her. He did not touch her; Rasa Belit never touched her casually. But he liked to stand close, to breathe in the scent of her.

'I saw men in bronze running through the streets. I saw blood on the desert sands. I saw a horse-head split in two.' She raised her gaze, fixing it on the mirror-shine of the cloudless sky. 'I saw smoke and gold. I heard the earth scream. There will be many deaths. There will be a miracle.' She heard the hissing intake of the priest's breath, but she did not add as she could have, I saw an eagle fly from the sun, and it came down over me and covered me with its wings, and then it lifted me up and carried me into the sky, with claws in my flesh that were fire and rapture. That was not something that Rasa Belit needed to know.

'Will Mulhanabin prevail?' he asked.

'I didn't see.' Her voice was as calm and detached as ever, but inwardly she nursed her secret, turning it over under her mind's eye. It intrigued her. She had woken from the dream heavy and wet with pleasure, her heart racing. She assumed it must have been Lappa Han, the sun god, visiting her as he had done so often in the past, to pour his golden seed into her aching body. Strange, then, that he had not spoken to her in familiar greeting, and that the eagle had been grey, not golden.

'It hurts me that those Irolian bastards must come into the city,' the priest muttered.

'You requested protection,' she reminded him, thinking, perhaps it had been some other god in disguise. But she had thought she was well acquainted with all the deities of earth and heaven.

'I know. But they're filth, those people. The one thing worse than an Irolian governor is an Irolian soldier. Murderers and sodomites, every man.'

'The divine light shines in them too,' she said mildly. Just thinking about the dream was drawing up an aching sweetness in her belly. She pressed her palms down hard on the rough sandstone.

'Yes – but I think of them strutting up and down the streets of the city, barging into homes and shrines, taking food from Yamani mouths. It makes me sick.'

'You should empty your heart of dark thoughts,' she reminded him.

He seemed suddenly to remember to whom he was speaking. 'Of course, Malia Shai. I shall go and wash in the tank. Then I must see to the sounding of the great horns.'

She nodded. 'And I wish to meditate, alone.'

She went, as soon as the priest had left her, to the shrine of Jekka the goddess of divination and visions. Jekka, a cthonic deity of caves and dark earth, was by derivation an obscure facet of Malia herself, so she was granted a large and windowless room very near the main shrine of the greater goddess, in the heart of the Outer Temple. The chamber would have been in total darkness if it had not had been for the banks of lamps burning near the pillars and the altar, but the light from the little wicks was swallowed by the stone and, despite their flickering flames, the room was filled with thick black shadow. The statue of Jekka herself was only partially illuminated, her shrivelled ascetic's features leering from the gloom, the coiled serpent upon which she sat glittering as the light danced off its carved jet scales.

There was no one else in the shrine. At this time of the day, most people hid from the sun and slept.

The Malia Shai decided to sit facing the statue but some little way to the side, in the darkness of an aisle. She sank into position on the bare stone floor, cross-legged with her palms open upon her thighs, her back straight. She breathed in slowly through her nostrils, held the air for a heartbeat and then let it whisper out between her parted lips. Her vision blurred as she relaxed, the bright flames becoming a shimmering orange pool, while she concentrated on her breathing, in and out; on the fragile moment between exhalation and inhalation when time was suspended, in and out, until she should achieve the correct mental state of perfect emptiness. Then, detached from the world and her body, she should be able to merge her soul with Jekka's and thus unravel the meaning of her dream.

She was almost there when someone entered the room. Without moving an inch she brought her consciousness gently back and focused on the figure pacing in front of the altar. It was a man, well dressed and at that peak of physical attributes attained once youth is passed. From his trimmed moustache and his oiled hair she judged him to be of the scholarly class; the sort of man who once had administered the affairs of Yamani kings and debated with the loftiest intellects, but who under the Irolian yoke was reduced to petty clerical scribblings. He ducked a bow briefly to the statue but seemed intent on something more urgent. He kept looking around the shrine although his frequent glances at the flames must have been ruining his ability to see into the dark corners and he didn't seem to notice her there. Clearly he was waiting for someone.

That someone did not keep him impatient for long. A second figure slipped through the door into the glow of lamplight, and this one was dressed in the yellow robes of a priestess. The Malia Shai even recognised her and could, after a moment, put a name to the round face with the dark and flashing eyes. Ayhan. She was only of moderate status; something to do with washing the statues. Her hair was of course cropped to a dark fuzz, but that did not detract from the lively gleam in her eyes nor the wicked smile that curved her lips.

The Malia Shai supposed she should be surprised at this assignation. But she did not move.

The man certainly seemed pleased to see the priestess. He rubbed his hands on his thighs. Ayhan cocked one hip and looked up at him appraisingly. The yellow cotton of her dress was strained across the curve of her ample behind. The man put his hands, a little hesitantly, on her shoulders. They spoke, but their voices were too low for the Malia Shai to catch the words. Some kind of negotiation seemed to be going on.

Soon Ayhan bared her teeth in a carnivorous grin and

stepped back, raising her arms over her head to display her whole body as she wriggled her hips. The man grabbed after her, seizing on her plump breasts and squeezing them through the layers of her dress. She put her back to a pillar and let him grope her up and down, her face a picture of anticipation. Quickly the man raised her skirt, bunching it up to her rounded belly. He put his hand down there, and his gasp of discovery was loud in the silent room. At once he sank to his knees in order to explore this new terrain at eye level. Although his dark head obscured her view, the Malia Shai knew what it was he had found; the shaven mound, the tightly pursed lips more chaste than the youngest virgin's.

Ayhan stared down at him intently and eased her thighs apart. He slid one hand in between them, and what he felt seemed to excite him even further.

'What do I do?' he whispered hoarsely.

Without replying, she pushed his hand away and brought her own palm up in a sharp slap against the prow of her pubic mound. She repeated the movement, and slowly he seemed to grasp what it was she wanted. He rose to his feet again, braced one hand on her shoulder and with the other smacked her firmly between the legs. Ayhan jumped and quivered at the blow, then looked at him with melting eyes. He began to beat upon her as if she were a drum, alternating slow heavy slaps with quick pattering strokes. She writhed her hips and opened herself wider to his palm, thrusting forward to meet each new impact, only his other arm holding her upright by the end. The room filled with the sound of skin on skin and the quickening of her breath until she finally jerked forward and cried out, her mouth slack.

The Malia Shai watched without blinking.

The man gave the priestess no time to recover, pushing her instead to her knees and fumbling frantically at his own trousers until he managed to release the stiff prong of his tool. Its moist tip glistened. He pumped it impatiently, though it seemed that it was physically impossible for the thick member to grow more erect, then pulled her head forward and fed the shaft between her unresisting lips. For a moment it looked as though she couldn't remember what she was supposed to do, then she fastened upon the turgid length eagerly, her lips flexing around the column as she sucked it further and further back into her mouth and throat. He put his hands on the soft velvet of her scalp and guided her in rising and falling on his swollen shaft. Her slurping was audible even from where the Malia Shai sat, and her pink tongue was perfectly visible lapping the darker flesh of his prick. It jerked and danced for her, begging her wet kisses.

The man leaned forward as he approached his crisis, jamming one hand against the pillar, holding his partner to his crotch with the other. His trousers slid down around his ankles, revealing sturdy legs that bulged with their straining muscles as he pumped and quivered in her hot suckling mouth. Then suddenly his thrusting tripled in speed and he spasmed, almost falling over her, ramming his cock so deep down her throat that she made muffled choking noises as he spurted his release.

When he pulled away she licked him clean, reluctant to finish.

Then the two stood up and readjusted their clothing, not looking at each other. Ayhan left first. The man smoothed back his hair, lit an extra lamp before the altar, then walked out only a little unsteadily.

The Malia Shai was left as before, unmoving and unmoved.

*　*　*

'General?'

The voice roused Veraine from his reverie and he looked round sharply. Rumayn, his new adviser, stood at his shoulder trying hard to look as if would never dream of interrupting the officer's thoughts.

'Yes?' said Veraine, pushing the memory of two warm and compliant bodies far down beneath the surface of his mind. The chances of him getting laid at all in the next few months, he told himself sourly, were as remote as water in this desert. So much for the privileges of rank.

Rumayn cleared his throat. He was the only civilian present with the Eighth Host and his manner showed how ill at ease he felt among all the soldiers. He wore his hair close-cropped to a stubble and even that was receding from his temples, so that when he faced any officer it was the back of his head he had to rub nervously. 'We're within sight of the city, General. We'll reach it tonight, if you keep your men marching.'

'Yes. Not before dark, though.' Veraine looked at him thoughtfully. Despite his awkwardness – the man was only the third or fourth son of some merchant, and could hardly be used to moving in military circles – Rumayn had an open, pleasant face and a keen mind. Even on their brief acquaintance Veraine rather appreciated his presence. 'I'm going to send a messenger ahead to announce our arrival. Who is it that I should address? Who'll be in charge in Mulhanabin – this Malia Shai woman?'

Rumayn looked pleased to be of use. 'No, General. The Malia Shai is secluded from worldly affairs, I understand. You'll be dealing with the High Priest.'

'What's his name, then? Do you know?'

Rumayn shook his head. 'Not his personal name. You

should address him as "Rasa". It means "pure one". He'll be a eunuch.'

Veraine stood, stretching his calves, and frowned out into the desert below. 'Is that normal for Yamani priests?' he asked with a grimace of distaste.

'No, General, just for this temple. The Malia Shai is a goddess of the desert and the barren earth. So her priests must be barren too, both men and women.'

'Sun's blood. How do you castrate a woman?' Veraine asked.

'I believe, General, that they are . . . sewn up.'

'That's disgusting.' Veraine shook his head.

'May I have your permission to speak freely, General?' the adviser asked.

Veraine met his gaze squarely, though the other man looked at once to his sandals. 'That's why you're here, Rumayn,' he said. 'You've got the right to speak to me freely at any time. In fact I expect it of you. Yamani sacred cities are not exactly familiar territory, and I rely on you to smooth the path for me.'

'I'll try, General,' said Rumayn, bowing his head. 'Though it won't be easy for you to avoid pitfalls. These places – isolated, filled with ancient tradition – are like wasps' nests, with every poisonous inhabitant ready to sting every other. One wrong move and you can set the whole swarm on your head. And they will resent you, General. We Irolians have hardly touched the big temples and the priesthood still clings to what power it can. They underestimate the authority of the Eternal Empire beyond their sacred precincts. You may find, General, that you will have as many enemies within the walls of Mulhanabin as without.'

'I had guessed that much. Thank you for stating it clearly.'

'I understand that you're fluent in Yamani?' Rumayn almost flinched as he said this.

'Yes. I don't read it.'

'Well, speaking it is more useful than reading. You never know what you might overhear, General. And I'm able to translate the script if that's ever necessary.'

It sounded to Veraine as if what he really needed was a squad of assassin-bodyguards, but he didn't voice his pessimism. 'Very well. I want you to instruct the herald to the Rasa, straight away,' he said. 'He'll ride ahead now.'

'That's another thing, General. I haven't been to Mulhanabin myself, you understand, but if it conforms to the old western Yamani city-fortress architecture then I'd advise you not to ride your chariot into the city. They often made the city roads very narrow – so narrow you can hardly get two men abreast – and labyrinthine, for defensive purposes. You might find you won't be able to get your chariot as far as the temple. You'd end up wedged between the walls. If you want my advice, I'd suggest that you enter Mulhanabin on horseback, General. The Yamani won't know any better.'

For the first time, Veraine smiled at his adviser – a small dry smile. 'At last some good news,' he said. 'I shall be delighted to enter the city on horseback. And by the way, Rumayn, your freedom to speak your mind applies to me only. With others, I want you to keep your eyes open and your mouth closed.' Trailing the other man behind him, he set off back towards his officers.

I stand in darkness. It is not night, for without day there cannot be night. There is no day. No sun, nor moon. No earth beneath my feet. There is only me, and I stand naked and alone.

I lay my hands on myself. My belly is warm and a little

rounded, spreading to cooler hips. I feel the bones firm beneath my skin. I feel the sun, unborn, burning in my belly. It must be the source of that heat.

My skin is soft. It yields to gentle pressure, but there is strength and resistance beneath that softness. I imagine there must be tiny hairs on that skin, but they are so fine that I cannot discern them with my stroking fingertips. Above my hips my body narrows to the waist. My hands can span half its circumference. Ribs lie close under the skin above that, their ridges curving in to meet at the mouth of a steep valley, my breasts rising to shadow that cleft. Cautiously I raise my hands to those breasts, cupping them. I cannot cover their whole surface in my grip. Are my hands small or my breasts large? My hands feel cool. If I heft them, I can feel the weight of my own flesh.

My cold forefinger and thumb frame each nipple. I pinch the teats and stir them in magical circles. They are soft to begin with, softer than the mass of the breast and I can push them right beneath the surface. Just touching them opens little paths of pleasure over the surface of those globes, down to my belly again. But playing with them makes those soft nipples harden and pucker. The areolae tighten to little ridges, and the nipples themselves stand out like fingertips reaching up to the fingers that stroke them. Pinching them is ... nice. The discomfort turns into joy at once; a restless excited joy that makes my stomach squirm. I pull the nipples high, hanging the whole weight of each breast from those nubbins of flesh, and the cold tracks of pleasure race right round to my shoulder blades.

Releasing the nipples at last, my hands continue their exploration, finding first the sensitive skin at the top of the breastbone that loves to be tickled, then the column of my throat. My pulse is thick and strong. I trace a web of sensation over my features, trying to picture what I might *look like, if there were any to see me, and any light to see by. Chin, lips, nose, cheeks, eyelids, forehead. My lashes brush stiffly at my fingers, and a wet tongue awaits behind my lips to ensnare them as they pass. I can feel the breath fluttering in my chest and out of my nose. If I blow steadily I can create a cool breeze that stirs my breasts still further with prickles of gooseflesh.*

I draw my fingers through my hair, massaging my scalp right down to the nape of my neck. My hair is long. It lies softly on my shoulders and strokes my spine. My palms glide across the rounded muscles of my shoulders, back down over my breasts – torturing my hard nipples on the way with the brevity of their caress – and back to my belly. I find the tiny mouth of my navel in the centre of my belly. Below it is a padded mound of flesh over the pubic bone, the coarse silky hairs there sticking out in tufts and swirls. I touch that mound. Surely the sun is not in my belly at all; it burns between my closed legs.

For a moment I force my hands away from my groin, back over my hips to knead and caress the cool curves of my buttocks. My arse is solid and muscular, and it likes the heavy grasp of demanding palms and fingers. The cleft between the cheeks is a crevasse that invites invasion. But my hands are drawn back, irresistibly, to the tight crease at the top of my thighs, to the lips pressed so firmly together. I cannot delve within while my legs are closed, ankle against ankle, so I am forced simply to press and stroke, tugging sometimes at the short hairs, tickling their wiry locks.

Quickly, the sensation becomes unbearable. I wriggle my hips, but it is not enough. I have to part my thighs, taking a single step to the right, and with that movement completed I feel rock beneath my bare foot. Now my fingers can pour down into the cleft beneath, finding plump, swollen lips, a humidity and a heat among the coarse vegetation of my hair. I think of jungles, and my fingers prowl like tigers through the forest. I brace one hand on my thigh, crouching slightly to part my limbs. My legs are strong and my knees flex easily, taking the strain. I rise and fall, letting my hand slide further into the secret valley. Where the softness of my labia end, I find smooth tight skin leading to the muscular hole of my arse. That little mouth tightens and pouts at my touch. Stroking it is pleasurable, but not to be compared with the sensations awoken by the pressure of my palm on my turgid lips. I return to them, and find a trace of moisture. I smell the musk of my sex. There is a well there, hidden deep within the valley.

Impatience overwhelms me at last; I have to spread my thighs further and devote my concentration to the task of my fingers, and this is impossible standing. I shuffle my feet, feeling wet sand shift between my toes, then I sink to my knees, thighs splayed. My shins rest among grasses, and some reaches up to tickle the underneath of my buttocks and my sensitive perineum. The tendons of my groin are rope-tight. Little sparks of light fill my mind with every flutter of my fingers, and these stars linger until they fill the sky. Faintly now I can see my own body, the jut of my breasts and the curves of my braced thighs. But I am not interested in looking out. My soul is concentrated in my fingertips, where they are probing for moisture and spreading the plump, wet petals of my sex. I find layers within layers; a complex flower of flesh. Within them is nested the void at the heart of the mystery; my hole, my vagina, my cunt. It is full of liquid as slippery as the finest oil, and with this lubrication I enter and explore, finding rings of muscle that grip my digits tightly, the curved grip of a canal that pulses and sucks at me. I am astonished to find that I not only have lips down there, a second mouth, but a throat, too, one that longs to swallow *my straining fingers. I push deeper, and the light opens in my head, the white clear light of a full moon. I can see my other hand spread on my thigh, now. I can see the stiff points of my nipples.*

But the heel of my hand, pressed against my pubic mound, shudders a drumbeat that echoes up my spine. Enchanted by my cunt as I am, I recognise a stronger demand from that place and I have to respond. I withdraw from the liquid well and ease that moisture up the folds of flesh until I find it; the spider in the rose; the pearl in the oyster. I begin to rub my clitoris and the light grows, and with it the heat. I can feel the sun boil in my groin. It is filling my sex and the first rays of its brilliant light are touching the horizon. I spread myself wide for that sunrise. I am radiant with power.

Everything rests on me as pearls are strung on a thread. I am the fragrance of the earth. I am the taste in water. I am the heat in fire and the sound in space. I am the light of the sun and moon and the life of all that lives.

My hand pumps, my muscles lock. I feel the sun burst from my body in a storm of light that tears me into a million motes of incandescent dust. I am shattered irrevocably. I have become everything, and nothing. I have come.

Well after nightfall the Eighth Host of the Imperial Irolian Army entered the city of Mulhanabin, General Veraine riding at its head. They entered by torchlight, through the only gate to the city. The men were tired and ill at ease, their legs caked with the mineral crust that coated the miles of ground they had covered, but they marched in tight formation, their steps precise. Veraine was proud of them. He was proud of their grim faces on heads held high, and of their disciplined silence, and of the ordered rattle of their hobnailed sandals on the stone underfoot as he raised his hand and ordered them to halt in the square just within the gate.

The people of Mulhanabin were not silent. They crowded every alleyway and every window of the buildings that walled the square, their dark faces shining in the torchlight, and while they stared they talked in a continuous murmur, nervous as the cackle of hens.

Veraine swivelled around in the saddle, searching the shadows for the bright yellow robes of a Yamani priest, or for signs of trouble. He was wearing full armour and the bronze helmet restricted his vision.

'Good place for an ambush, sir,' muttered Loy in an undertone. 'A real bottleneck, this.'

Veraine nodded. All the streets that led from the square were narrow and all seemed to lead upwards. They had entered the city at the lowest point, right at the base of the cliff. The rest of Mulhanabin towered above and before them, wall after wall and window above window, all the way to the top of the hill, steep as a cresting wave. Even the stars overhead were invisible past the glare from the torches. It felt very claustrophobic.

'Tell the men to take up positions around this square, Commander,' Veraine ordered. 'They may stand at ease but they are not to break formation. Where's that herald?'

The outrider sent previously to the city steered his horse through the lines of soldiers and saluted.

'You, lead the way to the Temple,' said Veraine. 'Commander, Rumayn, Arioc; you come with me. Sron, you are to remain in charge down here. Commander, I want twelve men on foot to accompany us. The trumpeters are to stay with Sron and signal in case of trouble.'

Slowly the small party of mounted men and their retinue made their way up the heights of the city.

Slowly, because the road wound back and forth across the face of the cliff, sometimes disappearing into tunnels behind the houses that clustered and teetered over the drop, and because the outrider was picking his way carefully, hesitating at each junction. There was no one wider route, rather a maze of passages that could lead anywhere. However, Veraine quickly noticed that it was the path with the most worn and eroded footing that they seemed to follow every time.

'You were right about the chariot,' he told Rumayn as his horse slithered yet again on the steep and concave pathway. 'This city is a death trap.'

'It's extraordinary,' Rumayn said with enthusiasm. 'Have you noticed how few of the buildings actually have courses of stones in the walls? They've just been carved out of the rock itself, from the cliff face. I've never seen anything like this! General,' he remembered at last.

They reached a point where the jumble of houses washed up against the bank of a huge wall, and the road plunged beneath a wedge-shaped tower through a tunnel several horse-lengths deep before emerging in an area where the gradient seemed less steep, the buildings larger and further apart. Clearly they were at the brow of the hill now, or close to it.

'Ah,' said Rumayn, twisting round to look back at the gateway with its looming *gopuram* tower. The soldiers marching at their heels were audibly panting with the strain of the climb. 'I think we've left the secular part of the city. This is the temple Citadel, the sacred area. That below is where the people live; the ones who aren't priests.'

'What do they live on?' Veraine asked with feeling. 'There wasn't a cultivatable furlong of soil out there on that plain.'

'Pilgrims, mostly, I think, General,' Rumayn said.

'Many many thousands of them every year, all wanting food and drink and accommodation.' He waved his hand at a large building close by, pierced with uncountable tiny windows. 'Look, that's a pilgrim hostel, I should think.'

Veraine reined in his horse briefly. 'It'll make an admirable barracks for the men then,' he said. 'Commander Loy, when we have made our introductions you can billet them up here. And keep them under a tight rein. I want you to make it very plain to the men that we're here to save this place, not to sack it. I don't want any trouble with the inhabitants. Misbehaviour will be severely punished.'

'Yes, sir.'

They moved up the broad street that sloped in front of them. The shadows around them were alive with movement and the sound of cymbals clashing. Scented smoke wafted from doorways along with the drone of chanting voices. Rumayn stared round him with the fascination of a hound on the hunt, remarking on each new feature. The buildings here were not modest domestic dwellings but squat towers, sloping as they rose in a pyramidal shape that echoed the hillside they had already climbed, to barrel-shaped roofs from which long pennons hung, hissing in the breeze. Every wall and sill was decorated in this part of the city, crowded with the statues of myriad gods and heroes that none of the Irolians could hope to identify. Here the polished sandstone was plastered and stuccoed over and every sculpture was painted in the most garish of colours. Monsters and demons, twenty-headed and bright blue or red, leered from niches all about them, while divine lovers clung to the columns, entwined in passionate embraces; all the soldiers stared furtively at these as they passed. They circled a huge sunken tank of water, glittering with the light of a thousand tiny lamps that floated in parchment boats on the surface. It was like entering a dream. Shadowy forms, eyes glinting in the light of their votive lamps, hovered on every side. Veraine, used to the simple lines of Irolian architecture and the uncluttered world of the soldier, found himself recoiling inwardly from the glitter and the colour and the visual confusion. He had deliberately to remind himself that this alien place did not represent menace; after all, the Yamani people had been subjugated for decades.

Passing through this glinting, visionary place, watched at every pace but never accosted, they reached the highest point of Mulhanabin; a great broad building whose multi-towered roof rose in ranks like the peaks of a distant mountain range up to the tallest central tower. Above that was only the field of the stars. A wide stairway ascended to the door of this building and down these steps, at last, a priest hurried towards them, his yellow silk robes billowing against his portly frame. The priest lowered himself to flagstones before the horses' hooves and pressed his forehead to the stone.

'General Veraine, scion of the Eternal Empire, has entered Mulhanabin,' said the herald sternly, in badly accented Yamani that made Rumayn wince. 'Your high priest is commanded to receive him at once.'

'Of course the Rasa awaits with pleasure the arrival of the Irolian General,' the priest said from his crouch. 'Let the temple guests follow me and enter the halls of Malia.'

They dismounted and Veraine threw his reins to Arioc. 'Wait here until we return,' he said. Arioc, a slim and strikingly handsome youth, was a mystery to Veraine. The Eighth Host was a small army of seasoned soldiers, conspicuous for the lack of nobility posing around as officers. Yet Arioc, the eldest son of a family so refined that there were probably rubies in his veins rather than blood, had requested a transfer to this army as Veraine's chariot-driver. Bearing in mind the young man's lineage, Veraine felt it safer not to demur. He had been as surprised as he was pleased to find that Arioc was a skilful driver and a conscientious horseman.

'And you,' he added to the herald.

They let the priest lead them into the dark interior of the temple, along several corridors and eventually to a door. 'Please enter. The Rasa will meet you,' he said with another bow.

Veraine strode through the door, followed closely by the foot soldiers who fanned out at either side in a protective guard. Then he halted and stared about him. It was a large room with painted walls, made larger by its comparative emptiness. There were thick carpets on the floor, but the only furnishing was a low platform around the walls covered with more rugs and fat cushions. Lamps burning clarified butter shed a low light.

'Well, he's certainly not here to greet us,' Veraine snapped. 'What in hell does he think he's doing?'

'No, General, please,' said Rumayn hurriedly. 'It doesn't carry the significance among the Yamani that it does with us. Please be patient. I'm sure the Rasa will be here shortly.'

Veraine grunted, but accepted this. 'Wait outside the door,' he told the foot soldiers. 'Let me know when the priest shows up.' He walked restlessly around the room, then to the tall window. It was made of stone intricately carved into filigree, and he stared out through the petrified lacework into the void beyond. This room apparently overlooked the desert, and he could see nothing but darkness. The cool night wind fluttered on his face. He stood brooding, trying to curb his impatience and spinning through his head over and over again, as he always did, the options that lay before him, the probabilities, the likely outcomes.

Rumayn's little pleased noise of interest recalled him from his reverie. He turned, to find the adviser examining the wall paintings.

'Amusing?' he asked.

'Depictions of the goddess Malia, General.'

'Shit,' said Loy, facing another wall. Veraine took the helmet with the horsehair plume off his head and crossed the room to look over his shoulder.

The paint on the plastered walls was faded and peeling in places, but the scenes were still vivid. The figures were slightly larger than life-size and Malia was, like all Yamani goddesses, wasp-waisted with opulent breasts and snug hips. There was no denying that Yamani artists knew how to depict women; breasts like ripe fruit, waists as pliant as willows; the curves on their goddesses would make any man burn. And Malia stood in this particular scene with her knees spread, straddling the prone man on the ground beneath her, so that the uncompromising slash of her sex gaped at the viewers. But her skin was the grey-blue of a corpse, her eyes bulged from her face and her long hair writhed about her head like a nest of snakes. And from the slit abdomen of the man at her feet she was hauling the ropy green loops of his entrails, stuffing them into her slavering mouth.

Veraine felt a coldness run up between his shoulders. 'Can I assume she's not a benevolent deity?' he said dryly.

'*Hail Malia, mother of misfortune,*' Rumayn replied, reading slowly from the border of script painted above the pictures, running right around the room. Yamani writing was so florid that Veraine found it difficult to identify from abstract decoration, but Rumayn seemed able to pick it out. *'Thou who gives birth to the earth-quake. Thou who sends forth the famine. Thou who brings the plague at Thy heel. In Thy shadow lie a thousand curses. In Thy hearing sound the lamentations of the world. Thy breath is sickness; Thy footstep is the withering of the harvest; Thy wrath is doom. The burning-grounds of the innocent send forth a sweet savour in Thy nostrils. Bitter are Thy kisses. Unbearable are Thy caresses. Oh Thou who dances in the wastelands and in the marshes, Thou who dries up the womb, Thou who pulls the empty teat from the hungry mouth; we bow before Thee.'*

There was a moment's silence.

'Some bitch,' commented Loy.

'She's one of the great earth goddesses,' Rumayn answered. 'The killing earth. The soil that refuses to yield harvest. She's part of the great triad of goddesses. Gelewi, the fertile earth, has her temple at Jalatabin in the south. Vahendra, the underpinning rock, is worshipped on the mountain of Bebi.'

'We could have been sent to Jalatabin,' Loy sighed.

Veraine shook his head. 'I don't think so, Commander. It's out of bounds to the army.' He started to circumnavigate the room, examining each picture just long enough to understand its contents.

'I wasn't complaining, sir,' Loy said dutifully.

'Understood, Commander.' Veraine noted Malia in a rainbow of colours and with varying numbers of arms, but always performing some revolting act; she danced amid funeral pyres, she squatted among the contents of ossuaries. She fell ravening upon cities with swords and firebrands, and she crouched filthy and emaciated beneath the laden table, reaching up to snatch the food. She cradled children in arms that were pocked with weeping sores. One particularly vivid tableau depicted her straddling the hips of a decapitated man, accepting the thrusts of his member even as she gulped at the jets of blood gushing from his neck.

'What do they want to worship a goddess like that for?' Veraine asked with distaste. The Irolian people, with their eternal confidence in their destiny, had a pantheon composed purely of benevolent deities.

'I should imagine, General, in the hope that she leaves them well alone,' Rumayn said.

'Well, I find I would like to leave this room alone. I think we've been kept here long enough waiting for the Rasa. Do you disagree, Rumayn?'

'No, General,' he shook his head. 'You were right. He is insulting you.'

'Time to leave, then. I feel like a walk, Commander.' Veraine threw open the door and handed his helmet to one of the soldiers outside. 'Two of you stay here. If the Rasa should show his face, you may tell him that I am looking round the building to find suitable accommodation for my officers and myself. This city is now under the jurisdiction of the Irolian army. This temple will be my headquarters. He may report to me for further information. Is that clear?'

Without any further delay he set off into the bowels of the temple, his entourage marching hard to keep up with him. Part of his intention was practical, as stated; part was a burning desire to scout out the building and find what was happening here, to gain some feeling of control over the chaotic mess he had been thrown into. A large part was just anger and the resulting restless need for action. The small party crashed through room after room, some clearly sacred, some administrative. There were surprisingly few people around for such a large building, and every priest they saw fled from them before they could close in. It would have been impossible to sneak up on any of them – not in full armour, with their bronze kilts clanking on their thighs. Hall followed hall in their progress, each seemingly darker and emptier than the last despite the frescos and the lurid shrines to the man-eating goddess. Even when they found what they judged to be the main chamber of the temple, with a gold-painted statue twenty feet high towering over the altar, there was no sign of the high priest.

Taking a line roughly down the spine of the complex towards the rear, they eventually went rattling out of the front part of the temple and through an enclosed court-yard thick with scented bushes and even, to everyone's surprise, a few trees. In the centre was a raised pool and Veraine scooped a handful of water up to his lips.

'Fresh,' he said. 'That's useful. I'll want to know every water source in this city by nightfall tomorrow, Commander.'

'Sir,' Loy acknowledged.

The back half of the temple was lit by lamps just as was the front, but it was immediately obvious that this place was different. The floor was not smooth flagstones but rough virgin rock, not even level. There was little decoration, and the walls appeared to be made of limed mud-brick. It was as if someone had decided simply to roof over the top of the hill. Directly in front of the entrance was a steep flight of steps leading up to two huge interior double doors made of ancient timber, grey with age and studded with bronze. The stairs and the facing wall were carved all of a piece from the rock of the hilltop. Veraine headed straight up the centre of the steps.

'You can't enter there,' said a servant girl sitting on the stairs.

'No?' said Veraine, not even slowing.

'General!' Rumayn called anxiously. 'Please, a

moment.' He turned to the girl and demanded in her own language, 'What's in there?'

She stood. 'It's the *Garbhagria*. No one may go in except the priests.'

'It's the womb-house; the Innermost Temple,' Rumayn translated into Irolian. Veraine hesitated and turned back to glare at his adviser, who said with considerable emphasis, 'General, I believe this would be one of the worst possible rules to break. To go crashing in on sacred ground; that would not be acceptable.'

Veraine snorted in exasperation but stopped where he was. He could see that his adviser was pale despite the exertion of their progress through the halls.

'Sothot's balls. Ask her if the Rasa is in there.'

'The Rasa?' the girl said. 'No. He's not inside.' She walked, barefoot, towards Veraine and stopped two steps above him, which put them roughly on eye-level. 'You're General Veraine. I'd heard you were coming here.'

'Well, I'm glad someone has,' he replied, falling into the Yamani tongue, but he spoke without great harshness because despite everything and even in her undyed homespun she was quite pretty.

'You are going to save us,' she said.

There was no time for Rumayn to comment on this or for Veraine to work out exactly what it was about her that troubled him, before a flock of yellow-clad priests burst through the outside doors and dropped to the ground at the foot of the steps. They were followed into the vestibule by two of Veraine's bodyguards. The man at the front pressed his forehead to the floor and cried, 'Mother of a thousand torments, forgive our abrupt entry, for no impiety was intended!'

Veraine felt as if the earth had fallen away from beneath his feet.

'Oh shit,' said Rumayn, not quite under his breath.

Veraine swung back to face the girl, wondering how in the world to rescue this situation. She met his gaze without flinching. He found it hard to believe what had just happened; she was only a young woman in the roughest of cotton dresses, her hair bundled up and hidden in a cloth wrap like any other Yamani peasant girl. Fine featured, in a way that Veraine considered slightly underfed. He was relieved to see that she did not look either amused or haughty. And it was that which made her strange.

'Malia Shai,' he said in a low voice that only she could hear. He did not dare apologise to her. 'I didn't realise it was you. I've never met a goddess.'

She did not acknowledge his words in any way. 'You may rise, Rasa Belit,' she said. 'This is General Veraine.'

The priest scrambled to his feet and glared up the stairs. His eyes were bulging from his face in barely suppressed fury. 'General, what do you think you are doing?' he snarled in Yamani.

'He will save us from the Horse-eaters,' said the Malia Shai.

Rasa Belit shut his mouth like a trap and Veraine felt a little flash of triumph. He walked without haste down the steps towards the theocrat, sizing the man up rapidly. He was certainly surprised by how tall the eunuch was; tall and big-boned, but with a softness to his flesh as if it had melted on his frame. His eyes were deeply bagged and his mouth was a thin, hard line. I'm not going to get along with this one, Veraine thought, without regret.

'Rasa Belit,' he said flatly, in Yamani. 'So sorry we missed you when we arrived.'

'I was detained by important rituals,' the priest hissed.

'Of course. I have no intention of interrupting the ritual life of this temple. The customs of our subject peoples are of importance to us.'

Rasa Belit pursed his lips.

'That is why you will be pleased that I shall be taking on the burden of defending this city from our foreign enemies. I require the minimum of your effort at this point, so that you may concentrate your own thoughts entirely upon theological matters. Merely room to set up a headquarters here. Space and supplies for myself, my officers and my men. Your full co-operation with any access or information we require. Maps of the city, if you have them. Inventories. I will be organising this city to withstand siege, Rasa. There'll be a number of changes. But rest assured, your rituals may carry on as if we weren't here at all.'

The high priest made a noise like cold water on hot stones.

'Of course I realise that we may inadvertently cause you a certain amount of inconvenience. This city is after all facing a major military crisis. But please take my word for it, Rasa; any small irritation your co-operation may cause will be trifling compared to the discomfort afforded by any of the alternatives I can imagine.'

There was a brittle silence. Rasa Belit, with obvious effort, swallowed, blinked and nodded. 'Very well, General,' he said.

'I am pleased we have an understanding.'

'Nonetheless, General,' he said with a fair semblance of politeness, 'you stand in the presence of the Malia Shai, on sacred ground. You haven't prostrated yourself before her as is correct.'

'And I won't. Neither will my men.'

'She is the goddess,' he smiled through clenched teeth.

'A Yamani goddess. We don't bow to your gods, high priest, no matter how immanent. I give the Malia Shai the honour that she's due as a figurehead of your people.'

Rasa Belit closed his heavy-lidded eyes as if unable to contemplate such a thought. 'You damn yourself to a hundred lifetimes of torment,' he whispered, with transparently insincere compassion.

'My current concern is the month before us,' Veraine said coolly.

'Oh, I understand that, General.' The priest's smile was sardonic. 'I am sure it will present you with many challenges.'

The two men locked gazes.

'You should offer them food, Rasa,' the Malia Shai suggested into the unpleasant silence. 'They've travelled a long way.'

Startled, both men turned and looked at her. She descended between them, pausing for a moment to look into Veraine's face before passing lightly through the door. Her eyes were clear and brown, with very dark, soft lashes. But her expression troubled him. He had known women of every kind look at him in all sorts of ways; with pleasure, or contempt, or calculation, or wariness. He felt that he could understand those people. But the Malia Shai looked at him with an expression he could not even name. He groped for a word and came up with 'expectancy', but even that he rejected. He wondered if she were slightly simple.

'Follow me, General,' said Rasa Belit through set teeth. 'I will find you suitable rooms in the Outer Temple. And you shall eat with us this very hour. This way.'

The priests preceded the military men back out into the courtyard. Loy and Rumayn fell in line immediately behind Veraine, who let his steps lag for a moment.

'That could have gone better,' he admitted in an undertone. He knew that was what both of them were thinking.

'You made your point, sir,' said Loy, who'd been rapidly updated by the adviser.

'So that was the Malia Shai,' Rumayn muttered.

'She was smaller than I expected,' Loy said. 'Nice arse, though.'

3 Foreign Gods

They did not emerge from the promised repast until many hours later, when the assembled priests departed for some nocturnal ritual and they found themselves free to return to the room which had been hastily designated as the military headquarters for the Irolian forces. Rather to their dismay, it turned out to be the painted room in which they had originally waited. Their actual sleeping quarters had been arranged in adjoining chambers but, stuffed with many variations on the theme of steamed wheat and spiced meat, the command staff of the occupying forces were too replete to retire straight away. The four men – Arioc was included in their number, though the other officers of the Eighth Host had been left to organise and find billets with the men elsewhere in the temple complex – stumbled into the room befuddled with physical exhaustion and, in Rumayn's case at least, with alcohol. Throughout the meal a fiery plum brandy had been served and the civilian adviser was still carrying a pottery jug of the liquor.

'What a hospitable people,' he enthused, slumping onto the mounded cushions.

'They certainly eat well,' Loy grunted as he sat back, 'if you like the taste of goat. Did you see them? All as plump as puppies.'

Rumayn smiled a beatific smile; 'Yes. Those ... ample priestesses.'

'There's not much use to be had from a locked box,' Veraine reminded him. 'Not when the key has been thrown away. Sun's blood, Arioc, help me off with this lot.' He began to unbuckle the heavy formal armour that he had been forced to wear all evening, dropping the *pteurges* from his hips to the floor with a crash. Arioc hurried to loose the straps that secured his breastplate at the back.

Rumayn frowned.

'There's always a hole of one sort or another,' Loy advised comfortingly.

'Gods, that's better,' Veraine muttered as he escaped from his bronze greaves. 'Put them in my room, Arioc. Get them cleaned tomorrow.' He had drunk the least of anybody at dinner, only a thimble-sized cup of the brandy, trying to keep a clear head, but it was now swimming with fatigue. For most of the meal he had picked at his food and stared down the length of the cavernous refectory at the ranks of priests, catching only snatches of the conversation around him. Rasa Belit had been in no mood to converse with the general. However, Rumayn, under the influence of increasing quantities of alcohol, had interrogated the high priest enthusiastically about the temple theology. Veraine had not bothered to overhear that conversation, assuming that his adviser would pass on any relevant information at some later point.

'I'm not impressed by this,' he said as he lowered himself onto cushions down almost at floor level. 'No chairs. No furniture.' He stretched his legs out in front of him one at a time. They were painful from the hours spent kneeling in armour while he ate at the low sandstone dais that served as a table for the priests. Arioc kneeled in front of him without having to be ordered; he knew his duties well.

'No wood, General,' Rumayn finished, 'not around here.'

'Not good enough,' Veraine growled as Arioc began to massage his calves, fingers digging deep into the hard muscles. 'I can't run a military campaign squatting on the floor like a Yamani stone-breaker. Somewhere in this nest there has to be a proper table. Find it tomorrow.'

'Yes sir,' Loy acknowledged.

'The priestesses have to be fat,' Rumayn said happily, 'so that they can sit comfortably on the hard ground all day while they pray.'

Veraine nodded, thinking of the priests in the refectory, who had certainly looked well fed and used to the sedentary life. There was no sign of any asceticism among the devoted of Mulhanabin, unless you counted the segregation of the sexes, in that the priestesses had, after serving all the male diners, sat at their own table at the far end of the room. Veraine stifled a wince as Arioc's fingers probed deeper. The Malia Shai had not been present during the meal.

'How are the men settled, Commander?'

'Plenty of space, sir, and comfortable quarters. They like that. They don't like the place. It puts the wind up them. Every room in the hall has a statue of that witchgoddess.'

Veraine lay back among the cushions. 'Full inspection and parade tomorrow, Commander. At noon. I want to address them.'

'Yes, sir.'

'They'll get used to being in a temple. And the statue's only a Yamani hag. Sothot knows they must have seen enough of them.'

'Just a pity the Horse-eaters aren't marching on Jalatabin instead, sir,' Loy said lightly. The Temple of the Abundant Goddess was a byword among Irolian soldiers for its rumoured debauches.

Veraine snorted. 'No, Commander – I need them to be in a state capable of fighting!'

'I've been to Jalatabin,' Rumayn offered, sitting up again so that he could drink more.

'Right,' Loy grunted.

'No. I mean it. I've visited the temple of Gelewi.'

'Really?' Veraine rolled himself on to one elbow. 'How did you manage that? It's forbidden to Irolians.'

'I was young, and piss-stupid.' Rumayn shook his head wonderingly. 'And in disguise. I wore Yamani clothes and wrapped a *shesh* around my face.'

'Is it true about the women?'

'Oh yes.' Rumayn widened his eyes and smiled. The effect was more of alarm than lechery.

'What happened?'

'Well.' He gazed down into the pitcher of brandy. 'I was in Jalatabin on business. My family is in the spice trade and one of the big pepper markets is held there. I was sent by my brothers to oversee our agents. You know the sort of thing. Well, I could speak Yamani by then and fake the accent too. You have to speak to them if you're in trade. It's not like being a noble and having slaves to order around; your sort only have to learn a few words – "go there, pick up this, suck that" –'

'Get on with it,' Veraine growled.

'Of course, General. I ramble, you know that. Too many things in my head. Well, I wanted to see the temple of Gelewi – who wouldn't? We've all heard of it. I traded a silk hood to get some old clothes that looked right. I told the washer-boy that it was for a servant, but I don't know if he believed me. It was strange, wearing Yamani clothes. The men have to put up with these baggy trousers that flap around the knees. Disconcerting. Anyway, I chose a quiet morning when I wouldn't be missed and I just walked in past the guards through the men's gate. The temple is huge, you see, but it has a wall all the way around the enclosure and enormous gates in each of the four walls –'

'I'm not interested in hearing about the architecture!'

'Ah, it matters. You see, there are four gates into the temple: one for women, one for priests, one through which only gods can go, and one for men. And when you walk in through that you're in a courtyard, straight away. The courtyard is closed, you can't see the rest of the temple. But all around that square there are women sitting on benches against the walls. Maybe a hundred women. They wear these red silk veils that cover them from head to foot and you can hardly see the features beneath. There are men in the courtyard, too, walking around, looking at the women.

'Well, I was lost at first. I hardly knew what to do. The women sit so still, only the men move. I thought, every woman in the city has been in here, or will be here before she marries. I could find anyone. A beggar or a princess. Well – I know they have no royalty left, but I was young and romantic then. Such a choice of women. I was nervous, I admit, but I was so excited too. I began to walk around the perimeter of the courtyard. When you get close you see the women making little move-ments, turning their heads. They're watching you through their veils. But you can't see anything, just the shape of the body beneath. She might be beautiful, or the plainest snag-toothed drab; you can't tell. She is – all of them are – just female. That's the point of the temple.

'Most of them are young, of course. They're getting this over with so that they can marry, paying their duty to the goddess Gelewi. You can see that, after a while. They're slim little things – well, you know how young Yamani girls are married off. I didn't want that. Even then, I wasn't interested in some skinny virgin. I wanted a real woman, one with ... curves.' Rumayn put down the jug long enough for his hands to describe extravagant shapes tenderly in the air.

'There are women there like that, you know. I'd been told about them by the merchants as we sat drinking and talking. Sometimes a woman gets a taste for Gelewi's service and she comes back to make the gift of the goddess again to some stranger. She can't be stopped. It's an act of piety. That's what I was looking for; some woman who'd found her husband couldn't satisfy her and was hoping for something younger to step her way. I thought I would give her some Irolian cock, see if that could fill her properly.

'I was lucky, I thought. I stopped in front of one who was sitting a little separated from the others. I think some of the young girls were scared about being picked and clustered together, but this one wanted to be seen. She had curves like a cloud. As I stopped over her she pulled the veil a little tighter from within so that I could see how tight her waist was under the jut of her breasts. And I saw her finger crook under the cloth. She was beckoning me. I felt my cock jump at that moment.

'I had with me the two big silver coins that are the traditional price, and I dropped those in her lap straight away. I didn't need to look at any more women. The coins go to the temple of course. She folded them in her veil, stood up and led me across the courtyard. We went through a door into the interior of the temple and I had to stop, I couldn't go any further. It was dark inside, and narrow; a passage full of shadows and perfume, and it had been so bright outside with the marble of the courtyard shining in the sunlight that I was blinded. She took me by the hand and drew me down the corridor. I don't know how she found the way. By touch, I suppose.

'She took me into a small room. It was tiny. Just space

for a bed and a shelf in one corner. The room smelled of incense and sex; it was a real whore's room. On the shelf was a little wooden statue of Gelewi the Fertile Earth, with a lamp burning in front of it. And there was a cup.

'The woman took the cup and gave it to me. The liquid inside was sweet and sticky. I didn't recognise it. I didn't like it much, either, but she motioned me to drink it all and I did. I would have done just about anything by that point. She didn't speak a word. Not ever, all the time I was there.

'When I had drained the cup she lifted her veil and pushed it back over her shoulders, so that it still covered her face but showed her body. She was wearing a robe underneath that opened down the front, and she parted that and took the robe off. She had a wonderful body. Not a little girl's body. Great big breasts, big as my head, brown and heavy, and the biggest nipples I have ever seen in my life. And a round, firm belly crossed with silvery stretch marks. She'd been a mother at least once. Her thatch was coarse and dark, almost black. She folded up the robe and laid it at one end of the bed as a pillow, then she climbed up and lay on her back, waiting for me.

'It was an awesome sight to a young man. In the lamplight her brown body gleamed with oil, but there was no face to be seen, only this splash of crimson, the veil. She began to move her hips, inviting me. It was too much. I dropped those trousers on the floor and just about threw myself down between her legs. My cock was like a spear flying into a target. She wrapped her arms around me and drew her knees right up to my shoulders, so that I was thrusting into this enormous soft cushion of her arse and her gash and her thighs. She was as wet as a swamp and had a grip like a python – I didn't think she would be tight but she was. Her heels drummed on my back. We fucked, I don't know for how long. My head was pounding. I remember ripping off the *shesh* that swaddled my head because I couldn't breathe. I could hear her singing. Under the veil, as she panted, she was moaning some wordless tune. The sweat from my forehead was dropping on the silk veil and making little dark spots. Her nails were digging into my shoulders. I just kept fucking. There was a roaring in my ears. I lost track of time, I forgot who I was, I couldn't see or think or stop. I was just one enormous cock eternally fucking into the wet, hot darkness. I forgot to be human.

'It might have gone on for ever, but it didn't, because I came back to myself to find that I had spent and finished. I didn't remember the spasm; I must have blacked out entirely. I lay on the soft cushion of her body and she wrapped her thighs around my hips until I'd stopped gasping for air. I was glad she did that, because I was scared, and I've never been scared after sex before. I felt as if I'd been cut adrift from my body. The room was spinning around me.

'As my panting slowed she slipped out from under me, retrieved her robe and left the room. I lay face down on that stained sheet and felt the bed throbbing to my pulse. I remembered, then, the drink she had given me. It was the drink that was doing this. I tried to sit up but my muscles had no strength left in them and it took several goes. In the end I more or less slid off the bed onto my knees.

'And just as the room had stopped swinging back and forth beneath me, the door flew open again and in marched the priestesses of Gelewi. I knew they were priestesses because they wore yellow robes and no veils. I wasn't up to any further mental leaps, and I was certainly in no shape to resist them. They put a rope around my neck and dragged me forward to the feet of the eldest. She crouched down to face me, lifted my head by the hair and propped my chin up on the point of her dagger. Well, it wasn't a dagger; it had three points and the handle wrapped around her knuckles, but I couldn't remember the right word for it just then. I knew that one push would send that tip up through my jaw and into my skull.

'"I will kill you now, Irolian shit," she snarled at me, "and no one will ever know what happened to you. You can't be here – this is the temple of Gelewi. So where will they look for your body?"

'I think I stammered that I hadn't done anything wrong. She laughed and spat in my face. "Listen to him talking in Yamani!" she cried. "You speak a few words of our language and you dress up and you think this means you can come into our holy temple! You pollute this shrine, Irolian shit. You think you can come here and fuck Yamani women like it was some brothel?"

'As that was in fact exactly what I had thought I could not answer her except to shake my head.

'"You think these women are whores, Irolian shit? You think they do it for gain? They're the vessels of the great goddess; they're givers and receivers of life. Now you are going to give your life to her, and when we feed your corpse to the pigs perhaps you'll have made reparation for your blasphemy."

'She stood up and kicked me in the face. Luckily for me her feet were bare and I only lost one tooth. I put my bleeding lips down on her other foot and kissed it. I don't know why I did that. It just happened. She froze, but she didn't recoil from me.

'"Every man who comes into this temple," she said, "no matter how base his motive, is Yamani born. He has known the goddess since his soul was hatched at the dawn of time. He has bowed his head to her lifetime

57

after lifetime. But you're an Irolian. You spit upon the goddess. Your soul is so unclean that you haven't even begun the journey to the divine."

'I protested then that I didn't spit upon their goddess, that I would learn. I have never been so scared in my life as I was in that room. I've never been so close to death. I'm not a warrior and courage is not my virtue, I don't need to pretend that. I would've said anything to save my life at that moment.

'But it was in vain. She took up the rope around my neck like it was a dog's leash. "Bring him," she told the others and they fastened other ropes to my wrists. The ropes were made of plaited leather. They hauled me out and down the corridor, my knees and feet scraping along the floor. I crashed to my elbows when they slowed and they yanked me upright again. I felt the darkness throbbing around me like a heart. And I saw that, despite everything, the pain and the fear and the helplessness, that I still had a hard-on. It must've been that drink the woman gave me.

'They took me into a great hall. I have no idea how large it was; it was in darkness except for islands of glimmering votive lamps. The hall was full of wooden pillars painted red. I could hear the chiming of gongs.

'They dragged me up in front of the great idol of Gelewi and, you know, it's strange: she was beautiful – so beautiful that she struck me with a kind of horror. She was painted green, and she was far bigger than any human, so big that I might have comfortably rested in the crook of her raised arm. In the dancing light those arms, one holding a sheaf of wheat and one with palm open in blessing, looked as if they were moving. Her face, almost in shadow at the edge of the golden haze of lamplight, was serene. She had wide eyes, and features more perfect than any human woman's. Her breasts were as round as moons, the nipples painted scarlet, and they hovered over a waist so pliant and lithe that my arms begged to encircle it, though they would have been completely inadequate to span such a round. That divine waist flared to hips that promised richness beyond my dreams. She kneeled on her left leg, the right knee drawn up. Because she was raised upon an arched pedestal (and that itself was almost smothered in banks of marigolds), I found that I was gazing up between her parted thighs into the depths of her yoni.

'My poor knob rose up in salutation to her awesome beauty and slapped against my belly. My head swam with delight and despair. I could anticipate no pity in such perfection. The priestesses took my hands and roped them to two pillars, then tied my straining legs to two more columns behind me. I had to clench my toes to keep a purchase on the marble floor. It was slippery under my skin. They cut the remains of my clothes off my back so that I was exposed to the smoke-laden air. I was hung spreadeagled, my weight pulling down through my bound wrists and pressing down through the balls of my feet. The priestess, my chief prosecutor and tormentor, stood in front of me and showed me two objects, though I had to strain my neck up to look at her. The first was a small copper cup, which she slipped over the swollen head of my cock. The weight wasn't great but it felt cold on my feverish skin. It bobbed to my movements.

'"Let that fall, and we will beat you to death," she murmured, displaying to me the length of split cane she held in her other hand. It was the heavy kind used for executions and I knew it would be as sharp as a knife-edge. Sweat was standing out on my shoulders already, and I could feel it starting to trickle down my spine.

'She stepped to one side then and nodded to one of

the women behind me. I heard something hiss through the air before I felt the blow, but when it landed I think I was struck momentarily deaf and blind. The pain was so intense that I did not even scream. The lash had branded itself across the top of my arse and it felt like it was burning. I was sure I could feel blood running from the wound. My whole body became a rigid board tensed for the next blow, and when that landed, a hand-span further down, that was worse. I started to scream then, yelling my lungs ragged, but as strike after strike came down on my shoulders and back and arse, and then down the back of my legs, too, I found I couldn't both scream and breathe and I had to alternate. Gods, I have never been through anything like that before or since. There was nowhere to run from the pain, that was the worst of it. I couldn't struggle or flee or fight or hide. Clenching made it worse. In the end I had to give way to it and let it carry me. My vision blurred with the sweat running into my eyes, but I fixed my gaze on that beautiful implacable goddess, on her face, then her breasts, and finally on her yawning cunt. That pit, filled with shadows deeper than any other in the hall, seemed to gape and pulse under my glazed stare. I felt as if the whipping was thrusting me closer and closer to its carmine lips. Maybe it was the drugs I'd taken, maybe just the pain. All I know is that for me the rest of the world vanished and I was left only with the agony and that cunt, wide enough to crawl into, insatiable as a shark's maw, that seemed to be opening wider and wider until I could fall into it. I felt that Gelewi was the whole universe, and that I loved her with the last rag of my tattered soul.

'Eventually I realised that the blows had ceased. I don't know what signal was given; maybe the whip broke, maybe the priestess just got too tired to strike any more. I hung limply in my bonds. It felt like my back was on fire, except that I could see the sweat that was pouring out of every pore on my body was dripping off my balls onto the floor. But my cock was still as erect as a club, and the cup dangled lazily from the knob-end. My whole back was throbbing with pain, like another blow stinging me at every beat of my heart, and my cock was jerking with that same rhythm.

'The priestess came in close to me, close enough to breathe in the stink of my sweat and fear. She took hold of my balls and then she rolled my stiff dick between her finger and thumb. I came at once. It was as if that was what I had been waiting for. My jism splashed into the cup and she rescued it quickly as I juddered in my traces.

'"Maybe even an Irolian can learn a lesson," she sneered. She took the cup up to the altar plinth directly beneath the goddess and placed it carefully there, like an offering.

'They kicked me out of the temple gate after nightfall, and I wasn't so badly hurt that I couldn't walk back to my lodgings. They were welts, not wounds. No blood. They'd switched to a lighter cane behind my back, I guess. I've still got some of the scars, though.'

Rumayn looked around him as his story concluded, wondering drunkenly what response the others would make. But Arioc had long since sidled out to prepare the general's quarters, Loy sat with his chin sunk on his chest, snores rumbling softly down his nose, and Veraine was laid out flat on his back, eyes closed, his breathing as deep and regular and insensible as the sigh of the sea.

'These are the two places where we can hold them,' Veraine said, putting his finger onto the charcoal lines of the map. 'The city gate and the temple gate.'

'The temple is better in many ways, sir,' Loy said. 'The gate into the Citadel is bronze, not wood, and they could only come at it a few at a time up that steep path.'

They were seated by the pool in the courtyard that separated the Outer and Inner Temples, partly because it was cool and shaded from the late afternoon glare, mostly because this was as far as their walking inspection of the Citadel had taken them.

'No. I want to use the temple gate as a fall-back position, not the first line of defence,' said Veraine, shaking his head. 'If we let the Horse-eaters into the lower city then they have access to food and water. We don't give them that.' He drummed his fingers on the map. 'What about the city gate? What state is that in?'

'Well, it's not the gate itself so much, sir,' Loy said. 'The city was built as a fortress by the looks of things, so the gate is easily defensible. The trouble is that over the years people have got used to being secure and they've knocked windows in the outer walls.'

'Then we get them walled up again, as a priority. Get the engineers on it. You've got as much stone as you could want; we can make mortar. Give them as many men as they need.'

'Yes, sir.'

'And we need quicker access up on to the top of the Citadel wall from this side. Stairs there and there. Mud-bricks will do. We can use Yamani labour.'

Loy scratched his stubble and made a squiggle on the wax tablet he was carrying, as he acknowledged the order.

'How far have your teams got in locating water sources? There are wells in the lowest levels, aren't there?'

'Apparently, sir. I've got men trying to find them all. The locals aren't co-operating fully – I gather a lot of the wells dug into the bedrock are family secrets. Water is precious here. Every drop of water that falls in the wet season is collected off the roofs – I've never seen gutters like they have here! The engineering beggars belief.'

'You're starting to sound like Rumayn,' the General observed.

Loy recovered his poise. 'There's a covered cistern in the lower city here, sir,' he pointed out, 'that's the main supply for the population. It's used for drinking and washing and livestock so at the moment it's low. It may not last until the Rains even without a siege. Up here in the Citadel is the temple tank. That's uncovered, and the water is sacred, for what that's worth. Pilgrims use it to wash away their sins. It's the biggest remaining source of water in the city – a good job it's up here with us. Most of the drinking water for the priests comes from catchment cisterns on the roof and in the walls, but those are very nearly empty. And then there's the smaller pool here.' He indicated the water they sat next to.

Veraine sucked his teeth as he studied the map. 'We need those wells.'

'You'll have them, sir.'

'What about other ways into the city?'

'As far as we know, sir, there aren't any. The Citadel wall goes right around the temple complex. And behind that building –' he pointed to the Inner Temple over Veraine's shoulder '– the cliff drops away sheer. It's un-scaleable. The whole place is the perfect bolt hole. The problem is that there are too many rats in this particular bolt hole. That's our weakness, sir. Too many people.'

'Well we certainly can't keep them all in the Citadel, not for more than a few days. On the other hand,' Veraine said, making a small gesture with his wrist as if flicking an insect off the back of his hand, 'I was not sent here to protect the population; just the temple and the Malia Shai. Which is why we need that second line of defence. If it comes down to it, we make our stand with the Eighth Host behind it and every other poor bastard outside.'

Loy nodded curtly. His eyes slipped to the water beside them.

'There're fish in that pool, sir,' he said. 'I'd have them caught if I were you. Nothing taints water faster than a dead fish.'

'Good point,' Veraine agreed, then he saw his officer's eyes fix on something beyond him. He twisted round in time to see the Malia Shai descend the last steps from the Inner Temple and walk towards their pool. Both men watched her without speaking or moving. Veraine had no intention of genuflecting to any Yamani.

For her part the priestess looked levelly at them once, without hurry or hesitation, before turning her attention to the water. She was carrying a wooden platter with crumbs on. She put one knee up on the low tank wall and called out softly, 'Whaha, whaha.' It was the cry used by every village girl calling in the livestock to the byre, and the sound plunged Veraine into old memories of dusk and lamplight and the clatter of hooves in a walled yard. The great dark fish in the pool rose to the summons, their slick bodies seething in the water as she bestowed the crumbs among them.

'Any problem with the priests so far?' Veraine asked in a low voice. He assumed she did not speak Irolian but he was not going to risk it.

'Not yet, sir.'

When she had finished she walked around and looked down at the map spread on the stone kerb. Feeling slightly uncomfortable, Veraine rose to his feet and Loy followed his lead.

'Priestess,' he said, politely enough.

'You've been busy planning, General,' she observed. 'Will you be able to defeat the Horse-eaters?'

'We're not intending to battle them, Malia Shai; just to hold the city.'

'And can you do that?' she asked, meeting his gaze squarely. There was no coyness or studied modesty in her attitude, despite the quietness of her voice. 'Is Mulhanabin going to be saved?'

'No city is entirely safe from siege,' he said gently. 'But Mulhanabin is more defensible than most.'

She considered this. 'Why can't you be sure?'

'If the enemy can keep the siege up for long enough, then any stronghold can be starved out in the end, no matter how thick the walls,' he explained. 'And there is always the problem of treachery from within. But we assume the Horse-eaters are not good at being patient, and the desert is against them. Even the Rains should work against them, when they come. My advisers tell me that the plain below becomes a sea of mud in the Wet Season, with quagmires deep enough to drown an army in. You might like to pray that the Rains hit us hard this year, Malia Shai.'

'I don't pray,' she said.

He felt again that stab of uneasiness, as if caught on the wrong foot in a fight. 'Of course not,' he acknowledged with a wry smile. He couldn't read her body language or her expression at all, and he did not like that. But her lips were drawn full and her intense eyes were dark enough not to need kohl to heighten their drama as other Yamani women's did. He did like that.

'You don't speak like a confident man.'

He folded his arms. 'I don't believe in certainties, Malia Shai. But,' he concluded, 'I'm confident that Mulhanabin will not fall. In fact, I'm staking my own life on it.' He looked sideways at Loy, who could not have been following the conversation in the Yamani language and was looking studiously blank. But Veraine knew exactly what thoughts concerning the young priestess the commander was entertaining, and suddenly found himself irritated by it.

'You have orders to pass on to the ranks, Commander,' he said coolly.

Loy snapped a salute and bowed out of the courtyard.

Veraine glanced down at his sketches of the Citadel layout. 'Can you tell me what's inside the *Garbhagria*? I need to know about all the buildings.'

'The *Garbhagria*? You can't include that in your tactics. It's holy ground.'

'Well, I'm sure that will keep the Horse-eaters out.'

She tilted her head and seemed to concede the point. 'It's a big open chamber. There is the altar and my throne and a small room for relics.'

'Is there any access except those doors just inside? Any stairs down, or way out onto the cliff face behind?'

She shook her head slowly. 'No. Not even any windows.'

'What about other rooms in the Inner Temple?'

'There are the chambers of the Malia Shai. My bedroom. The library. Rooms for different rituals and activities. Some of them have windows, but you couldn't climb out. Not unless you could fly.'

'Oh, you do sleep, then?' asked Veraine. 'I would have thought it difficult for you to find the time, in between blighting harvests and destroying cities.' He tried to soften his cynicism with a smile, but he found it hard to see this young woman as a living goddess. The notion was preposterous.

But she took his jocular words seriously, it seemed. 'The goddess Malia is outside time,' she explained, eyes bright under lowered lashes. 'I am eternal and unchanging, I am the dark face of the earth. But I am also incarnate in flesh and time. So I can take action, and grow older, and I do have to sleep. And eat. And all other things.'

'Please don't take offence,' Veraine countered soothingly, though he had no idea whether she had. 'These things are novel to me, and they seem strange.'

She nodded. 'I understand. I'm not offended. You Irolians seem very strange to me, after all.'

He was amused. 'Mm? How so?'

She looked him up and down quite openly. 'Well. You're men, but you grow your hair long. And what you're wearing, it looks like a dress to me. If you were Yamani, those would be things women did. Except that it's a very short dress. It would be against all law and decency.'

Veraine didn't quite manage to stifle his smile. 'The long hair is a warrior tradition; it marks out soldiers. It comes from the time before we were a nation, before we had conquered this land. Then we were always fighting each other, and when you killed a man you took his head and hung it from a pole outside your house. To wear long hair is to show you're not afraid of battle, to defy your enemies to take your head.'

'I see.'

'And we do wear trousers for riding. Otherwise it ... um, rubs.' He raised his eyebrows.

'There, it makes sense when you explain,' she pronounced gravely. 'Anyway, you don't look like a woman.'

Veraine laughed out loud, unable to help himself. Then he was delighted and somehow moved to see his own easy grin raise the faintest of echoes in her face, the ghost of a smile warming her lips. It did not look as if she was used to smiling.

If she wasn't a goddess, some treacherous part of his mind said, she would let me tumble her, eventually. And I would be willing to put effort into that seduction.

Then once again she threw him off balance with a glance, a few innocent words. 'I need to ask you. I've never met your gods, General Veraine. Tell me about them; I might need to recognise them.'

He was nonplussed, but willing enough to indulge her. 'Well ... Irolians worship the Seven,' he said. 'They are gods of sky and fire. We see them above us, in the heavens or on the mountaintops. Shuga is the greatest of them, the sun himself, the celestial king. But soldiers pray to Sothot, who hurls the lightning.' He shrugged. 'We have altars to the moon, and the smithy-fire, and the tempest, and the stars, and the darkness between the stars. You Yamani have a million gods; we make do with seven. It's plenty.'

'Haven't you any goddesses?'

'Some of the Seven have wives. Women pray to them. There's Ay, the goddess of children. And Tesub, who makes mortals fall in love.' He smiled, teasingly. 'The goddesses handle trivial things like that.'

'I see. But your great deities are all male?'

'Our priests are all male,' he said dryly. 'They may be prone to a little bias.'

She stared at him.

Nice eyes, he thought. Nice mouth and arse and ... this is going to be a long couple of months.

'You,' she observed, 'are not reverent. You don't like priests.'

He nodded. 'Do you think Rasa Belit noticed?'

Her solemn expression did not crack, but she looked away sharply for a moment as if in confusion. 'You're not like I was led to expect,' she said. 'People say foul things about Irolian soldiers. Terrible stories. They say when you sacked the palace of King Elendram you hung the eaves with the flayed skins of the inhabitants.'

'I'm not like most soldiers,' he answered, suddenly sober. 'Believe me, most of the stories are true.'

Veraine ran that strange, brief conversation through his mind that night, as he sat alone in his chamber. He suspected he should have treated the Malia Shai with greater formality, but it was difficult when he kept being distracted by her youth, and by the full curve of her unpainted lips. She was so young. And so serious, so intense. It was like being confronted by some precocious child.

With a sigh he dismissed the thought and turned another palm-leaf sheet. Each of the dry, brittle pages under his hand was covered with neat black ink-marks, listing the first rough inventory of the city. He was sitting up late to work, long after his men had been dismissed, and the notes were scattered all around him over the bed-sheet. At least it was a comfortable bed, though irritatingly low to the floor, and the room was pleasant. The walls in this chamber were painted with a frieze of peacocks, now softly illuminated by a dozen little lamps. It was a warm night and Veraine was naked, glad that out here in the desert there were none of the blood-sucking insects that plagued the wetter parts of the Empire.

He bent over the palm-leaves, brushing back behind his ears the stray hair that had escaped from the binding at his nape.

The slightest sound broke the silence of the temple's night. Even as he looked up, Veraine's hand was on the hilt of the short-sword beneath his pillow. It had been the sound of the door falling quietly shut, and someone was in the room with him. Blood jumped in his veins and conflicting emotions warred for supremacy as heart-beat succeeded heartbeat. The first was outrage that anyone could have opened the woven cane door without it creaking and alerting him sooner – if he had realised it possible he would have posted a guard. The second was confusion as he realised that it was the Malia Shai standing in the doorway. And then he thought, I'm bollock-naked, I hope this is what she was expecting, and with that came a thrill of surprised but real pleasure.

She did not appear to be shocked. She looked quickly around the room and then at him, her expression unfathomable but her finger raised to her lips in a gesture of silence. Then, stepping forward into the room, she reached up and tugged loose the end of her head-cloth, bringing the fabric down and discarding it on the floor. Her dark, slightly curling hair tumbled over her shoulders.

Veraine released his grip on the sword-hilt. His mouth seemed to have gone dry.

She moved forward into the room, taking tiny slow steps. As she passed a lamp her hair seemed to flare into life, and Veraine realised that it was the colour of rose-wood, a rare feature among the Yamani people. His abdominal muscles tightened.

In the centre of the room was a mud-brick dais that might have once supported one of the repulsive statues but which now acted as a repository for Veraine's armour and kit. She circled this slowly, throwing quick glances towards him. Eventually she came to a halt facing him and lowered herself to sit on the edge of the platform. She moistened her lips hungrily.

Veraine felt he should say something but could not imagine what. His anticipation was only too obvious to her, the thickening length of cock rising between his thighs making any comment redundant. She smiled the slightest of smiles, making desire stab his guts.

Slowly her hands moved down the length of her body in a languid caress that pressed and explored her breasts and stomach and thighs. Her dark skin stood out against the pale cloth. Like any ordinary Yamani woman, she wore a simple robe over which was wrapped a spiralling length of fabric that gripped her tightly from just beneath her arms to just across her hips, simultaneously constraining and defining the curves of her body. When she reached the loose material of the skirt she began to gather it up, lifting the hem span by span to show the long, slender lines of her legs. She raised the dress until it only just covered her pubic mound; another finger's breadth and he would be able to see the fuzz of her most intimate fur. But she did not raise it, tantalising him with what remained hidden.

'Come here,' he managed to whisper. She ignored the command. Instead she groped behind her on the dais and brought out a slim object; it was Veraine's fighting knife, still in its leather scabbard but free of the belt it normally hung from. She gripped it by the sheath and raised the ivory pommel to brush her cheeks and lips. Then she lowered it between her thighs and pressed the bulbous knob against her mons, first through the cloth and then slipping it up under the hem.

Veraine, kneeling bolt upright, watched as she stirred herself to the boil, sliding the hilt up and down a furrow that he could not quite see. But he read her pleasure in the way her eyes glazed over, and in the soft slackening of her lips, and in the flush that rose to her cheeks. Her other hand flexed and gripped on the edge of the dais while she rolled her hips, grinding her pubis back and forth. The sight made him hard, as rigid as any sword-hilt. His fingers bit into his own thigh muscles.

She was obviously needy and soon roused beyond return, but she rode her orgasm silently, her thighs jerking to an inner beat. Veraine clenched his teeth and felt his breath hissing shallowly between them, savouring every nuance of her spasm and putting it to memory. When she finally opened her eyes again she met his gaze with a heat he scarcely believed. She dropped the slick knife and slipped the top of the sash free from under her arm. As she began to unwind it she rose and started to dance. Her movements were the stylised postures of temple ritual, in which the subtle angles of hand and ankle and head were decreed by rules millennia old, simultaneously abrupt and fluid in their procession. The strangeness of the dance struck Veraine with a force that both repulsed and excited him; he was acutely aware how the curve of her hip and arse were emphasised by each alien motion. The only sound was the drumming of her bare heels on the carpet. Slowly she unravelled the length of cloth, twisting and turning each way, hardly an arm's length from him. He missed no nuance of her movement.

When she was reduced to the crumpled under-dress he caught her round the waist and pulled her up against him, hard enough to let her know how much he had appreciated the display, and hard enough to demonstrate that he could tolerate no further teasing. Her back flexed under his hands; she felt lithe and yet infinitely fragile against his own rigid frame. Her eyes, staring into his, were huge. He could see the sheen of moisture on her lip and neck, the legacy of her masturbation, and he stooped to taste the perspiration on her throat, using his tongue to draw out a low cry of arousal from her. Her hair smelled of the incense that burned everywhere in the temple, but her skin smelled of honey.

Still holding her in one arm, he slid the other hand up

under her dress, up the inside of her thighs. They were soft as silk. His fingers found the coarser pelt at the junction of her thighs and she nestled eagerly upon his palm. Gently he probed further, and it was with unutterable relief that he found that his fingers encountered no obstacle, no obstacle at all. They slid easily into the rich hot wetness there. She was tight and muscular, and he could feel the pulse thumping through her loins. With two fingers he entered and prised wider that hole. She wriggled on him, trying to drive him deeper. His hand was soaked in her juices.

Slowly he withdrew, ignoring her whimpers of frustration, his expression not quite cruel. He lifted his slippery fingers to his nostrils, breathing in the mingled scents of her sex – the sweet musk of her natural moisture and the sharper tang of her orgasm. Then he smeared that wetness on her soft lips and kissed it off again, tasting her, deep and unhurried. She yielded under lips and tongue with total abandon, and while he explored her, his hands gathered up the coarse cotton dress.

When they broke off to gasp for air, he contrived with one pull to wriggle her free of the robe and she was abruptly coppery and naked under his eyes. He ran his palms over her from breasts to hips, entranced and ravenous. The tight sash had flattened the sweetness of her curves and now, unbound, she was more delicious than he could have believed. Between her breasts and around her navel, barely visible against her skin tone, delicate henna spirals traced paths that his tongue was thirsting to follow.

'You're beautiful,' he murmured, though his voice was thick with lust. For the first time, she did look like a goddess.

She too stared down at their nearly touching bodies,

and reached in to take his pole-hard cock in her hand. Her grip was frustratingly soft, with a gentleness he could only interpret as inexperience, so he closed his hand around hers and showed her how hard to squeeze. When she improvised on this by biting his earlobe as well, his growl of desire nearly choked him.

He lifted her up and laid her on the bed, desperate to enter her, his cock throbbing with a savage impatience. She stretched out beneath his gaze, reaching up to him. He wanted more than anything to dive into that embrace, but he stooped first to suckle on each of the nipples – so dark they were nearly black – that jutted from the glorious mounts of her tits. She moaned with pleasure and knotted her fingers in his hair, undulating beneath him, and with that he could not bear it any longer. Parting her thighs wide with the weight of his own, he entered her sex with his whole inexorable length.

Heat fused them. The warmth of the night, the warmth of their naked skins, the warmth of their flesh where it joined in wet darkness. Veraine felt her arms wrap around his ribs and her legs twine about him, her bare feet on the back of his calves. He laid his cheek against hers and, his eyes closed and his face buried in her hair, he thrust into her to the rhythm of her gusting breath and the moans that spilled from her throat. Even past his own straining muscles and galloping heartbeat he felt her tighten up to orgasm, her whole body finally locking against the thunderous current that swept over her and through her. Triumphantly he leaped after her into that dark river and let himself be carried away.

When he opened his eyes the afterglow was fading, sweat was tickling his jawline and he was very much awake. He stared at the palm-leaf page resting in front of his nose and groaned, 'Oh no.' The sticky wetness beneath him was his spilled semen, but there was no slender body between his own and the mounded cushions. The sheet was rucked up under his hands. He raised his head disbelievingly and looked about him. The last of the lamps were burning low, but by their shuddering illumination he became certain that there was no Malia Shai in the room, neither were her clothes scattered on the floor where impatience had discarded them. His weapons lay undisturbed on the dais where Arioc had left them that evening. There was no scent upon his cramped hands except his own. She had never been in the room.

Veraine rolled over onto his back and raked his fingers through his scalp. The dream of ecstasy, so vivid at the time, was an ebbing tide that had washed him up on the shores of reality with nothing but a spent cock as proof of the pleasure he had taken. He pressed his hands against his eyeballs, but it did not dispel the harsh truth.

For a long time he could do little but stare at the ceiling and the little green geckos stitching their way across its shadowed expanse.

4 Jilaya

'The library, General,' Rasa Belit said, waving one hand
at the room before them. 'For whatever use it may be to
you. I don't suppose that you can read?'

'He can,' Veraine answered, jerking his head at the
third man.

Rumayn was rigid with excitement, like a leashed
hound shown a deer. 'What have you got in here?' he
asked in a husky voice.

'Temple records; the annals of the Yamani kings;
architecture; geometry; astrology; poetry. Gifts from
every corner of the world, in twenty different languages.
Copies of the sacred scriptures and legends of our people.
Medical texts. A thousand years of history; that's what's
in this room.' The priest's litany seemed to rise in the
dim chamber like smoke. From every one of the shelves
that covered the walls, palm-leaf books and parchment
scrolls peered out from under their patina of dust at the
men standing below.

Rumayn made a small incoherent noise and lurched
forward among the stacks, as if unable to articulate any
meaningful request. The priest and the soldier watched
him with matched airs of cynical detachment as he took
down book after book and concertinaed them out to read
the arabesques within.

'This is the not the greatest of the temple archives,
but it is one of the oldest,' Rasa Belit remarked. 'Of course
you Irolians burned the great collections at Margaybi
and Halghat.'

'That was a long time ago.'

Rasa Belit snorted. 'That was barely yesterday! You can't imagine the depths of history, any more than you can imagine the wastes of time stretching before us. You hardly remember your own past. How could you? Your people couldn't even read and write before we taught them, General. Did you know that?'

'I knew it.' Veraine was not going to be riled.

Rasa Belit kept his voice low and even, but he did not soften the stinging edge as he said, 'It was like giving language to apes. Do you know what the Irolian people were, General, before they stole civilisation from the bloodied remnants of the people they butchered? Before they learned to write, and build, and farm? They were Horse-eaters. They lived in tents and ate their meat raw and slept with their animals. Those are your brothers out there in the desert.' He sniggered.

'Would you like us to let them in?' Veraine asked.

The priest sucked his teeth. The derision did not leave his eyes. He clapped his hands, and a yellow-robed acolyte scurried in from the corridor.

'Fetch Muth,' instructed Rasa Belit.

Veraine walked slowly through the library, pausing only to look out of the windows for possible access. It was not a large room, compared to others in the temple, but it certainly held more books than he had ever contemplated existing.

'I've called the priestess Muth to show you the remaining rooms of the Inner Temple,' Rasa Belit said, reappearing at his elbow. 'She's responsible for overseeing the upkeep of the chambers. She's well qualified to guide you on your tour, General; whereas I have duties elsewhere, you understand, of a ritual nature. Our sacred task cannot falter even at times such as these.'

'The gods forfend. You've been doing this for a thou-

sand years, high priest; don't let me get in the way.'
Veraine's willingness to let the other man go was
entirely sincere.

Again those lips narrowed. 'Far longer than a thousand years, General. That's only as far back as our writ-
ings go. There was worship here before the first letter
was ever scratched in clay – before there ever was a
temple in Mulhanabin. On the bare rock, when man was
first created, he kneeled here to pray and make sacrifice.'

Veraine raised his eyes to the ceiling, saying, 'I know;
I was told. You believe that the human race was created
here.'

Rasa Belit shook his head coldly. 'Not the human race,
Irolian. You've been misinformed. The universe.'

Veraine decided that remaining silent would be
politest.

'Before man, before the world, before the gods, there
was only the divine essence, and it chose to dance. To
dance is to take form, to step, and to step requires that
there must be a firm place to set the foot. Thus the earth
came into being. The hill of Mulhanabin is the first
footfall of God.'

The soldier blinked, trying to take it in. 'I see.'

'That's why this place is sacred. All matter was spun
from nothingness at this place. It is the centre of the
universe. And this is where the last of the earth will
stand when the dance of destruction is danced and the
world is unmade. Everything will end here too. That's
why the pious send their ashes here to be scattered upon
the hill. That's why the Malia Shai is born here every
lifetime.'

'You've lost me now. What has it to do with her?'

Rasa Belit made an impatient gesture. 'Doesn't your
councillor talk to you? I've wasted my breath upon him.
What are the gods, Irolian?'

He shook his head. 'The gods are the gods. How can I say more than that?'

'The gods are pieces of the divine essence. They are facets of the ultimate reality, that's all. When the world came into being the gods took form with it. They are manifestations of finite parts of the godhead. They can be named and described; yet the divine itself is beyond name and form. They are tied to the world. They are separated from their true nature, which is the totality of existence. You follow, General?'

'Perhaps.'

'The goddess Malia craves to return to the godhead, so she must sever her links with the world. She must become *sunyata*; void, emptiness. So she has chosen to undergo three hundred and thirty-three fleshly incarnations, to purge and to prove herself. In these lives she must not give in to passion, because it's the chains of passion that tie us to the world. If she can achieve this then she will be reunited with the infinite, and for the earth there will be no more famine or flood or drought, because Malia ceases to be a part of the world.'

'I see,' said Veraine, with the expression of someone presented with a novel and potentially indigestible dish at dinner. 'Has she a long way to go?'

'Don't hold your breath,' said the priest, with a thin smile.

A woman walked into the library, and it was like the entry of a small sun into the twilit space. She was broad shouldered and fat with it, and the ample swathes of her yellow robes seemed to glow. Only her face detracted from the solar impression. The expression on it was sour, and her cheek was marred by two large and hairy moles. She bowed to Rasa Belit, and from the grunt she made this cost her some discomfort.

'This is the priestess Muth,' he said, 'highest among

the priestesses, who will show you the rest of the rooms. You will excuse me, General.'

Muth looked at the younger man coldly, with no pretence of politeness.

'You can stay here, Rumayn, if you want,' Veraine sighed. Rumayn, who had not even looked up from the documents, nodded enthusiastically.

'What can I show you?' asked Muth, when they had left the room.

'I need to see the layout of the Inner Temple, and I need to look in any room with any access to the outside walls.'

Muth shrugged massively and led the way. They did not linger, nor did it take too long. The main corridor of the building was an inverted U-shape with the *Garbhagria* nestled in the cup. The rooms on the outside of the curve backed right on to the edge of the cliff, and the windows were mostly too narrow for anyone to climb through. The sense of age in this part of the temple complex was palpable; everything from the raw rock floor worn smooth in the doorways to the blistered plaster behind which colonies of bats nestled and squeaked, spoke of the dead weight of centuries. There were no domestic or comfortable rooms. The priests' own chambers were in the Outer Temple; this was a place set apart for the gods. Shrines to the deities associated with Malia – or perhaps deities who were themselves aspects of that great goddess; Veraine had only a vague grasp of the vast and labyrinthine hierarchy of Yamani spirituality and could not tell – predominated; most other rooms seemed empty. The wind at this end of the building moaned constantly at the unshuttered windows.

Eventually they came to a curtained doorway. Muth stopped outside and seemed to hesitate.

'What's this one?' Veraine asked.

'The Malia Shai's chamber,' she growled. She had a deep voice for a woman.

Veraine felt a prick of curiosity. 'Is she in?'

Muth swung her head. 'Not at the moment. She is asperging the gateways.'

'Then there's no reason I shouldn't look,' he said, and lifted the curtain.

He was not sure what he had expected, but the actuality stopped him dead in his tracks. The room was large and high ceilinged, and it totally dwarfed the contents. Just under the central window was a narrow straw pallet with one sheet, and next to that on the floor a single lamp and a wooden platter. There was nothing else in the room. Veraine looked around at the walls. They were grey with the indefinable grime of years, and completely featureless. He walked across and looked at the platter. It held a loaf of bread, a frond of some herb, and a clay cup of water. The meal did not look like enough to feed a child. He thought about the Malia Shai lying on that thin mattress and whatever it was that had knotted up his guts gave them a sharp tug.

He went to the window and stared out. The view was as he had expected from here; a sheer fall to the scrub-speckled desert plain hundreds of feet below. Birds flew past beneath him. Not too far distant was another dusty cliff face; the main plateau of which Mulhanabin formed the lone outpost. It was only a few hours' walk away, but separated from his window by an immeasurable gulf of air. That plateau was his bane because at the base, so his scouts informed him, slow springs leaked from the cliff face and fed pockets of vegetation.

He should be thinking about these things, about strategy and resources, not about some half-crazy Yamani priestess. He had glimpsed her only once since the night of his dream. He had been riding out past the tank of

81

sacred water in the middle of the Citadel. It was a large pool and had been surrounded by pilgrims all jostling for position. The Malia Shai had been wading into the pool, chanting, with arms upraised. He didn't know what it had been about, but he had seen the way the wet cloth of her skirt clung to her thighs and it had brought back the force of his dream with dizzying power. He'd had to hurry away.

'Why do you make her live like this?' he asked, turning back into the room.

'What?' Muth said.

'You priests live in plenty. You eat, you drink...' He gestured at the pitiful accoutrements on the floor. 'But she...'

'She's the Malia Shai. Not a priestess.'

'I wouldn't keep a kennel slave like this.'

Muth grinned slowly, revealing stained teeth. 'Your compassion is touching, General. I wonder if you would care so much if she were old and ugly.'

'Do they get to grow old?' he said sharply.

Amusement glittered in Muth's eyes. 'Sometimes. She might, this time round. Or maybe not. She's still young enough to give into temptation. There's a lot of it about, even for the Malia Shai.'

For a moment Veraine was silent. Then he asked, 'And what happens if she fails?'

She smiled poisonously. 'You know, I bet you were thinking, "I wonder if her cunt-lips have been sealed." I bet you thought that the first time you set eyes on her. Well, they haven't. Doesn't that please you?'

'You have a filthy mind, for a priestess,' he said coldly.

'Oh, wrong again, General. When they sew you up, it doesn't change the way you think. It just means you can't do much about the feelings you have.' She looked him up and down lingeringly, as if to prove her point.

'Now the Malia Shai, she's different. Unlike us poor priestesses, she doesn't have a dirty impulse in her bones. Or any other kind, come to that.'

'What do you mean?'

'I mean, she doesn't feel anything, soldier. You could plant the imperial standard in her slit and she'd just blink at you.'

The hair crawled on Veraine's spine. 'What are you talking about? Belit said she had to stay a virgin all her life.'

Muth laughed out loud at that. 'A virgin? I'll bet he didn't. The Malia Shai has to reject passion if she is to ascend, that's what the Rasa will have told you. Not just lechery, soldier – there you go, thinking about sex again – what's wrong with you? *Any* passion, General; greed, fear, pain, anger – and pity, and affection, and joy. All are types of desire that can attach you to the world. They're traps and illusions. You have to let them go if you want to escape the bonds of Earth. Very hard for most of us, but she has an advantage, being a goddess. Her will is greater than ours ever could be.'

He did not bother to hide his derision. 'You think I'm going to believe that?'

'You think you know everything, don't you? You're not a priest of the Malia Shai, soldier; you haven't seen what we have seen. I was there the last time she died and the priests went looking for her new incarnation down in the city. She didn't cry, even when they took her from her mother. She has never cried, or been afraid, or lost her temper. That was how they knew who she was.'

'I find that impossible to believe.'

'Well, you might,' she said smugly.

'There's no such thing as a child who doesn't cry. Not unless it's witless.'

'No natural child. The Malia Shai is not a human being. She's a goddess on a spiritual journey.' She smirked. 'We assist where we can.'

'Oh yes? How?'

'We teach her the illusory nature of pain and self-pity.'

'I see.' The urge to strike the gloating cruelty from Muth's face was rising in him like a tide.

'It's our holy calling.'

Veraine had to turn his face away.

'Does it trouble you, General?'

'It disgusts me,' he told her, his voice flat.

'You do surprise me. I thought that an Irolian soldier would be on familiar terms with the many causes of pain.'

He didn't reply.

'The Malia Shai isn't like you and me,' Muth said serenely. 'You can't treat her like a normal girl.'

'And what happens if she doesn't keep the standards you've set?' he repeated. 'What if she acts like a human woman?'

'What is it to you?'

'Indulge me,' Veraine said, his throat tight. 'I'm searching for enlightenment too.'

'Well, if she's failed then in that incarnation she has no further purpose on the earth. She must complete the allotted number of lifetimes in a state of purity and detachment, and if she's wasted her chance, then it's better for her to die and be reborn. She's walled up alive, usually. It only takes a few days for her to die, but she has time to meditate on her next attempt.'

Veraine decided it was a good thing that years in the army had instilled in him the self-discipline to refrain from striking the woman. Just the sound of her voice, gloating and thick, made his skin crawl. 'I've seen enough,' he said flatly. 'Let me take up no more of your time.'

The Malia Shai pulled her dress over her head and handed it to the priest waiting at her side. He bowed low over the garment, folded it carefully and then backed into his place in the circle as she, naked, stepped carefully over the lip of the bronze basin and kneeled down in the tepid water.

The circle of twenty priests began to intone, in a soft murmur, the prescribed prayer for the ablutions of the living goddess. She listened to the rising and falling cadences without interest, as she had listened to them at sunset every day of her life. The water was pleasantly cool after the heat of the day, but she hardly noticed the pleasurable sensation of its touch on her thighs and sex, any more than she had noticed the burning of the sun on her skin, or the ache of her muscles as she had stood for an hour, completely motionless, before the altar. She looked at the faces that ringed her. They were as blank as masks, only the men's lips moving in the chant.

She looked down at her knees in the clear water, and slowly began to sluice the liquid up over her belly and breasts. A small cloth of white silk aided her in her cleansing. Her dark skin was gleaming in the light of the lamps all around her bath, and when wet it reflected the golden flames. She was in no hurry. This was a time of day when she was able to let her thoughts run idly free. There was no hymn for her to sing, no god to invoke. Only the ceaseless watching of the men around her, and the cool caress of the water.

Her nipples hardened as she wet them. There was no break in the murmured praises, no flicker of interest on their faces as she rubbed the cloth over each firm orb. She had no way of telling whether they had noticed, or whether they cared. She wondered about that. The priests were all eunuchs, but they had been emasculated after they had reached manhood, as no children of any sort were permitted within the Temple. So they had presumably known all the pangs of adolescent desire, and perhaps some of them had known what it was like to satiate that desire in a woman's body. What did they feel now, watching her bathe? Did they remember what it was to lust?

She slopped the water over her shoulder, feeling it run down her back. The silk clung to her skin. Perhaps long familiarity with the rite had bred indifference in them, she thought. Perhaps they had seen her tits and arse so often that it meant no more to them than some carving on a wall, passed every day with such regularity that it became invisible. Her body was not that of a normal woman; not a private thing of mystery and potential. It was holy, and a public object of veneration. It was a tool of temple ritual.

She reached between her legs and smoothed the silk up and down her sex. What would an entire man do, if he were to see such a thing? She knew what a god would do. If the Sun Lord was here, or the Thunder Bull, or Yami the god of Darkness and Fear, any of them would be stricken with desire and they would seize and ravish her – if they could. There were a hundred myths to tell her so. If she sought in her mind, she could remember every incident, every pursuit and struggle, every wooing and every surrender. All gods are one God, and she knew the history of each deity intimately. But the memories of her mortal lives were blurred and unclear; like her present incarnation, the days ran into one another without incident or differentiation. She could not remember what it was like to lie with a human man. She had hardly even met with any in this life, not counting the priests, until the Irolian general.

General Veraine, she pondered. What would he do if he saw her like this? Her hand, delving between her thighs, lost its languid rhythm. She pictured his face; the intent dark eyes, the sudden warmth of his smile when it broke through that serious mask. Would he grin at her if he saw her naked? Or would his lips set into that thin, hard line? What would he say? She could not begin to guess.

What would he be like if he took her in his arms and laid her beneath him? He would never be as good as the gods she had copulated with, she was certain; he certainly was not as beautiful as them. There was that long Irolian nose for a start. Nor would their mating be as perfect, as fiery, as effortlessly erotic. There could not be that blaze of spiritual ecstasy she knew when two divine essences merged momentarily, god and goddess, each perfect in every movement and every word. If Veraine bedded her it would be clumsy and coarse like all mortal sex, an exchange of fumbling and confusion and sweaty contortion. He would not carry her up into the heavens, he would lie upon her like a dead weight, crushing her flesh against her bones. It would be more akin to two animals rutting in a field than anything else.

The Malia Shai suddenly became aware that she had fallen still as she kneeled, her lips parted and the hand that lingered between her thighs pressed firmly against her pubic mound. With the slightest shiver she managed to resume her washing. She detected no change in the priests' demeanour, but that did not mean they had noticed nothing.

Despite resolving to contemplate the nature of the void in an unhurried fashion, she found that she finished her ablutions rather quickly. She crushed a handful of aromatic, astringent leaves in her hands, rubbed them through her scalp and bent forward to rinse the sap clear in the water. The curve of her back glistened in the lamplight. She flipped her long hair back as she stood and then stepped out from the basin. The water cascaded down her tawny body onto the bare stone floor.

A priest was instantly at her side, wrapping a robe around her slender figure. The cloth clung to her wet skin. Four more priests stooped to lift the bronze basin. The water she had washed in had started in the rooftop cisterns and now would be poured out into the public tank in the Citadel, thus maintaining the pool's sanctity. Every drop of water she drank or used had fallen direct from the heavens, and now that it had touched her it would, she knew, make soil barren as surely as if it were brine, but for the pilgrims who bathed there it would wash away the accumulated worldly cares of a thousand lifetimes.

'I have cleansed myself of all desire,' she said, as she said every day over that water. 'So shall you be cleansed.' The words were in a dialect so ancient that common people would scarcely be able to understand them, devised in an age when temples were still open to the sky and the rich earth was pierced only by wooden ploughshares.

The priests chanted in unison the ancient response, 'And so shall we be made free.'

Rumayn found the General that evening, staring gloomily out of the headquarters window and slowly running his knifepoint through the thick plaster of the wall next to him. The deep lines scored through the fresco, mutilating a delicate painting of blighted wheat, testified that he had been engaged in the practice for some time. He did not turn when Rumayn entered.

'What's happened?' Rumayn whispered to Arioc, who stood in attendance just inside the door.

'I have no idea,' the youth shrugged, the crisp white linen of his tunic riding his bronzed muscles.

Rumayn frowned. There was a livid bruise on Arioc's cheek and a bloody scab on his lower lip. 'Has he hit you?'

Arioc cast the shorter man a look of undisguised contempt. 'No,' he said, and that was enough to close the subject.

'Is there something wrong, General?' the adviser asked, coming cautiously up to stand at his side.

Veraine seemed to rouse himself out of a daydream. 'No.' He sighed down his nose. 'I was thinking about the Imperial Virtues. You know?'

'Of course, General. Loyalty, piety, pride. Courage in warriors, ambition in men, compassion in women. Personally I think a little of each is not a bad mixture in anyone, but I know that most people won't see it like that.'

'You're right, Rumayn. You do talk too much.' Veraine smiled bleakly, adding, 'I was wondering, could indifference ever be a virtue?'

Rumayn raised his eyebrows. 'Indifference? I don't see how. Fortitude, perhaps. But we only have one life, General, and it's a short one at that for most of us. We have to shine.'

Veraine nodded, though his expression was far away.

'I was thinking, General, that I would go into Mulhanabin tonight. Loy has been checking up on the facilities for the men. He says there is a silk-house just a few streets down that would do for officers. A bit expensive,

89

he says, but clean and you get quality for your money. I was going to try it out tonight. I thought, if you were interested, you might want to come too?'

Veraine snapped his fingers. 'That sounds like a very good idea.' He raised his voice, a little smile pulling at the corner of his mouth. 'What about you, Arioc? Want to visit a silk-house tonight?'

The handsome chariot-driver shook his head. 'No, thank you, sir.' His dark eyes were unclouded by embarrassment.

Veraine nodded, unsurprised. 'Let's go then, Rumayn.'

Rather to Rumayn's alarm, Veraine refused to commandeer a full bodyguard and enlisted only Captain Sron for their recreational trip into the night. The three men walked down into the city armed with no more than the officers' own swords. The establishment they sought was easily found; light streaming into the narrow street from an open door illuminated also a swathe of red silk that fluttered from the lintel. Two Yamani men hung about in the doorway, arms folded over their chests, but they pulled themselves back out of the way after a moment's startled scrutiny of the visitors. Veraine took the lead up a narrow flight of stairs, encouraged by the sound of music spilling down from above.

He emerged into a large room, warm and humid and perfumed. A swift glance around took in a panorama of low couches with men sprawled or sat upon them, rather more young women attending the men, brass lamps, polished mahogany chessboards, a trio of seated musicians, rich embroidered drapes, all wrapped in a haze of blue smoke. The glitter and the colour was Yamani to the core, but the scent and the sound and the atmosphere of the place – musk and hashish, vibrant music and pleasant chatter, the open proffering of sexual pleasure – was nothing like the temple at all. Praise all the gods, thought Veraine.

Several young women, their long hair unbound, started forward from their places near the door, where they had seemingly been waiting with no other intent than to welcome him. But when they saw who it was that had entered, they hesitated and fell back. Veraine wondered whether it had been the best idea to bring the hatchet-faced Sron, whose right eyebrow was bisected by a thick white scar and who would never look anything but menacing.

Rumayn spread his hands appeasingly and smiled. 'Ladies!'

Several of the clients on the couches turned to look at the new visitors and a ripple of unease ran visibly through the room.

'May we be seated?' Veraine asked the girl nearest to him, as gently as he could. Her eyes were huge with consternation, but she managed to force a smile.

Then another woman walked across the floor straight up to them, inclined her head and spoke directly at the General. 'Honoured guests, welcome to the House of Jilaya.' She spread her hands gracefully. 'I am Jilaya. The comforts of this house are yours tonight.'

'We're delighted to hear it,' Veraine replied. 'Thank you.'

'An evening in the public room here will cost you six silver moons apiece. We serve delicacies spiced for the palate and the soul; our pleasure is to stimulate the appetite and inspire the senses. If you should require a private room to satisfy more demanding requirements, there will be an additional charge; ask any of my girls.'

'That will be fine,' said Veraine, as Rumayn winced at the price and Sron, who could not follow any of the conversation, looked blank. He dug into the pouch at his belt and paid the madam for all three of them. She smiled at him as her fingers closed over the coins. Although she was, he guessed, slightly older than him she was still good looking and had a wide, appealing mouth. She reminded him of someone, but he did not have time to pursue that thought.

'This way,' she said, and led them through the shoals of couches to an empty one near the open space in the very centre of the room.

'Loy wasn't wrong about this place,' Rumayn murmured in Irolian. 'Have you seen the clients? This is for people who only count the gold coins.'

'Which is why Loy isn't here himself,' Sron laughed, low in his throat. 'I saw him head off to the House of the White Goat hours ago.'

'Well, they'll have to close the place down once he's finished,' Veraine smiled, 'to give the girls time to recover.'

Jilaya swept her hand over their couch, which was big enough to accommodate them with room to spare. At her signal several of her girls duly appeared, and the three men found themselves, as they sat down, the centre of a small flurry of attention. Sron was joined on the cushions by two young women – presumably operating on the theory that there was safety in numbers – while the superior officer and the civilian adviser merited merely one smiling houri apiece. Veraine turned to take stock of the one who had materialised against his shoulder. She was very small, but, in that way that Yamani women seemed to have, her slenderness was offset by a curvaceousness of hip and breast that was quite enchanting.

'What's your name?' he asked.

'Vandi.' She faked shyness rather well. 'Would you eat,

lord?' She indicated a tray of sweetmeats that was being presented by yet another girl kneeling in front to him. The array included silvered almonds, paralysingly sweet cakes of pistachio, honeyed fennel seeds and tiny leaf parcels decorated with slivers of fruit peel and petals carved from nuts, that looked appetising but were actually *paan*, a mild narcotic commonly used across the Empire. Veraine did not much like it because it stained the teeth red. He picked out a syrupy dough ball no bigger than a knuckle bone and waved the tray away.

'Would you like a water-pipe, lord?' Vandi asked.

'No.' He put the sweet between her lips and watched as she ate it. 'I had something more energetic in mind.'

She slid one hand up his thigh as she licked her lips. It brushed his sword-hilt. 'Are you going to wear that all night?'

Smiling, he unclasped his sword-belt and tucked the weapon away at his feet. Vandi giggled with satisfaction and went back to tracing playful patterns up his bare leg. She wore her hair loose and uncovered; something no respectable Yamani girl would do in public. In fact the only woman in the room who affected a headcloth was Jilaya herself, and hers was little but a token veil of silk designed not to conceal anything but to mark her out as a woman of rank. Vandi's hair was thick and as dark as the kohl around her eyes. Her dress, in contrast, was a pale lemon silk and, he noted, woven of so sheer a material as to be almost completely transparent. This seemed, he decided after a confirmatory glance around the room, to be the uniform of Jilaya's girls. Although the rainbow-hued dresses were worn in the normal style, even the double or triple layers of sash-over-shift did not conceal the coppery flesh beneath. And the single layer of the skirt, he was delighted to see, did not hide at all Vandi's nest of curls.

A very young girl, barely more than a child and ornamented with ankle-bracelets made up of scores of tiny silver bells, bowed gracefully in front of them and offered him a tray of drinks. Veraine chose a brass goblet of wine, took a few sips and then amused himself by brushing the cold metal against Vandi's nipples. He could see as well as feel them harden. Vandi giggled again.

'I hope I am not tickling you, lord,' she said, her dextrous fingers stroking further and further up the inside of his thigh.

'No, I'm not ticklish,' he said. 'Not there.'

'Oh. That's good. I just thought I felt you shiver, lord. Shall I stop?'

He hissed a wry acknowledgement of her talents. 'No . . . I find it quite pleasant. Please carry on.'

She was still engaged in the dextrous exploration of his groin when the trio of musicians in the corner suddenly fell quiet, and the cessation of noise distracted Veraine where none of their melodies could have. He looked round the room, aware once more of the presence of others. The buzz of conversation seemed to grow louder. Sron, he noticed, was flat on his back with his head cradled in the lap of one girl, while the other fed him dates. Rumayn had his companion sat in his lap and was clasping her tightly, all the better to squeeze her breasts. Veraine was pleased for his sake that the girl was quite plump and that she kept wriggling pleasurably. But some of the regular clients were sitting up or easing themselves to their elbows with an expectant air. Veraine's gaze was drawn into the centre of the room, where there was an open space free of couches but circumscribed by a number of tall brass lamp-holders. Jilaya was currently walking that perimeter, carefully lighting each lamp in turn. As she bent over the flames the uncovered ends of her hair turned from umber to mahogany, and Veraine felt his heart turn over.

'Ah, you're feeling quite lively tonight, lord,' said Vandi, whose hand was by now on his cock and who could hardly have failed to notice.

'What's happening?'

She eased her fingers under his balls and rippled the fingertips experimentally. 'Some of the girls are going to perform a story-dance,' she murmured. 'Our clients expect entertainment. You're a big handful, lord.'

Veraine made himself more comfortable by putting his right arm around her and slipping his palm over the curve of her breast. She nestled in closer to him. The musicians, after conferring, struck up again, drum and flute and some lap-held stringed instrument the General couldn't identify. The drummer also began to sing, though there were no words to his ululation. Jilaya finished with the lamps and stepped back out of the lit area.

Her place was taken at once by a tall woman dressed in a tight silk sheath that had been put on wet; it clung to every line of her body. She raised her arms over her head, tilted back her chin and began to dance, her feet hardly moving but her body undulating with serpentine flexibility.

The caressing of Vandi's fingers was sending little bolts of pleasure up Veraine's spine and this new apparition did little to soothe him. His cock was already pushing up hard against the cloth that constrained it. 'What is she supposed to be doing?' he murmured.

Vandi glanced at the tall dancer then snuggled her chin onto his shoulder and said, 'She's a tree. This is the story of Goppi getting lost in the forest. Do you know about Goppi?'

He did. Goppi was a folk-figure who was the subject of every Yamani risqué story and the butt of almost every dirty joke. Eternally naïve, she blundered into unlikely sexual encounters over and over again with an expression of pained surprise.

'That girl is the forest,' Vandi breathed into his ear. 'She's dancing the trees. Do you see?'

It took concentration, but he could see it. Not precisely imitative, the dance somehow suggested the swaying of branches, the slender pillars of the tree trunks. But it was a lot easier to see only the way the transparent silk clung wetly to the dancer's breasts and arse, to her firmly toned legs and the taut convexity of her belly. Her nipples were big and hard, rubbed into alertness by the moist cloth. She moved with a confident sensuality that made Veraine's cock dance too.

'It's night,' Vandi translated as the dancer's hand described the moon rising over the trees. 'The forest is very quiet.'

The tree-dancer grew still. Veraine could feel his breath pulsing all the way down to the root of his cock.

'Here's Goppi. She's lost in the forest.' Another dancer emerged into the centre of the room. This one moved quickly, her every action suggesting nervousness and confusion. Her small breasts were high and pouting under the same wet silk. 'She was looking after the cows and one has strayed into the forest. She doesn't want to go back to her mother without it. But she has forgotten the way back, and it has grown dark. She's afraid of the forest.'

Goppi circled the tree, looking this way and that but failing to find any comfort. Eventually, exhausted, she leaned against the tree. The taller dancer undulated against her, but Goppi did not seem to notice. She rested her head on the tree's breasts.

'She's tired. She lies down to sleep.'

Goppi slid very slowly down the other woman's body to the carpeted floor, rolling over onto her back in a pool of her own dark tresses. Once she had grown still, the tree-dancer took a step back and lowered her arms, twisting sideways, and her legs, suddenly splayed in the exaggerated step, split the fabric of her dress to the thighs.

'In the forest is a tiger-spirit.' Vandi's voice was a tickling murmur in his ear as her palm rubbed over his cock. 'He's hunting.'

The tall woman, a forest no longer, prowled among trees that the audience only saw in their mind's eye. Her movements were sensual and catlike, but they also conveyed a masculine menace. Veraine was forced to admire her skill, though half his mind was more concerned with Vandi's talents.

'He sees Goppi asleep.' This comment was unnecessary, as with lightning speed the tiger-dancer turned from pacing the floor to looming over the supine form of the sleeping girl. She fell on her, breast to breast, catching her weight at the last moment on toe-tips and hands. Goppi's eyes shot open in an agony of fear. The tiger-spirit bared her teeth.

Goppi convulsed, and in a single movement had slid from under her assailant and was lunging for the edge of the circle. But she did not reach it. A supernaturally strong hand seized her and pulled her back, bringing the two dancers into a clasp. The tiger gripped her fragile garment at the throat and ripped it from her, leaving her naked to the avid view of the audience. The pieces of torn silk fell to the floor. Still Goppi was not prepared to submit without a struggle and she fled again, and once again the tiger leaped and seized her. The two dancers began an extraordinary interplay that was partly dance and partly an undisguised display of sex. Every time the tiger-dancer had the other woman in her arms she pressed up against her, crushing her victim's round arse against her groin, thrusting against her thighs, mouthing her breasts. Goppi fought, but her strength was insufficient to resist her bestial attacker. The tiger bit her throat and squeezed her breasts and groped with inhibited directness between her thighs, while Goppi twisted and shook and mimed her distress. Eventually the tiger flung the naked girl flat upon the carpet and straddled her, pinning her wrists beside her head. Goppi arched her back, but this only brought her unprotected nipples up to the tiger's cruel lips. Goppi gasped and grew still.

Without releasing her, the tiger bent and nuzzled her body, then began to lick the whole length of her torso. Her rough tongue left glistening trails on the abused flesh. The tiger's arse twisted in the air as if her tail was lashing. Then the music and singing stopped, all but the drum, and the beat of that drum carried on as the tiger-dancer spread her victim's thighs, lowered herself between them and began to thrust. It was a parody of ravishment, the tiger's penis invisible and non-existent, but the drumbeat pounded on and the tiger's arse flexed and clenched, and if there was a slack cock in the audience Veraine could not believe it belonged to any man who was not a eunuch. Vandi's hand gripped his own shaft like she was trying to hold it down.

The drumbeats built to a crescendo, the tiger-spirit threw back its head and spasmed, and suddenly Goppi cried out. In the wake of her cry there was silence. For a moment the tableau was frozen, then the tiger dancer bowed her head, rose up and slunk away, hips rolling in feline contentment. There was a smattering of applause, but most of the men were too wrapped up in themselves to praise the performers.

Veraine glanced sideways and saw that Rumayn was sat very still, a look of terrible concentration on his face. Veraine was instantly certain that under the rumple of silk skirts, the Irolian had managed to slip his cock up the wet hole of the girl in his lap. But now she stopped wriggling, and the immobility must have been an agonising strain. Veraine's own member felt like a lead cosh. He looked back at the stage. Goppi had not moved.

Slowly it dawned on the audience that there was something wrong. The Goppi-dancer still lay with her legs splayed, her thighs slightly raised. Veraine was close enough to see not just the sheen of sweat on her belly and the flush of blood in her cheeks, but also the wetness coating her thighs. Her breasts were heaving and they looked swollen. Her eyes were half-lidded, as if in pain. It was not pain. Helplessly, her hands slid over her hips to her groin.

'Somebody put the girl out of her misery,' Sron called. He spoke in Irolian and it was doubtful anyone understood a word, but the gist was obvious and several other men made similar suggestions. The Goppi-dancer, her sopping cunt spread wide for anyone to see, pressed down on her mons and gave a little moan.

The other dancer stepped back into the arena, looking around hesitantly. Masculine cries of encouragement greeted her. She looked down at her erstwhile victim with a strange expression on her face, then turned away. Swiftly she crossed to the musicians, snatched the drumstick from its owner's hand and returned to kneel over the Goppi-dancer – whose eyes at last focused. The tall woman reached in with the stick and ploughed Goppi's wet furrow from top to bottom, bringing it out shiny with sex-juices. Goppi gasped and bucked her hips, and did it again when the tiger-dancer slipped the wooden stem in and stirred her cauldron like a boiling pot. Something was certainly boiling.

Next she took the stick, nine inches long and polished smooth with loving use, and fed it into Goppi's mouth. The small woman opened her throat and took right it to the back, while every man in the room felt his cock jump with jealousy. Then she brushed it down over the girl's lips and tapped it on her breastbone, as if softly beating a drum. The real drummer, forgotten in his corner, patted out a heartbeat on his hourglass-shaped *damaru* in time to the beat. Slowly she worked her way down the girl's supine body in time to the drummer's fingers, from breastbone to belly and navel and pubis. There she stayed, beating out an insistent and quickening pulse. The Goppi-dancer jerked and spread and thrashed, but it was as if she were being nailed to the floor by that drumstick striking her barely concealed clitoris. She pressed the soles of her feet together, thrust her pelvis up and came with a shuddering cry.

This time, the applause was loud and enthusiastic. The Goppi-dancer had to be helped off the stage by her partner.

'You liked that,' Vandi observed, her hand squeezing Veraine's tumescent length. 'Do you want to take me somewhere private?'

Veraine had to clear his throat before he could speak. 'I want you to find me Jilaya.'

A little surprised, Vandi released him and left the couch. Veraine tried to collect his wits and ignore the fumbling going on at his left, where Rumayn was exploring the depths of frustration.

Vandi returned in a short time with her mistress, and Jilaya kneeled down to come face to face with him. Her expression was polite but cool. 'Can I help you, General Veraine? Do you require a private room with Vandi?'

'I want a room,' he said in a low voice. 'But I want you to go with me.'

A flicker of surprise showed in her eyes, but her lips stretched in only the tiniest of cold smiles. 'I own this house,' she said, 'I don't work the floor. I retired a long time ago.'

'Well, that's what I want,' he said reasonably. 'How much does Vandi cost?'

'A gold sunwheel, unless you're going to leave bruises. That will cost you a lot more.'

'I will pay you seven,' he offered. 'No bruises.'

She said nothing, but after staring hard at him for a moment she stood and turned and with the smallest flick of her wrist indicated that he should follow her. He picked up his sword and walked out of the room without a glance at Vandi.

Jilaya led him down a long corridor with many doors opening off it, then up a short flight of stairs at the end. She paused outside the door there. 'I'd like to see your money first,' she said. 'It's a rule of the house, I'm afraid.'

He opened his pouch and laid out seven small gold coins in her hand. She smiled and opened the door for him. The room within was no working room, but a beautifully furnished bedchamber. The walls were painted with huge sprays of flowers and, to judge from the several large items of wooden furniture present, all inlaid with mother-of-pearl, a large amount of money had been spent on the contents. 'My room,' Jilaya said.

Veraine glanced around. Jilaya obviously was fond of fur; the whole floor was covered in thick pelts rather than the more usual carpets. 'You've done well for yourself,' he observed.

She smiled. 'I worked hard for it. And I came into some money.' A small boy, probably only seven years old, was curled up asleep at the foot of the bed. Jilaya clapped her hands sharply and he woke up with a start. 'Leave us,' she ordered. The boy fled. She closed the door behind him and fixed her guest with an appraising look. 'If you don't mind me asking, why did you want me?'

'You remind me of a dream I had.'

This seemed to amuse her. 'Different. Would you like some wine, General?'

'No.'

She nodded acknowledgement and reached up to loosen her dress.

'Turn round,' he said softly. She raised an eyebrow but obeyed, turning her back on him as she removed her sash and tugged her dress down over her arms. He watched her brown shoulders come into view, then he stretched out a hand and tugged the silk scarf from her head. As she dropped her dress on the floor he stroked the length of her hair from crown to tip, twisting it softly round his fingers. It burned in his hand, the red of fresh-peeled chestnuts. Then he laid his hands on her waist. Her body was well kept for a woman of her age, and if her arse was a little broader than Vandi's would have been, then it did not matter to Veraine.

'Don't move,' he said. He stripped off his own clothes with soldierly efficiency, then pressed himself against her back, burying his face in her hair even as his hands reached for her heavy breasts. She smelled of patchouli oil, not honey, but the illusion was sufficient for the moment. His cock had quickly hardened again and he pressed it between her buttocks, searching for the heat and wetness of her cleft.

'Like it up my arse?' she said. 'So it is true what they say about Irolian men.'

'If it were true,' he grinned, squeezing her breasts together, 'then I wouldn't be here at all, would I?' But she was so short compared to him that without crouching he was finding it hard to angle anywhere lower than the small of her back. He grasped her firmly around the middle and lifted her feet right off the floor, her weight resting easily on him, so that he could tuck himself into the slot between her thighs. His cockhead skidded up and down in that slippery groove.

'Wah!' she gasped. 'You take my breath away, General, but I'm sure we could find a more comfortable position. Perhaps on the bed.'

He slid inside her quickly, like a blade into a wound, then pulled out again as smoothly and set her carefully on the floor. The thick fur of a tiger was under his feet, the tiger's pulse throbbing in his veins. She turned around and looked at him from under her dark lashes; her expression suggested she was pleasantly surprised.

'Very nice,' she complimented him. 'Nice enough to eat. Shall I?'

Veraine spread his hands politely. 'If you insist,' he mocked. He took one step over to the timber-framed bed and set himself on the edge of the thick mattress. Jilaya lowered herself between his splayed thighs.

She was a masterful fellatrix. From the moment her lips brushed his swollen cockhead he felt himself enraptured, captivated by the near unbearable pleasure she was able to wring from every nerve in his skin. She tickled and caressed and probed with lips and tongue-tip, then took his length right down her throat and held him imprisoned there. Her mouth was like hot velvet, rough and then smooth in turns, demanding then gentle. She teased, and then she punished. Where her mouth could not reach because it was busy elsewhere, there she sent her fingertips stroking and tormenting. In moments she had roused him to an apex of desire, then her grip would clamp around his root and she would curb him in tightly, forcing him to back down; only then he would realise that this was no peak of pleasure, but a plateau on the slope of some sky-piercing mountain which she was forcing him to ascend stage by stage. She made him sweat and she made him keen with frustration. He had never experienced a mouth as muscular and capacious and clever as hers. It was a vampire's mouth, draining the world dry of its reality until there was nothing under the sun but that rapacious orifice.

Veraine felt himself grow deaf and blind to everything else, and he did not care. In a moment of pause he caught up handfuls of her hair and spread the glowing locks over his thighs. Her head rose and fell on his turgid member. His fantasy was solidifying about him. He tried to imagine it was the Malia Shai's face he glimpsed sucking and nuzzling, her full lips swollen and dark around the pillar of his flesh. The superimposition was surprisingly easy; perhaps only because Jilaya had the same skin tone, perhaps because of some angle of her brows or flash of her eyes that brought to mind the goddess he wanted. Veraine could picture that cool, passionless avatar flushed and straining as she nursed upon his cock. His balls were filled to bursting. He fell back upon the bed, white lightning building from his loins up his spine.

Jilaya paused and pulled her mouth from him. Her cruelty made him gasp, and suddenly cool air rushed into his empty lungs. In a moment she was straddling him, her body dipping to meet his, but his head had cleared somewhat as she let go and he was not helpless any more. 'Turn around,' he told her, before her sex and his could meld.

She raised her eyebrows, letting the moment hang with great deliberation. But she swung around the other way and kneeled down over him with her back turned to his face. 'You really are an arse man,' he heard her observe.

He was not going to argue with her. Her backside was not something he wanted to deny anyway. As it slid up and down, her buttocks squashing on his stomach then rising just clear of him, he found the diminution in sensation more than compensated for by the view she offered him. He reached down and laid his hands on her hips and cheeks. She was hardly Jilaya at all to him. All he could see was a tumble of red-brown waves that came down from her head to the mid-point of her spine, the swell of her hips and arse from that point a perfect flow of curves. He traced the small bumps of her lower vertebrae with one finger, then pushed her forward slightly and spread her cheeks with his palms. Looking down the length of his body he could see, framed by her thighs, his cock sliding into her wet sex, her stretched labia, the wetness of her curls, the little brown bud of her arsehole pouting at him. He teased that hole with his thumb and was rewarded by feeling her quiver. His cock went in and out of her with the implacability of a boulder cleaving the torrent of a river. He would not let the river sweep him away.

He ran his fingers through her hair. 'You're beautiful,' he said, as he had in the dream. He was talking to the woman in his head, and did not particularly mean Jilaya to hear.

She swivelled her hips, breaking the rhythm of her ride with deliberate malice. 'You've got a thing about my hair, haven't you?' she grunted.

'It's a rare colour,' he murmured. 'Don't you like it?' He was deliberately prolonging the chase now, savouring the sensations and the scene before him. And he was not going to let her choose the moment.

'They say,' Jilaya replied, reaching down between her own thighs and stroking his tight bollocks, 'that it means your mother was a slut who showed her arse to the sun.'

Veraine smiled slowly. 'So what about your children?' he asked. 'Did they get it from you?'

Her rhythm faltered slightly. 'My eldest daughter did,' she said.

'Does she work here?' For a moment he entertained himself with the thought of having the daughter next, after he had finished with Jilaya. Then he felt her spine stiffen under his hands. She stopped riding him.

'What's up?' he said to her back. His thumb pressed against her arsehole.

'I lost her when she was a baby.'

'Lost her?'

'She died.' Jilaya thrust down on him and clenched her inner muscles with the resignation of the professional.

'Right.' His imagination was running out of control, and he was so drunk on his own pleasure that he did not guard his tongue. 'Are you sure you didn't sell her to the temple? I bet they'd have paid you enough to buy a place of your own. Like this.'

She moved fast, but his reactions were faster. She was off his cock and in mid-air but he caught her round the waist and impaled her again, his teeth bared against her ear. 'I haven't finished yet,' he admonished. She swung her elbow back to jab him and he rolled her easily over, dropping her face down on the bed and following her weight with his own. For a few moments she braced her arms under her and tried to push against him, but he was far too heavy and it was like trying to fight a rock. He spread her cheeks and in three or four hard thrusts he took himself to the edge of orgasm and over, spending his seed in her quim as if he were hurling some weapon.

Slowly he came back to himself, his own breath ringing loud in his ears. Jilaya lay under him like a log. Even when he rolled away from her she did not move. He raked his nails across the flushed skin on his chest and stared at the roof.

Under the buzz of his satisfaction he felt guilt prick at him, like a thorn in the sole. He should not have baited her about her children, he thought; it was a cruel thing to do to any woman, and an unworthy one. He turned his head to look at her, groping towards an apology. Then she rolled on to her back and he saw her upturned face, blank as a mask. It was a familiar face. He saw her, and his stomach turned over.

Jilaya sat up without a word and slowly put her clothes on. Veraine felt like there was a stake through his guts, pinning him to the bed. When she had finished she looked at him for the first time. 'Let yourself out, General,' she said. Her voice was flat, without any trace of emotion. 'You're not welcome in the House of Jilaya. Don't come back.'

5 The Slave

There were no fish left in the tank now. It did not stop
Veraine staring into the water, but it was not fish he
was looking for. He often sat, as now, in the garden
courtyard between the Inner and Outer Temples. He
liked it because it was almost always deserted, and
because it was cool in the daytime. He liked the trees
and bushes that gave it an air of peace and ease a
thousand miles removed from the harsh desert and
harsher city around it. And he liked the pool, because he
could parade the pictures in his mind's eye across its
milky green depths.

At this moment he was supposed to be working, but
those pictures kept interrupting. He had intended to
allocate work details, apportioning men between building duties and foraging, training and maintenance, but
the wax tablet rested idly in his fingers as he sat on the
pool's edge. Messengers had ridden in from the east,
bringing the intelligence of the day. The bridge over the
Amal Bhad had been severed. No more pilgrims would
be arriving, and no further supplies or military aid. They
were cut off from the Eternal Empire.

I hate the waiting, he thought. I'm like a man who
has trained all his life to run a race, and now has to wait
for hours in the stadium. This place makes my skin
creep. I'm not afraid to fight. I'm not afraid to lead men
into danger. I'm not afraid to face death. I've done these
things before. But Mulhanabin gets into my bones and
makes me distrust myself.

From deep within the buildings a muffled gong chimed the passing of some sacred hour.

I should not be thinking these thoughts, he told himself. I should not be acting this way. I should not be brooding over some poor broken chit of a girl. An Irolian warrior should be impervious to these things.

He smiled contemptuously to himself, and as he did so a door opened in the courtyard and Rasa Belit emerged at the head of half a dozen priests, all bearing staves. Veraine watched them draw level with the water tank.

'I need to speak with you, General Veraine,' the priest said, slowing his pace.

Veraine nodded.

Rasa Belit turned to his acolytes and said something to them. He spoke in a low voice and an archaic dialect so Veraine could not make out the sentence, but he did hear one word and he understood that very well. When the priest turned back he found Veraine's iron short-sword levelled at his throat.

'One more move, high priest, and it will not need the Horse-eaters to reduce Mulhanabin to ashes,' said the soldier coldly.

The priests with the staves twitched and surged forward and hesitated. Rasa Belit threw up his hand to hold them back.

At that moment the Malia Shai stepped out of the door to the Inner Temple. She took in the tableau before her: the frozen gang of priests, the weapon threatening her chief votary, the looks of black fury on both his and Veraine's faces. 'What is happening?' she asked.

Rasa Belit bared his teeth down the length of the blade, took a deliberate step back and sideways out of range, and bowed to the ground in her direction.

'Mother of pestilence,' he said as he climbed to his feet again, 'I was about to ask the General to go with me out of the Temple. Information has been brought to me. It seems he shouldn't be here.'

'What information?' she asked, coming up and looking at both of them with mild wonder. Veraine lowered his sword to a side guard position, keeping an eye on the priests.

'His presence is in contravention of the sacred laws.'

'What laws?' Veraine said derisively, though he could have taken a guess.

Rasa Belit swung round and glared at him like a vulture. 'There are laws of cleanliness for every Yamani temple,' he said down his nose, 'to keep out the tainted. Those who are not permitted into any sacred precinct except the shrine of Hu, the lord of outcasts. Those who have slipped down the ladder of incarnation even lower than the heathen Irolians.'

'How kind of you to say so,' Veraine murmured.

'I'm talking about lepers, and the children of slaves, and those born deformed. And this man,' he concluded triumphantly, turning back to the Malia Shai, 'was born a slave.'

She blinked. 'Is this true?' she asked Veraine.

'It's true.' He felt no need to justify himself. Deal with it, he thought.

'He admits his shame,' Rasa Belit said, smiling through tight lips.

'Screw your shame, and your laws, priest. I have my orders and I will fulfil them, with or without your approval. If you cannot be grateful, at any rate you will not obstruct me.'

Rasa Belit would not even turn to look at him now. 'He's an abomination in this place,' he told his goddess.

She blinked again. 'It doesn't matter,' she told the

eunuch. 'He's here to save Mulhanabin. I give him dispensation to enter the Temple.'

'Merciless Mother,' he reproached her, 'you cannot put aside the scriptures. This man's presence desecrates this temple. He pollutes the stones he walks upon.'

She frowned slightly. 'How can he, when I am here?' she asked. 'He's only a man, but I am the living goddess. I bless Mulhanabin with every step.'

Rasa Belit grimaced. 'Nevertheless, it's the law,' he said softly. 'The law was written at the dawn of history. I do not need to remind you of the sacred duty we bear, Malia Shai.'

'But I am older than the law. I'm older than the stones of the Temple. The walls of Mulhanabin were raised to furnish me a dwelling place on the Earth, Rasa, and the scriptures were written to instruct my worshippers how to behave. Not to instruct me.' She spread her hands. 'If my house is to be saved from the barbarians, then I will invite its defender within the walls.'

Rasa Belit's face was a picture of frustration, little muscles tightening and twitching all over it. Veraine wondered if the Malia Shai had ever before defied her high priest. Very slowly, he inclined his head.

'If it's your will, Malia Shai,' he murmured. 'Perhaps an exception could be made.'

'In this situation, it is only reasonable.'

'Reason and wise action are great,' he said, bowing, 'but *sunyata* is greater.'

'*Sunyata* is my only desire,' she replied.

Rasa Belit did not contradict this. Silently, the priests withdrew from the courtyard. Veraine let out a long, relieved breath, then sat down slowly on the broad rim of the pool. Under the satisfaction of seeing his opponent back down – and the surprise of being defended by the

Malia Shai herself – he felt a familiar queasiness. He told himself it had only been a matter of time before the high priest found out. It was common knowledge among the Eighth Host, after all.

'I thought you were the son of a great general,' the Malia Shai said. She had not moved. She did not, it seemed, use posture or gesture much in conversation.

'I am. My father was a hero of the Irolian people. But my mother was a slave.'

'What had she done wrong?'

Veraine looked up at her from under his brows and for a long moment was silent. 'Nothing,' he said at last. 'We make more use of slaves than you do. It's not a form of punishment.'

'She belonged to your father?'

Again, he hesitated. 'She was of the class of – there is no word for it in Yamani. Listen; your men can take several wives, can't they?'

'Yes. If they can afford it.'

'Well, an Irolian may take only one. But rich men are expected to keep a stable of female slaves for their entertainment. Like ... pets.'

The Malia Shai's gaze revealed neither disgust nor pity. 'If you were born a slave,' she said slowly, 'then how did you rise to be a general?'

Veraine swallowed, though his throat felt dry. He had never discussed the subject with anyone, not in his whole life. In fact, when younger he had terminated a number of attempted conversations on the subject with violence. Why should he tell this girl now? He kept meeting her dark, level stare and wondering what lurked behind it.

'When I was fourteen,' he said, his voice a little hoarse, 'my father's attention was drawn to my existence. It then amused him to have me adopted.'

'You . . . you don't sound proud. Aren't you pleased not to be a slave now?'

Veraine stared over at a trumpet-flower bush, his eyes tracking the tiny dances of the blue butterflies that haunted it. He exhaled slowly. 'I was born on my father's estate. It was a big one, right in the middle of the countryside.' The words rose slowly to his lips, and he heard his own voice as if from far away. 'The Glorious General Morin raised horses and cattle as every nobleman should, and needed a lot of land and many slaves. He didn't farm himself, of course. In Irolian families the right thing is to present the eldest son to the Eternal Empire as a warrior. He inherits the land, but it's the younger brothers who manage the herds and run the business for him. My father very rarely visited us. Our estate was run by Morin's third brother, Darphan. He was a bullying, miserly man. The Lady Morin lived there too. She was never particularly cruel to me, though she gave my mother a great deal of pain, I think. It's considered correct for a man's wife to have his slave women whipped when he is away. Not hard enough to damage them, just enough to express a proper jealousy of her husband's affections. Lady Morin ordered beatings that left my mother unable to walk for days.'

He paused. The Malia Shai waited silently. 'I grew up as a herd boy and stable lad. I ran a little wild, I suppose. I didn't have any real friends of my own age. The other slaves didn't like me because I was the lord's get, and his legitimate children wouldn't look at a slave. And I think Lady Morin did her best to ensure there were not too many of my sort born.' He shrugged. 'So I was kicked and beaten a lot until I was old enough to run off, then later to hit back. And I would spend the time I could in the women's court, where my mother lived with the other slaves.' Warm memories flickered among the ashes

113

in his mind; music and perfume and giggling laughter. 'They liked me. Especially as I grew up. They treated me as a pet, and they got me to run errands and do jobs for them. They couldn't leave the court without permission.'

They had enjoyed teasing him, too, getting him to comb out their hair or rub perfume into their backs after they had bathed. They had enjoyed the boyish pleasure and confusion they had been able to wring from him. And some of them, by the end, had not been teasing. Not entirely.

'But when I was fourteen, the Lady Morin bought herself a new maid, a little older than me. Her name was Zura. She was very shy; I hardly even got to speak to her. But I fell in love. She had huge brown eyes. I used to sneak around the house, trying to get a glimpse of her.' Veraine smiled painfully. 'She was ... unusually pretty. Unfortunately this brought her to Darphan's attention. I saw what was happening, that he was trying to get her on her own. I started to shadow him, to make sure he never got the chance. Then one day he grabbed hold of her, and I attacked him. I know it was a stupid thing to do. But I was young, and it was the first time I had fallen in love.'

'I don't think it was stupid,' the Malia Shai said levelly.

He bit his lip, looking at her.

'What happened?'

'Oh, Darphan called for help, and servants came running. I was grabbed and held down. Darphan would normally have had me whipped. To death. That's the punishment for a slave attacking a free Irolian. But it so happened that General Morin was in residence at the time, so instead of doing it himself he brought me up in front of my father for punishment.'

'He pardoned you?'

'Mm.' Veraine looked at the floor. 'You see, at fourteen my hair had just started to go grey. Like it had for Morin when he was a boy. He saw this for the first time. And none of his legitimate children had ever shown the trait. He was moved by ... sentiment, to lay claim to me. He let me off the whipping, and he had me officially adopted as his son, and he sent me off to the barracks at Antoth to train as a warrior of the Empire. And if I had thought being a slave was harsh, I had a whole world of pain to learn there.'

The Malia Shai tilted her head. He assumed it was meant to be interrogative.

'I had grown up among women,' he explained. 'But these boys, most of them had been in barracks since they were seven or eight. They had forgotten the world outside. I wasn't one of them. And I was a bastard, they knew that. I was not good enough for those firstborns, so they went for me like a pack of dogs. Day after day, until the time I smashed one of the older lad's skulls. I didn't kill him, but ... he lost one eye and all of his wits for ever. After that they let me alone.'

'What about Zura?'

Veraine felt his mouth go dry again. Despite all the years, the pain had not entirely eased. He at last said hoarsely, 'My father made me watch while Darphan had her. To teach me my place, he said. To render me callous, as a soldier should be. And after I left the estate, I never got to go back. My mother died two years later. So did Morin, before I was twenty.'

The buzzing of bees sounded loud in the courtyard. 'So,' he concluded, 'I have a hero for a father, and I have a regular income from my half-brother's lands, and now I'm a general of the Empire. But,' he said, looking her in the eye, 'I'm not ashamed of being born a slave. And I am not...' He hesitated and shook his head, 'I'm not proud, I think, of what I am now.'

And he wondered why he had admitted that, after all these years. Why to her?

I lie naked beneath the gaze of my golden lover, the Sun. The warmth of his body on my skin is like a caress even before he touches me. His smile lights up my heart. I feel my flesh respond even as he reaches out to lay one hand upon the smooth plain of my belly, his golden palm upon my rich brown skin. I see his lips part softly. My pulse beats through his flat palm up into his veins. His heat suffuses my limbs, loosening them in the strangest ways so that my thighs part without my conscious direction, as if they were drifting asunder. I feel so light that I might float in the air, yet so heavy that I cannot stir. His hand is heavy, but not heavy enough. I press against it, my eyes filled with pleading.

Come to me, I beg him.

He kneels down between my thighs, nudging them gently apart with his own. I feel the roughness of the hairs on his legs, the firmness of the taut muscle. His member rises like the dawning of a new day. He bends forward over me as if kneeling to pray, his face coming down to worship my body, and I writhe in anticipation of that contact. His beard is soft and tickling, his lips soft and hot. He kisses my breasts, he kisses my belly. I cry out for pleasure and desire. I grab his hair with my hands and twine my fingers in it.

He moves down the length of my body, his tongue blazing a trail of fire. He licks around my navel. I am ready for him. So ready.

Yet without warning he lurches away from me, staggering to his feet, snatched by pale hands. I cry out. It is my other lover, the Rain, my grey and blue paramour with fists balled like thunderheads. They slam together, my two lovers, locked in a knot that has nothing to do with love though thigh strains against thigh and they grunt and gasp with passion. Hands claw and heave, scrabbling on sweat-slick skin to find purchase, to tear and rend. Back and forth they rock, the slap of flesh connecting with other flesh the only music to their dance. Muscles bulge and lock. Blow after blow is swung from both sides, to be blocked on rigid forearms or to land with hammering force on unprotected places.

They spin around each other like dancers. My lover the Sun is a warrior; strong, brutal, confident of his right and his ability to win both the fight and my body. My lover the Rain is a magician; subtle and cunning. He fights with the unscrupulous ferocity of the desperate.

At last they break apart, both crouched, both gasping for breath, both bloodied and bruised and snarling with rage, their eyes alight with jealousy. When they resume they will kill each other and I cannot let them do that. I step between, pushing both away as they try to snatch me. Then I kiss my storm-cloud lover on the swollen lips, tasting the salt of his sweat and his blood. His naked body is cold and shaking as I press myself against it. I hear my golden lover moan with fury behind me.

Then I turn from the Rain to the Sun and kiss him in turn. His skin burns like a furnace. Sweat is dripping from the fringe of hair over his eyes. Gently I unclench his fist and lay it upon my belly where it belongs. Then without breaking away I turn back to the Rain and spread his cool palm over my breast. At the touch of his icy fingers my nipples harden like ripening nuts.

Softly I coax them both against me, one on either side. Both cling to me as if afraid they had almost lost me.

I want you now, I whisper.

One on my right, one on my left. Then one before and one behind me. They take it in turns to kiss my hungry mouth and their hands are all over my body, teasing and caressing and possessing each curve and each cleft. I feel as if I am melting in their moisture, their warmth. My limbs soften. I yield entirely.

They lift me up between them and spread my thighs, taking my weight on their hard muscular frames. Then they both enter me at once. One from in front, one from behind, yet both sliding into the same wet and pliant orifice. Member against member, both firm in my grasp. I gasp with pleasure, not realising until this moment that I was capable of taking so much. I am spread wide, my yoni an aching void that only they can fill.

They move, slowly at first, rocking me back and forth with their rhythm. My own eager moisture lubricates their motion, each sliding muscular thrust stretching me further, hard cock grinding against hard cock and soft cunt simultaneously. In me they are joined. They grab each other for balance, for leverage, as they churn deeper and deeper into me. I am tossed up and around like a boat on battering waves. I moan and they both kiss me, bloodied lips scouring my throat, tongues entering my mouth in turn. My golden lover holds my legs spread wide to facilitate his entry, and that of his rival. I am helpless. Their thrusts grow deeper.

I come, crying and shaking, pinned in the crush of their bodies and, feeling me buck between them, they at once spend their seed within me, groaning my name in the agony of their crisis. The foam of their desire runs down our legs like boiling milk overflowing a cauldron.

The Sun has risen upon me. The Rain has soaked my every pore.

And the Earth becomes fruitful.

* * *

The days passed, light and dark succeeding one another like sunlight flickering through the branches of a tree. No further news came from Antoth, though rumour rode in from the west on the pony of an imperial scout, fleeing from the storm wave that built, invisible, behind him. The Horse-eaters had taken the city-state of Oryon on the Western Spice Road, so it was said, and built a pyramid of the heads of its inhabitants. Veraine cracked his knuckles, ordered extra scouts out into the desert and strode up and down the Citadel wall, feeling as impotent as any of the sacred eunuchs in Mulhanabin. With the defences shored up, there was a limit to what he could set the Eighth Host to doing, apart from repeated drill. He got them to practise the defensive wedges that they would need to take on Horse-eater cavalry, over and over again until they must have been able to follow orders in their sleep. The men were restless and grumpy from inaction, and he was the worst of the lot.

The only time he mellowed was when he met the Malia Shai, as they passed in the corridors or in the sacred precincts on their way to their respective duties. He would incline his head and acknowledge her, always polite though never humble, and if she were not busy she would stop and exchange a few words with him, to the obvious dismay of her priests. Veraine found that highly amusing. He was also intrigued by the fact she seemed to welcome his conversation, though he searched her expression and her voice fruitlessly for any hint that she might be flirting with him. She never even smiled.

That didn't stop him fantasising that those dark eyes regarded him with more than casual interest. For that matter, his private fantasies ran the gamut of possibilities every night and in most idle moments; he didn't seem able to shake his imagination free of her.

'The body is an illusion,' she said.

'Really?' His eyes expressed a humorous scepticism. They were standing in a doorway somewhere in the interminable bowels of the Outer Temple and she was trying to explain to him some theological precept, oblivious to the fact that he was far less interested in the spiritual truth than the warm, curvaceous illusion only an arm's length from his own.

'Yes. Think of it as an actor's costume, that's discarded between scenes. Only the soul is eternal, and it takes on new bodies throughout its journey.'

'I see.' A shaft of sunlight was gilding the soft fuzz of her cheek and highlighting the ripe sweep of her breasts. Her cotton dress was far too light to disguise her charms. 'And the point of this journey would be?'

'To learn. To grow. To become ever more familiar with the whole universe in all its facets.' She shifted her stance slightly and the light caressed the slender column of her throat.

I would like to kiss her, just there, Veraine thought. Just where the pulse ripples her skin.

'You learn how unbalanced and harmful your flaws are. For example, if you were a man who used women thoughtlessly, for his own pleasure –'

Veraine raised his brows sharply, with a look of pain. He didn't quite make her laugh, but she stumbled a little in her speech.

'– If you did, I'm not saying that's true for you, then you might well be reborn as a woman to learn the suffering you'd caused.'

He briefly entertained the idea of being female and then decided not to think about what that might entail just at this moment. 'Would I remember what I was being chastised for?' he asked.

'Not consciously. But your soul would.'

He saw priests coming purposefully towards them

down the corridor and decided it was time to break away. Frustration tore at his guts with velvet claws. 'Well, if it's true, I have to conclude that in my last life I got everything I wanted far too easily,' he murmured. 'Malia Shai.' And he nodded his head to her as he withdrew.

Full-scale drill took place on the desert floor, under the beetling shadow of the city, but hand-to-hand combat was practised every day in the courtyard of their make-shift barracks. Veraine made sure he took part, too, mostly to burn off the excess of his tension. The thrust and slice of individual conflict gave him something more physical to focus on than the anticipated siege, and it helped clear his head.

Word came to him via Arioc one day, just as he was squaring up against a big Irolian soldier under the blistering afternoon sun. This was Veraine's third fight of the day and most of the other combatants had retired to the shade of the colonnade, but, though the sweat was stinging his eyes and there was a bruise on his right arm the size of his palm, he wanted to push it for one more round. His opponent was a notorious warrior among the men of the Eighth Host, not smart enough to have been promoted beyond *optio* but as heavyset as a small building and just as difficult to demolish. Both men were armed with short wooden staves instead of their iron swords, but Veraine, as an officer, carried his oval bronze shield rather than the larger, lighter wicker rectangle clutched by his foe. He had decided that in mock combat this actually put him at a disadvantage, but it would have been a point of shame noted by every soldier in the courtyard if he had discarded the metal shield.

Just as the two of them were walking out into a clear

space equidistant from the nearest sparring pairs, Arioc strode across the sand to his side. Arioc's tunic was a blazing white in the sunlight, unmarked by sweat or dust. The young man rarely fought, and as a member of the General's staff he was exempt from compulsory training. Veraine had noted that when he did get into combat, he did not have the bulk to parry very well but that he struck out with the speed and accuracy of a snake.

'Sir, the high priest is here. He has asked to speak with you.'

'Has he now? Where is he?' Following Arioc's nod, Veraine turned and looked at one of the many windows that opened onto the courtyard. Past the elaborately carved stone screen, in the darkness within the building, he thought he could make out the saffron blur of a priest's robes. He frowned. 'Tell Rasa Belit that he will have to wait a moment.'

He turned his attention back to the armed man in front of him, as Arioc strolled away. A nod from him brought the soldier into a guard position and the two men began to circle each other warily. Veraine gauged his opponent carefully, decided he kept his leg too far out of cover, feinted towards the shield and had to spring back to avoid a swinging response. The soldier's momentum carried him forward and Veraine twisted out of the way. They resumed their circling, like dogs facing each other off. He let the other lead the second time, catching the blow on his shield and swinging up from low down. His stave bounced off the other man's bronze greave with a clang. They jumped apart. The *optio* grunted and shook his head: a blow off armour did not count, of course.

Veraine decided to try for his opponent's head, since any touch there counted as a decisive wound. The only problem was that the soldier was taller than him and the weapon too short for an easy stroke. He jabbed at the man's sword-arm and then, when it was snatched wide, smacked his shield across it to keep it out of the way and closed in for a vicious strike to the head. The wicker shield was thrust high just in time to catch his stave, and a flurry of blows that felt like the kicks of a mule battered back on his own shield, jarring his arm to the shoulder. Veraine ducked, twisted aside and landed two blows on the exposed leg – but again on the greave that protected his shin. He pulled out, recovering the guard position just in time to prevent the delivery of what would have been a crippling blow at hip-height. The tip of the enemy weapon whacked off the bronze plates of his *pteurges*, but most of the force of the blow was caught on his shield once more.

Sweat was pouring down the soldier's face. He was a heavy man, and Veraine could see that he liked to use his bulk as momentum, like a wall falling. The General decided to try some more defensive moves, jumping out of the way of each attack, circling and side-stepping, letting the bigger man waste his energy in wild swipes and sudden lunges to regain balance. He liked fighting like this; being able to anticipate his foe at every move, deflecting the blows harmlessly. It was hard work, though, just because of the sheer strength of the other man, and Veraine was glad to seize the opportunity when it presented itself and catch the soldier's over-swing with a backhanded blow that cracked off his wrist like the sound of a whiplash. The *optio's* stave went flying from his paralysed hand, Veraine lashed out and kicked his leg from under him – careful to avoid the side of the knee, which would have broken that limb – and as the big man smacked onto the sand, tapped him sharply on the head with the tip of the stave.

He saluted the soldier before he walked off, wiping his arm across his forehead. He was very satisfied with the conclusion of the combat, and glad it had not lasted much longer. In this heat, every breath he took felt like it was scorching his throat. He walked over to the quartermaster on duty, handed in the battered stave and took a scoop of water from the vat waiting.

It tasted disgusting, as thick and silty as river-mud. Veraine spat it out on the sand. 'What in Shuga's name is wrong with this?' he asked.

'Sorry, sir,' the quartermaster snapped. 'The cistern on the roof is nearly empty.'

'Then send a party of men down into the city and requisition the best well. I'll not have my men drinking this! Ariot, go and get me something to drink that doesn't taste like it's been passed through an elephant first.'

The aide hurried off, and Veraine contented himself with splashing the tepid water over the back of his neck before crossing the length of the courtyard, as unhurriedly as he could, and entering into the building. Rasa Belit was ensconced in a room next to the door.

The interior of the barracks was almost impenetrably dark after the harsh sunlight outside, and Veraine paused in the doorway, blue lights dancing in front of his eyes. He forced his still-ragged breathing to quieten.

'A fine display of your prowess, General,' Rasa Belit's voice came from beside the window. The other priests in the room stirred and drew back as the soldier approached.

'We do our best to entertain,' Veraine said. 'What was it you wanted to talk to me about?'

The priest sighed. 'I have concerns about the treatment of pilgrims by your men.'

'Go on.'

'I understand they are being refused entry to the Citadel.'

'Only at night, high priest. I don't want civilians billeted in the Citadel. The space is too limited.'

'You understand that part of the temple income comes from provision of hospitality to pilgrims? We're suffering greatly this year because of the invasion, as it is.'

'And you'll suffer more. But I am sure you will survive.' He shook his head in disgust. 'Just what are those people thinking of anyway, priest – to come here in the face of an invasion?'

'Oh, normally there would be many more, General. We've reached the driest point of the year. The desert withers, the streams run dry. Crops all across your Empire fail. This is the time of fear and hardship, when the earth turns to dust. Plague festers in the slums. This is the time of the Malia Shai, her great festival. The people make their pilgrimage to her, and pray for mercy. If she is moved, then the Rains come early. If not, then there is real drought, and famine.'

'I see.'

'Normally at this time of the year, the streets would be packed with pilgrims. You wouldn't be able to move up the street for the press of bodies, General. They would camp in the alleys, in the desert – anywhere where there is room. The nights would be loud with prayer. In the cool of the evening, they come to the tank in the Citadel to bathe, and to light lamps, and make worship. They wash away the concerns and the illusions of this world here. They drink the water and they carry it home to their families. In this way they come a little closer to the goddess.'

'Your beliefs are not my responsibility, Rasa Belit.'

'No. You think they're a foolishness, don't you? You Irolians worship your dead, I understand.'

Veraine snorted. 'No. We revere our ancestors, we are told they watch over us still from the Field of Heaven. But we have faith in our gods.'

'Do you, General?' Rasa Belit's voice purred from the shadow of his face. 'Do you have faith in the gods? Because I think you'll need it here in Mulhanabin.'

Veraine frowned at him, but could see nothing but a silhouette against the glare from the window. He took a few steps closer, so that he was in the light himself. The priest turned to face him, his heavy-lidded eyes emerging from the gloom. He looks like some predatory lizard, Veraine thought.

'I don't need faith, priest. Not in any god that is supposed to sleep in a shrine, or eat the meat sacrificed to him, or father royal babies. And I do not,' he emphasised, though his voice was so low that only Rasa Belit could have heard it, 'believe that a goddess could be born as a girl.'

Rasa Belit licked his lips slowly. His tongue looked blue. 'You're a fool, General,' he breathed. 'You think the Malia Shai is an innocent maiden. You think that you can use her as a tool against me. No. You are making a great mistake there. She is the mother of torment, and she will bring you nothing but pain.'

Veraine blinked, shook his head and turned away. 'Tell your pilgrims,' he said flatly, 'that if it matters to them then they can come into the Citadel after nightfall. But they may not stay there, and if they are found camping in the streets they will be thrown out. Does that satisfy you?'

'It will do. So kind of you, General.'

Veraine grimaced.

'It now occurs to me, General,' the priest added, shifting his bulk from one thigh to the other, 'that you might like to attend the Drought Ceremony of the Malia Shai.

It's one of the few occasions upon which the populace are permitted within the *Garbhagria*. The rites are very holy, and you may find them instructive.'

Veraine was taken aback. 'Well,' he murmured, stalling.

'Ask your officers as well. They will all be welcome. After all, the Malia Shai seems to find no offence in your presence. I am sure the short one, your assistant, he'll find it fascinating.'

'I accept, on behalf of the Eighth Host,' he said slowly.

'At the full of the moon, then. At sunset.'

'Fine. Do we have anything else to discuss, priest?'

'No.' He waved a hand languidly. 'Our business is concluded.'

Veraine turned sharply on his heel and walked out. In the doorway he nearly bumped into Arioc, who was waiting with a cup. Veraine grabbed the vessel from his hand, knocked back the watered wine and strode off down the corridor, signalling the younger man to follow him. When they had reached the sanctuary of the room set aside for officers' ablutions, he slammed the wicker door shut with unnecessary emphasis.

'Is there something wrong, sir?' Arioc asked.

'I don't know,' Veraine said, dragging his stained tunic off over his head and slinging it into a corner. The loincloth beneath rapidly followed. 'I'm sure that bastard is up to something. I just don't know what. All these hints and warnings –'

He broke off as Arioc presented him with a bowl of water and a cloth, slopped the liquid into face, armpits and groin, and scrubbed himself briefly.

'He reminds me of a vulture,' Arioc ventured. 'Those eyes.'

'He reminds me of a scorpion under a rock,' countered Veraine, with feeling. 'He seems to be under the impression that I marched the entire Eighth Host here simply for the pleasure of pissing on his personal territory.' He turned to the dais in the centre of the room, a broad surface spread with clean cloth, and laid himself face down on it. Laying his forehead on his folded arms, he listened to the sound of Arioc moving around the room and tried to relax. It was far from easy: images of Rasa Belit and the Malia Shai, each in their own way as disturbing, kept intruding.

'Do you find this place gets on your nerves, Arioc?' he asked, as the youth laved oil down his spine and the backs of his legs.

'This room, sir?' Arioc asked, setting down the pot of oil and beginning to spread the slippery liquid across the General's shoulders with smooth, practised strokes.

'Mulhanabin. I find the place has an atmosphere of oppression.' Veraine finished the sentence with a long exhalation of breath.

Arioc was seeking out the aching muscles across the top of his neck and kneading them with strong thumbs. 'It's a Yamani city sir. They're all shit-heaps. The food tastes terrible, the natives stink, there's no such thing as a bath house or a theatre. I would rather be in Antoth. But it's no worse than I was expecting.'

A trickle of oil found its way down the crack of Veraine's arse and started to tickle his balls. It was not unpleasant, but he tried to ignore it. 'What are you doing here, Arioc?' he asked. 'You requested this transfer to an active unit. Shouldn't you be in Antoth?'

He ploughed parallel lines either side of the General's spine right down to the buttocks. 'My family wanted me out of the capital, sir. Certain of my activities were starting to cause them embarrassment.'

'Nothing political, I hope.'

'No, sir. It was a question of who I was fucking.'

'No shit,' Veraine sighed, his eyes shut, his nostrils filled with the green smell of the oil. 'You could have found a better billet than this one, though. Administration somewhere on the frontier.'

'I asked for this posting. I didn't want to sit in an office. Is there a problem with my work, sir?'

'No. No problem.'

'I pride myself on a job well done, sir,' Arioc pointed out, grunting slightly with the effort of massaging the big muscles of Veraine's thighs.

'Well. Ah. There's a knot in there. A bit harder. You're certainly bloody good at that.'

'Thank you, sir.'

'It's just you're a little different to the other officers. Most of them are not of such good family.' Veraine could clearly picture Arioc's face, the look of concentration, the set of his fine arched brows as he worked diligently at his task. He must have a fine view right up between my legs, he thought with amusement. No doubt the lad was enjoying it.

'I have no complaints, sir.'

Veraine snorted a smile to himself and lay silently as the other worked oil into the soles of his feet, rubbing the tightness from the heels and the instep. The youth had excellent hands, not to be faulted, and a dedication to his work that clearly sprang from a love of the masculine body.

'You know, sir,' Arioc ventured, after he had loosened the cords of the Achilles tendons and slid cupped hands right up the length of his legs, from rough-textured calves to the soft skin at the small of the spine, 'your back's like a board. You're too tense. If I might say so, sir, you could do with a bloody good fuck.'

'And you're offering, are you, Arioc?' Veraine grunted to the linen sheet under his face.

'No, sir. You're not my type. I'd suggest you go back to that silk-house though.'

'The silk-house just about threw me out last time,' Veraine growled. Then he added, 'What do you mean, I'm not your type? Don't tell me you do prefer pussy to arse, Arioc; four thousand men can't have all got it wrong.'

'Four thousand men are under the impression that I'm your mattress,' Arioc pointed out, digging into his ribs perhaps a shade too hard.

'Oh, great. Just great.' Veraine was not really surprised; he supposed he should have expected it.

'I do screw arse, sir,' Arioc continued conversationally, adding an extra drizzle of oil between the shoulder blades and running it out to the triceps. 'But you're not the kind I prefer. You're . . .'

'What?'

'You're a general, sir. You walk and act and think like a noble. You smell like a noble. You're rational, self-disciplined and courteous. Mostly,' he added as an afterthought. 'Not what I'm interested in.'

'You like something a bit less bland, I gather?'

'I can appreciate a good man, sir. It just doesn't get me hard.'

'So you fuck foot soldiers. Well, I can see that your family might want to keep that quiet.'

'Oh, you don't know the half of it, sir.' There was a clink as Arioc picked up the strigil he had prepared. He touched the bronze scraper firmly to Veraine's neck and the General jumped at the coldness of the metal.

'Go on, shock me,' he said grimly.

Arioc began to run the strigil across his body, bringing off a layer of oil, sweat and dirty skin, which he wiped off the bronze onto a handcloth. 'I fuck foot soldiers,' he said as he scraped Veraine clean. 'I take cock. I like it hard and nasty. I like it from a group of men. One isn't enough. I like it when they slap me about, and when they piss on me, and when they make me crawl. It's hard to keep that discreet. I've tried to tone it down, to make do with the lighter stuff. But it doesn't give me a rush the way being cluster-fucked in a latrine does.'

Veraine's eyes were suddenly wide open, though he said nothing.

'There was this time. This was the best time I ever had – I still think about it, though it left me terrified for weeks. I was in barracks at Antoth. It was late at night, and I was out in the city, just going from tavern to tavern, looking for action. I was crossing the road when I saw a soldier coming out of a wine-house, fumbling with himself. He was a big, rough-looking bloke, with a broken nose and scars all down one side of his face. He had an ear missing too. I didn't recognise him, he must have been from a different host. He caught sight of me and looked me over, long enough for me to be sure, then he stared right past me like I wasn't there. He turned away down an alley and I followed him. He went behind the tavern into what must have been a potter's yard; there were broken pots all over the floor and the ground was all dug up into humps of kilns. He stopped against the nearest one and lifted his tunic. I came in a little closer, and suddenly he turned round and glared at me, asked me why I'd been following him. He had his cock out in his hand and I couldn't stop staring at it. It was thick and knobbly and misshapen, just like him, with thick veins like snakes twined about it. I told him I wanted to watch him piss. He didn't say a thing, but he suddenly rushed at me and knocked me flat, then grabbed hold of my tunic and held me up as he straddled me, his legs set either side of my shoulders, my face stuck against his crotch. Then he lifted his tunic again and slapped his cock into my face and he pissed all over me, up my nose and in my eyes, and he stuffed it in my mouth and just kept pissing. I nearly drowned. He was snarling something about if I wanted to see it, here it was, but I couldn't really hear, I was so busy trying to swallow and breathe at the same time.

'Just as he finished a bunch of other men came up to us. Three men. His friends. They asked what the fuck was going on, and he told them he had found this little bitch-dog that was following him around. He whipped his belt off and looped it round my neck, then dragged me back and forth across the ground in front of his mates. They were laughing like they were going to burst. They made me bark and whimper, and then lick their feet. They liked the whimpering. Then one of them said he thought the bitch was on heat because she was flashing her ass for everyone to see. He pulled out his tackle and asked me if I wanted to lick at that. So I did, and he held me by the hair and fucked my throat. Then, while I crouched on hands and knees, they took it in turns to bugger me while their friends had their cocks sucked at the other end. They stank of alcohol and piss, and they were so fucking strong and brutal – I had a hard-on every moment of the ordeal. They laughed at that. They threatened to cut it off, because a bitch shouldn't have a pizzle. They stood round me when they had finished and made me bring myself off, and then eat my spunk off my hands. I was nearly shitting myself in fear. They all had knives.

'Finally they tied my wrists to my knees and left me crouched there in the potter's yard, unable to move. I was one huge bruise from head to foot. My commanding officer had to send a team of stretcher-bearers to get me back to barracks the next day. But I still had a hard-on. Turn over, sir.'

Without thinking, Veraine rolled onto his back, propping himself up on his elbows. Arioc had set down the strigil and his hands were cupped full of oil. He looked down at Veraine's body. Veraine followed the line of his gaze.

Arioc raised his eyebrows. Veraine looked uneasily at the tumescent length of his half-erect cock, stirring on his belly. As they watched a surge ran up it, and it visibly thickened.

The smile illuminated Arioc's beautiful features like a light. 'I told you, you were tense,' he murmured. Oil dripped from his long fingers. He reached out to touch the General's member.

'No,' said Veraine, very clearly.

The smile became mocking. 'Don't tell me you've never fucked a man, sir?'

'Not recently.'

'I didn't think you could be the only virgin in the Eighth Host.'

'I prefer women,' said Veraine through bared teeth.

'That's all right. I don't like officers.' Arioc looked down at his own quite obvious bulge. 'We can be flexible.'

Veraine sat bolt upright, trying to parry the reaching hand, but he was far too slow. And as Arioc's oiled fingers closed around his aching length, he forgot why he had any objections. A groan escaped from his throat. The muscles of his stomach clenched and jumped.

'That's better, sir,' Arioc said, kneeling up beside him to get both hands engaged. His grip was firm and knowing, as efficient as his massage. One slim patrician hand worked up and down the shaft, while the other cupped and flexed his scrotum. Veraine imagined hot lead had been poured into his balls; they felt heavy and fit to burst. Unhurriedly, Arioc worked his foreskin back down from the head of his cock, revealing the flushed and angry dome and the slitted eye from which milky fluid was already seeping. And Veraine, who had never intended or anticipated this, could only be grateful that somebody – anybody – was taking in hand the demanding, raging beast that jerked and danced between his legs. He leaned back against his braced arms, eyes closed, feeling the blood begin to boil in his veins.

'You're gagging for it,' Arioc observed.

Veraine forced his eyes open. The young man's head was bowed reverentially over his toil, his hand alternating between a blur of movement and slow, masterful strokes that made the General bite his lip in frustration. Arioc's glossy black curls quivered to the rhythm of his pumping muscles. Veraine struggled for speech.

'That's enough,' he managed to say.

Arioc looked up at him sharply and shook his head, the quirk of his lips expressing sheer wickedness.

'That's enough, soldier!' Veraine rasped, and this time his voice held the bite of command. 'Up against the wall!'

Arioc released him, crossed the room in two long strides and slapped his hands hard against the plaster, head bowed. Veraine rolled off the table to his feet, glanced around the room and found what he wanted; a short-bladed knife on the pile of linen to be used for rags. He walked up behind Arioc, his cock sticking out before him like a spear, surveyed the young man's back for a moment, then hitched the knee-length tunic up and cut through the cords of the loincloth beneath. He was sloppy with the knife, nicking Arioc's skin over the hip. The young man shuddered like a horse on the battlefield.

Veraine threw both blade and shredded cloth to the floor and placed both hands on the other man's arse, feeling the muscle hard under the sculpted planes of the skin.

'Spread your legs,' he growled. Arioc jerked his feet apart on the flagstones. Veraine slid his thumbs into the cleft of his buttocks, finding tight, shiny skin and wiry hairs and – very quickly – the clenched muscular ring of his anus. He guided the head of his own cock to that aperture and without pause or warning shoved nearly the full length of his member hard into it.

It was a good job that Arioc had slathered him in oil, because that orifice was far drier and tighter than a woman's sex. The chariot-driver jerked beneath him and made a noise that might have been a sob, but he did not cry out. Veraine rested for a moment against his back, bemused temporarily by its muscularity, by the narrowness of the hips under his hands. He laid his cheek against the youth's raven-black locks. 'Comfortable?' he asked sarcastically.

Arioc made a whining noise in his throat.

Veraine considered abusing him verbally, but impatience got the better of him. Though the young man would probably appreciate it, Veraine was not interested in giving a performance or indulging the other's tastes. He wanted to come. He wanted to shoot his load into that tight grip and fill the man's arrogant arse with his jism and that was all.

He reached round and found the other man's erection, proud as a battle-standard. He slapped it once, stingingly, with his flat palm and then let it fall back to rest there. It felt surprisingly good. Arioc's cock, like Arioc, was slim and elegant. Veraine gripped it firmly, knotted his other arm around the other man's belly and began to fuck him strong and hard. Arioc groaned, spread his legs wider and opened up to him, taking it to the hilt. The grip on Veraine's cock pulsed and clenched and new spaces unfurled about it, the incredible heat and softness and yielding caress of that interior world sending bolts of fire up the invading member and into his spine. He thrust pitilessly and came at last with a snarl, barely conscious of the alien prick spasming under his hand.

He pulled out after only a moment's rest, before his tumescence had subsided, and stood panting, surprised at the effort the act had wrung from his body. Arioc leaned against the wall, wiping the sweat from his face. Snail-trails glistened beside him on the plaster, where his own ejaculate had bespattered the wall.

'Well, I do feel better for a good fuck, you were right,' Veraine nodded, trying to calm his ragged breathing. 'But if you ever disobey an order again like that, soldier, I will have the chariot-pole rammed up your insubordinate arse. Understand?'

Arioc's brows shot up. 'Yes, sir,' he said soberly.

6 The Devouring Earth

'If you are ready, Malia Shai,' said Muth, picking up the paintbrush. It looked tiny in her broad hand.

The younger woman slipped off her dress and lay down on the plinth that occupied the centre of the Room of Writing. A single layer of cloth separated her from the block of stone and it was cool where it pressed on cheek and breasts, belly and thighs. She let out a long breath, composing herself.

'Forgive me, mistress of lamentation!' Muth said, and followed up with a swiftly chanted prayer in the priestly dialect, begging the cruel goddess of pestilence to forgive her profane touch. The goddess in question closed her eyes and tried to relax.

She was tense. It was undeniable. Despite her self-control, anticipation of the Drought Ceremony, only a matter of hours away, was making her nerves sing. It was not a rite that could be approached casually. The effort it demanded, both physically and spiritually, had to be garnered from every fibre.

Muth, finishing the prayer, offered the tiny pot containing pigment to the Malia Shai. She looked down at the powders, brown and black, then pursed her lips and spat into them. Her mouth was dry. That was not surprising in this, the height of summer. The earth was parched. Muth stirred the contents of the pot into a paste with the blunt end of the brush she held. Then she laid the clean end, the soft scut of fur, between the Malia Shai's bare shoulders and ran it slowly down her spine.

The brush tickled. As it reached the curve of her arse, the Malia Shai spread her thighs. The pigment that would be used to paint her body with the sacred sigils of the Drought Ceremony was composed of henna and earth and, to enhance its potency, her own body fluids. The soft brush slipped right down between the round hills of her buttocks into the valley between, paused to circle the dry well of her anus, then gently stroked the cleft of her labia. It found the narrow combe within moist.

The Malia Shai wiped her mind blank, stepping away from the inevitable bodily reactions to Muth's adroit questing. She listened to the sound of the priest on her other side, who she could not see, patiently grinding the dry ingredients of the paint. She thought about the ritual ahead of her. She felt the first warm trickle of her own wetness begin to gather and seep, but it seemed to be a distant event that had little to do with her.

Muth, for all her coarseness and her bulk, was an expert in the use of the brush. She wielded it with both delicacy and daring, easing the full fleshy lips apart to stir the pink bud within, then chasing off to tease the younger woman's anus and returning to probe the well-spring of her yoni. When she had gathered enough moisture on the deer-hair tuft, she wiped it into the paint pot and stirred it in. The dark lacework of the holy words she began to write onto the Malia Shai's flank were applied with the fine tip of the brush stick.

The goddess felt the first syllables scribed onto her flesh and caught her breath slightly. The ink seemed to burn coldly where it touched, and she could feel the patterns taking their shape in her mind. They spoke of power and destruction and a merciless purpose. She thought of the War of the Gods and her breathing became shallow and hard.

'Hold still, Mali Shai,' Muth grumbled. The stick dotted the ripples of her backbone. 'This is not easy.'

The young woman beneath her made a small noise of acknowledgement. She thought about the sun shining down on the desert rocks, his heat baking them into immobility, the dark lines on her back like cracks in sun-fired earth. The stick traced its ancient paths across her skin. The brush flicked and dipped, seeking moisture in her hot cleft. She thought of lizards running over the stones, sliding into any cracks that might offer shade or damp. She thought of their little flickering tongues and their tiny splayed hands. She thought of the warmth of the sun's body beating down on her smooth back and her coppery fleece. The brush licked at her clit, stoking the heat within it.

'It's too hot,' Muth muttered almost to herself, pausing to wipe the sweat from her brow. 'I will be glad when the Rains come, Malia Shai. Don't hold them off too long.'

She thought then of the rain falling on the baked rocks and the desiccated earth, the Rain Lord crouching over her, his grey hair falling on her back, beating and trickling its way into the crannies and the cracks. She smelled the bitter smell of rain on dust. She felt her cleft fill with moisture, brimming with it.

Muth clicked her tongue. 'You're wet, lady, all of a sudden.' She plunged her brush into the sopping well of the Malia Shai's sex, swirling the implement in the unexpected excess of moisture. 'What are you thinking about?'

'The rain,' she replied, eyes wide.

Muth made the smallest of snorts down her nose. She began to paint quickly, freely, using the bounty offered her.

The Malia Shai pictured the Rain Lord lowering himself over her parched and thirsty body, his lips on her neck and shoulders where the brush now licked. It was just like a tongue, first flickering over her skin then descending to lap at the rising spring of her sex juices. She spread her thighs a little wider to admit him. She wanted more than anything the long shaft of the lightning strike to stab into her wet earth. She wanted the flash and the burn of his spear to shake her to the core. She wanted his clouds to cover her, the lightning to lash her again and again.

She did not think about the brush. She was not concerned with Muth's tormenting strokes. Nevertheless, as the priestess dipped into the seeping cleft between her legs one more time, the touch of that fur on her clit drove her over the edge into orgasm. The Malia Shai gave no outward sign, not even by the slightest tremble or moan. Her body was too well disciplined for that. Perhaps if it had been Muth's fingers questing there and not the brush, she would have felt the pulse and the clenching of internal muscles rippling over them, but as it was the priestess did not notice. And the Mali Shai saw nothing but her inner vision of the Rain Lord entering her from behind and above, their bodies fused in fire and water and darkness.

'I have a bad feeling about this,' Rumayn muttered to no one in particular.

Veraine cast him a brief sideways glance before turning his gaze back on the river of pilgrims that was flowing past them, through the courtyard and into the Inner Temple. That river, which had its source in the lower city and was now flowing miraculously upwards, kept looking over at the three Irolian men as they lounged against the colonnade, but no challenge was offered to their presence. The pilgrims were too intent on shuffling forward down the line, craning their necks to see ahead.

'Why's that?' Loy asked.

Rumayn shrugged and stared about him. 'I don't know. I just have this feeling.'

'The only feeling you should have is in your knob,' the commander advised.

'It's the weather,' Veraine said, from where he stood with his back and one sole propped against a pillar. 'The Rains are on their way.'

All three men looked automatically into the sunset sky. There was no sign of any cloud from here, in the courtyard, but that morning the first grey clots had appeared briefly over the hills to the north, before being boiled away by the climbing sun.

'Maybe, General,' Rumayn said.

Veraine watched the pilgrims, dressed in their finest even when this was only rags, their hands cupped and full of grain in offering to their goddess. Men and women, young and old, some singing, most chattering, passed in a pageant of dark eyes and bright clothes. There were, however, no children among them; children and pregnant or nursing women were forbidden in the temple of She Who Makes the Womb a Desert.

'I hear there is sickness down in the city,' Veraine said.

'There is always sickness among the pilgrims,' Rumayn replied. 'Every year. The priests told me. It's called the Kiss of Malia.'

Veraine's face did not betray the thought that rose unbidden into his mind.

'To die of the plague here is supposed to release you from many incarnations,' Rumayn added cheerfully.

'As long as it hasn't appeared among the Host,' Veraine said.

'No, sir,' Loy reassured him. The rugged soldier looked ill at ease in his dress uniform, the fringed tunic somehow too clean and smooth. Veraine's version included a white, pleated overmantle. Neither man wore armour, though both carried swords at their sides. Veraine never went anywhere in Mulhanabin without his sword.

'I think they've stopped,' Rumayn observed, nodding at the pilgrims. The flow seemed to have choked.

'The Temple must be full by now,' said Loy. 'I thought it was a slow year.'

'This is. In normal years pilgrims are regularly crushed to death in the streets, according to the priests.'

Loy cracked a smile at this thought. Then he added, 'It's probably too full for us, sir. Maybe we shouldn't bother.'

'We wait for the priest, Commander.'

'Perhaps we should take the girl's advice, General,' Rumayn suggested. 'She should know.'

Veraine pulled in a long breath through his teeth but said nothing. He was only too aware of the Malia Shai's warning and it troubled him more than he would ever admit to his subordinates.

She had come to him days ago, in the middle of the evening meal he had been sharing with his command staff. All the higher officers had been there, sprawled upon the cushions of the headquarters room, goblets of wine at their elbows and bowls of food balanced on the brocade before them. Loy and Rumayn, the four captains including Sron their senior, the chief of surgeons, the master engineer, the *tesserius* who was responsible for paperwork and the procurement of supplies, Arioc and the eight other junior officers of good birth who were learning their vocation; all had been deep in their cups and loud with belligerent good humour.

Then the door had opened and she had walked

straight into the centre of the room. Silence had fallen like a stone. Only the Malia Shai could have stood in front of those men without a trace of self-consciousness, and only she could have failed to discern the hostility of their regard. She was like a cat walking into a kennel full of war-hounds. Veraine had been on his feet and in front of her before he even realised what he was doing. It had looked to the other men as if he were blocking her way; but only he had been aware of quite how strong his instinct to protect her was.

'What can I help you with, Malia Shai?' he had asked in Yamani, spreading his hands. If he could have shielded her bodily from the gaze of his men, he would have.

She had stared up at him, her face a mask of inscrutable purpose as she said, 'Do you like me?'

Veraine had felt the ground lurch under his feet. He had dimly heard Rumayn splutter into his wine as his own throat sought for an answer and found nothing. He had no idea what the Malia Shai could possibly mean by asking a question like that in public. From any other woman the inquiry could have had only one purpose, but it would have been posed in private, not in front of a coterie of men, of whom several were undoubtedly following at least the gist of the conversation.

'I'm sorry, I don't understand,' he had said at last.

She had frowned. 'You don't like Rasa Belit. Do you like me?'

Veraine had felt relief wash over him then. It had been a child's question, not a woman's. 'Well, yes, I like you,' he had admitted awkwardly.

'Rasa Belit is thinking of asking you to view the Drought Ceremony. If he does, say no.'

'Why?'

'You like me now. You will not like me after the Drought Ceremony.'

Veraine had tried to wet dry lips. 'He has already asked me, Malia Shai. I've accepted. I can't change my mind now.'

She had not argued with him, or looked upset, but only turned slowly away. He had not tried to stop her leaving, only stood perplexed and frowning while all around him the officers of the Eighth Host muttered and sniggered.

'I wonder what . . .?' Rumayn had begun, but then had caught the General's eye and thought better of it.

Now, in the courtyard, moments from the great ceremony, the Irolian adviser did manage to ask, 'I wonder what she meant? It must have been something bad to bring her to warn you, General.'

'Well, we're about to find out,' Veraine replied. 'Here's the priest.'

A yellow-robed priest wielding a wooden rattle finished beating his way clear of the crowd in the doorway and approached their small group. He bowed. 'General Veraine, please follow me to the *Garbhagria*.'

With some trepidation, the three obeyed.

I am armed and ready for war. Blood sings as it boils in my veins, and my hair stands out like the tail of a peacock. All around me the gods cower, afraid of what they have created almost as much as they fear the enemy I will now face in their name. I look upon them with unrestrained amusement, and when I laugh my tongue lolls past my tusks and down upon my naked breasts. My belly is tight with curbed power. I raise the weapons in each of my many hands, weapons the gods have gifted to me. I wield the earth-shattering thunderbolt and the sword that is death, the spear of pestilence and the flame that burns the impure, the drum whose beat sloughs flesh from bone and the flute whose note dissolves the marrow. I am ready, as they have willed it. I will face the demon Sorol Sek who has chosen to challenge the gods, who would try to destroy the firm and ordered Earth. I will defeat him in all his polymorphous, writhing shapes, as the mewling deities of the cosmos cannot. I will devour him and I will drink his blood. I am rage. I am destruction incarnate. They have brought me into being to defend the earth, they have armed me for this fight and gifted me with their strength, and my appetite will not be sated until I have consumed the demon that is Chaos. Fire runs in my veins. My yoni is wet for the pleasure of slaughter. I am Malia, the goddess above all gods, the salvation of the universe, the devourer of worlds.

The Innermost Temple, the womb-house, the forbidden heart of Mulhanabin behind the ancient doors – it pulsed with the beat of humanity, with their shuffling feet, their swaying shoulders, their softly clapping hands. The priest forced a path through the pressed crowd and Veraine followed directly behind him into a vast nave thick with incense and sweat. Somewhere a clutch of musicians were pounding drums and blowing conches, the howling sound of which ululated endlessly without melody or direction. Pilgrims pulled back reluctantly on either side to permit them to pass, turning to see who could be pushing; a few faces looked angry but most just stared.

They made their way with painful slowness to the left-hand side of the hall and then climbed upstairs, further into the crowd that teetered over them like the curve of a wave. There was a stone box or pavilion, its carved wall only waist-high, halfway up the flank of the room, and into that the three soldiers were urged. It gave them some space, though no privacy and nowhere to sit. Perhaps it had been originally constructed for royalty.

Veraine laid his hands on the top of the low wall and looked up and down the hall.

The *Gharbagria* was, as he had been told, a single great room, with tiers of steps rising on either side of the central floor. That floor was kept clear of pilgrims by a perimeter wall of priests armed with staves, although the press of devotees near the door threatened to buckle their line. The walls were carved in horizontal tiers, too, rising to a barrel-shaped roof which the torchlight barely revealed. In the centre of the room were a large altar and a brazier. The altar was heaped up and overflowing with grain and flowers, the offerings of those pilgrims lucky enough to have been able to get close to it. At the far end of the chamber was another flight of stairs, much steeper, at the top of which gold curtains screened off what seemed to be a room-within-a-room, like an enormous sculpted jewellery box.

'This stinks,' Loy said softly from his far right.

Every tier of the public stands was crammed with the sweating, jostling worshippers of the goddess, most of them wailing softly to the beat of the throbbing drums. Veraine looked down at a field of dark heads and up at the rising cliff of brightly clad bodies opposite. Outnumbered and cut off from escape – not a good situation, his soldier's mind nagged him, although the advice was now pointless. He automatically calculated the distance to the open floor and how fast he could climb over the shoulders of the suppliants to get there.

'Just try to look dignified,' Rumayn offered facetiously.

'There's Rasa Belit,' Veraine said, jerking his chin to point. The high priest was circling the wall of his underlings, thrusting his hands through into the crowd. The people on the other side were heaping his cupped hands with more offerings, so that he could turn and throw them onto the altar. Gemstones flashed among the wheat-seed as they fell. Most merely fed the slithering waterfall of grain spilling into a pool upon the floor.

'So what happens now?' Loy asked the adviser sandwiched between him and the General.

'I have no idea. No one's seen the Drought Ceremony before, as far as I know.'

'Well they had better hurry up about it,' Veraine said grimly. 'There are no windows in here and if it takes too long we're all going to suffocate.'

The Yamani seemed to be in no hurry, though the temperature built and the air in their lungs became wet and heavy. Rasa Belit grabbed handful after handful to throw on the heaped altar and the people sang louder and louder the distended syllables of their song, of which the Irolians could make out very little other than the word 'Malia'. The music tightened round Veraine's forehead like a ligature. The wall of noise seemed to be building to some kind of climax, though it was in the end impossible to discern what sign it was that made Rasa Belit drop the last offering at his own feet and swing to face the stairs, arms raised high. The musicians fell instantly silent and a great hush gripped the crowd by the throat.

The high priest filled his lungs with wet air and began an invocation and, even in this crowded chamber which should have smothered his voice, the deep mournful chant resonated through the hall.

'Come, come in haste, oh goddess, with thy locks bedraggled; Thou who hast three eyes, whose skin is dark, whose clothes are stained with blood, who hast rings in thy ears, who hast a thousand hands, who ridest upon a monster and wieldest in thy hands tridents, clubs, lances and shields. 'Come in haste, Thou who devourest thy children!'

At this signal the two priests by the curtain swept back the golden cloth to reveal the dais within.

The crowd gave a great, prolonged cry of acclamation, which fell away into a sudden and bottomless silence.

'Shuga's balls!' said Rumayn with feeling.

From their vantage point they had an excellent view of the whole hall. Behind the curtain on a throne as wide as a bed the Malia Shai sat cross-legged. Her legs were bare, though the rest of her seemed to be clad in armour. Veraine knew it was her. He knew the set of her shoulders and the shape of her jaw, though a spiked mask from which the dark pits of eyes stared out covered the rest of her face from the nose up. Oddly enough her hair, in the Yamani symbol of female intimacy permitted only to lovers and husbands, was unbound and streamed down across her shoulders.

Veraine felt his heart turn over. Her hair in the torch-light was the colour of rosewood.

It was only a dream! he told himself, his hands tightening on the stone. How did I know?

Slowly the Malia Shai uncoiled herself and stood upon the throne. She moved with a strange insectile grace. There was absolute silence from the throng, although the musicians lurched into a new tune, more complex and somehow more aggressive. It soon became apparent that she was wearing a skirt of the finest chain mail, though this was slashed to the waist on both sides to leave her movements unrestricted. There were elaborate vambraces on her forearms, yet her feet were bare. This was fantasist's armour – ritual and symbolic rather than practical. Her bronze body armour, like her mask, emphasised the contours of breasts and waist and hips beneath while at the same time transforming them into something threatening and terrible. Veraine felt his mouth go dry. The unarmoured parts of her skin were painted in swirling calligraphy. She moved with the jagged, swaying steps of a praying mantis, arms spread wide and legs akimbo. The strain on her thighs must have been terrible. The silver chain mail sparkled and swung between them.

Slowly, to the clashing and squealing of tortured musical instruments, the Malia Shai descended the steps to the floor area. There she suddenly stretched, reaching over her shoulders to the two crossed swords sheathed there and flourishing them in the flaring torchlight. She began to dance. It was not the slow measured dance of a Yamani temple priestess, though it was just as stylised in its way; it was the stamping, kicking display of the warrior possessed, all whipping legs and slashing blades that whirled within inches of her audience's faces. She leaped her own blades over and over, crouched and spun and clashed her weapons on the stone so that metal shrieked and sparks sprang. Veraine was astonished and impressed and appalled all at once. And the audience hung on her every movement.

The General felt the boiling heat of the air seep from his lungs into his blood and flow inexorably to his groin. The pounding rhythm of the alien music and the writhing gyrations of the woman he wanted, the sheen of sweat visible on her naked thighs, all these were conspiring to make him hard, even as his stomach tightened with revulsion. His balls felt as heavy as lead slingshot. This was nothing like what he had expected from the Malia Shai. It was a travesty of the serene calm she had presented on every occasion of their meeting, and he could hardly believe that it was her beneath that demonic armour. But that did not stop his cock thickening as he watched her twist on serpentine hips.

So intent was he on devouring every moment of the Malia Shai's performance that it took a sudden exclamation from Rumayn to make him realise that another actor had entered the stage below.

'Oh no,' said the military adviser, very low, very fast. 'No, no, no.'

He jerked his gaze away and saw that from somewhere the priests had produced a man and laid him across the altar, his belly stretched tight as his back was arched over the mound of grain. Four of them were holding his limbs, though he did not seem to be resisting. He had only the simplest of *fouta* loincloths wrapped around his wiry body.

Veraine opened his mouth to say something but nothing came out. He felt a wave of cold wash over him. Rumayn was staring at him, wide eyed.

'They can't do this, General!'

'Shut up,' Veraine said hoarsely. 'Don't make a sound. You don't have to watch.' He saw the Malia Shai leap and fall to a crouch like a tiger, the swords dashed to the ground. One of the blades shattered and a vicious shard flew across the floor into the crowd. Any cries of pain from them were drowned in the dull roar from thousands of throats as the dance froze in a moment of perfect stillness – perfect but for the heaving of her chest as she fought to draw enough air into her lungs. And now she was close enough that he could see that her breastplate was an elaborate filigree cage through which the sheen of her bare skin could be glimpsed, and desire and horror were at bloody war inside him.

She was facing the man on the altar, staring straight up between his splayed legs.

Veraine felt as though some great cold snake had coiled itself around his chest under the ribcage and was forcing its way up his throat, choking him. It tightened further when the Malia Shai stood and climbed up onto the altar between the man's thighs. She pulled the *fouta* off him with a single derisive jerk, then kneeled across his hips.

Veraine could feel that all the colour had run out of his face.

The priestess laid her hands on the man's bare chest and caressed the length of his torso. He was staring up at her, vacant of all expression. He's been drugged, the General thought, though his own mind seemed to be moving through a sluggish mass of half-frozen ice.

Her hand brushed her chainmail skirt aside from his belly and reached down into the hidden space between them, where his groin met hers. Veraine saw the muscles tighten in her arm.

The man screamed. It was a savage, guttural sound that wrenched a strange ululating wail from the audience. He bucked against the restraining grip of the four priests. Veraine watched what the Malia Shai did, glassy-eyed. He could not have looked away if his life had depended upon it, though his jaw ached from the pressure of his teeth grinding together and cold sweat was running down his temples.

Even after she finished the man beneath her would not stop screaming. She reached round to the small of her back, where a short, broad-bladed knife was sheathed among the plates of her armour. She slid herself further up his body to get the right angle and placed the tip of the blade on his breastbone.

Veraine managed to look to his right at his companions. Loy's face had set like mortar in the heavy, closed expression of a soldier who has seen more atrocities than he can remember. But Rumayn had turned ashy, was swaying, and looked as if he was going to faint.

'Look at the floor,' Veraine said. His voice seemed to him to come from very far away. 'If you fall I will kill you myself.'

He saw Rumayn sink his head upon his chest, then he raised his own gaze and watched. His hands gripped tight the stone wall, so that they would not be seen to shake. He watched until the man on the altar had stopped screaming for ever. He watched the Malia Shai stalk back to her throne and disappear again behind the curtain. He watched the congregation burst into a chaos of chanting, arms thrust high towards the throne, some whirling in circles, some falling to the floor and thrashing in convulsions. All around them the Yamani pilgrims shook in the transport of exultation, their faces wet with tears and sweat. The three Irolians clung to their perch and did not dare to move a muscle until the worshippers finally, still singing, filed out of the hall. He watched for what seemed like hours. His gaze followed the movements of the crowd automatically, but in his mind's eye all he saw was the blood. Blood soaking into the wheat. Blood on her beautiful coppery skin. Blood on her lips.

Only when the hall was almost empty did he give the order to the other two that they could move out. They slowly descended the steps towards the door. Rasa Belit was waiting there, though whether for them specifically it was impossible to say.

'I trust you found the ceremony educational,' he said with a lingering smile.

Veraine stared at him for a long moment. Then he cleared his throat. 'You know very well that human sacrifice hasn't been permitted since our conquest. Your balls must be made of brass, priest, wherever they are at this moment.' His voice was low but cold, as cold as steel on skin, and he was rewarded by the tiniest of flickers in the smirk before him.

'Well, if you intend to take it up with someone then I suggest the Provincial Governor,' countered the priest. 'He was the one who supplied us with the sacrifice, after all. And he has done for years. A goodwill gesture to the natives, I believe.'

Veraine drew breath in through his teeth. 'I'll be taking it up,' he agreed grimly.

'You're disgusting,' Rumayn butted in, his voice not quite steady.

The priest looked at him in mild surprise. 'I'm sorry?'

Veraine, who should have silenced his subordinate, said nothing.

'You priests. Your goddess. That girl ... she's insane. The gods don't need to drink human blood.'

Rasa Belit grinned. 'She's the Malia Shai. What offering do you think appropriate to the goddess? Flowers perhaps?' He snorted derisively. 'Maybe you Irolians don't take your gods seriously enough. Malia saved Heaven and Earth from Chaos. She is the rawest and strongest of powers, and no sacrifice less than a human being would be sufficient. What, are we to say no to her?'

Rumayn made a noise as if he were about to spit.

'That man was already condemned to death,' explained Rasa Belit. 'He was a convicted bandit. He'd robbed and raped scores of people. Do you still feel sorry for him?'

'Doesn't matter. What she did ...' Rumayn shook his head, grimacing. 'That was disgusting, beyond belief, beyond words.'

'Don't be ridiculous. She is the devouring earth and we are all her victims. She is famine and she is plague. If you forget that, Irolian, go look in the streets of any city.'

'We're leaving, Commander.' Veraine interrupted. He

betrayed it by no outward sign, but within him he could feel the anger mounting like a white sheet of flame. He could not listen to Rasa Belit any longer. The ceremony had left Loy discomfited and Rumayn shocked to the quick, but he felt like it had torn his guts out.

They brushed past the smirking priest and strode towards the doors.

'What are your orders for the evening, sir?' Loy asked as they emerged into the clean air.

'I need a drink,' Rumayn muttered.

'See to the men, Commander,' Veraine answered. 'I don't want to be disturbed.'

I am burning. I have destroyed the demon Sorol Sek, I have saved the gods, but his blood is churning in my belly and my wrath is burning in my veins. My skin is afire. With every step away from the battleground my feet flatten mountains. The froth from my distended lips poisons the seas as I stride over them, and the continents crack beneath my bare soles. My hands still weave their dance of destruction, and all creation hides itself in terror of my passing.

The gods seize me. Having created me, they must curb what they have let loose, or the earth will never survive. They bind my wrists in the long locks of the Rain's hair, they pin me beneath the weight of the Sky-Mountain, they pour upon my molten skin the pure waters of the Holy River. Innumerable hands caress me, soothing, distracting, the eight thousand gods and goddesses of the cosmos stroking and tending to me, the starry heavens rippling with music to calm my rage, the sweet kisses of the Sun warm upon my lips. My limbs tighten against their constraining hands, but they are determined and terrible in their gentleness, in their deft and loving manipulations, until my fury curdles imperceptibly to pleasure, and my

pleasure shakes my body in every thread. The unbearable
pressure of my power flows out of me like water down a
sluice, leaving me at last drained of violence and wrapped
in peace.

No one saw Veraine that night; he kept to his room and refused any dinner except a bottle of brandy. It was during weapons practice the next morning that officers and men began to notice that something was wrong. Veraine entered the lists without comment, then proceeded to beat his opponent to a pulp with the wooden stave, leaving the soldier with smashed ribs and a broken arm, continuing to strike at him even when the man was on the floor. Loy was the only one watching who had the courage to run in with a shield and physically intervene. The General threw down his stave and walked away without a word.

He was walking back to his quarters when the Malia Shai stepped out from an alcove. She had been waiting for him, knowing he was bound to walk down that particular corridor.

'General Veraine,' she said softly.

He turned to her. His eyes were as cold as shale. She had never seen him look at her like that. 'You've got blood on your mouth,' he said.

She raised one hand halfway to her face before she realised he couldn't be speaking the literal truth; she had cleansed herself thoroughly since the Drought Ceremony.

He turned away and walked off.

Back in his room, he ordered Arioc to prepare his chariot and horses. 'You won't be needed to drive.'

He took the chariot out into the flat desert at a gallop, unheeding of the goatherds who had to leap from in front of the hooves. He drove across the salt-encrusted plain in a plume of dust, whipping the horses to their utmost effort. He circumnavigated the whole hill of Mulhanabin and returned to the city to abandon the team at the gate, the once-fine animals heaving for breath and dripping bloody foam onto their sweat-soaked chests.

Returning to the Temple, he called for several bottles of brandy and shut himself in his private chamber.

'This isn't like him at all,' Arioc complained to his comrades. 'What's happened? He hardly drinks, normally.' And rumours of ill news and impending disaster ran rife among the Irolian host.

There was a very good reason Veraine only drank to moderation. He had learned long ago that alcohol exposed in him a black lode of bitterness that normally never saw daylight. He could be a vicious drunk, one who did not know when to curb the savage desire to lash out; a liability to himself and others.

This time he did not care. He sat himself in front of the window and slowly, meticulously, drank his way through the fiery liquor. For a while it dulled the pain, for a while he passed into a daze where he did not have to relive the events of the Drought Ceremony over and over again, but he did not manage to sleep, any more than he had managed to sleep the previous night. Eventually he came back to himself, and the goblets of brandy no longer seemed to have the power to affect his head or his memory. His mind, like a leopard pacing in a cage, could not cease contemplating the thing that tormented it.

He had been utterly betrayed. By her or by himself, he could not tell. He had imagined he saw in her something he had never recognised in any other woman; a purity that had nothing to do with naïvety. An otherworldliness;

an inhuman innocence. He had seen it, and for all his cynicism about priests and gods he had wanted so very much to believe in that. He could hardly believe now that he had been such a fool. He had cherished an image of the Malia Shai, and she had smashed it to shards, in performing an act so foul that only a monster or a lunatic could believe it acceptable. Veraine's stomach cramped with loathing.

Only an idiot could still desire her.

As he returned to full awareness of his surroundings he realised that deep night had fallen on the city. No sounds of life or activity filtered into his room from within or without the temple. His room was in almost total darkness. He heaved himself to his feet and walked to the door, carrying with him the small bronze cup of intricate design that had been brought all the way from Antoth with his baggage.

Outside in the corridor a single Irolian guard was leaning against the wall and he jerked hurriedly to attention when Veraine appeared.

'What watch is this?'

'The third, General.'

The depths of night, then, when even soldiers and whores slept. 'Going for a slash,' Veraine muttered, and set off down the corridor. However, he did not get as far as the latrine room that overhung the cliff-edge. Two junctions away was a niche holding one of the omnipresent statues of Malia, her corpse-features leering in the flicker of a single lamp. Veraine paused mid-stride and glanced around him. There was no one else in sight. He put his cup down carefully, pulled up his tunic and, with great deliberation, pissed on the idol until he could not force another drop. Stepping back, he readjusted his clothing and smiled a sour smile at the goddess.

'Priestess,' he murmured. The smile died. After a moment he retrieved his cup and, still taking sips of brandy, set off walking.

Sometime in the afternoon he must have removed his hobnailed sandals. Barefoot, he moved silently across floorboards and flagstones. He met no one and heard nothing; it was as if he moved through a dream. The cup hung loosely from his fingers. Crossing the inner court-yard he glanced up at the sky and saw that the full moon was shining through clouds as if veiled in rags. The stars were muffled from sight, and a heavy feeling had settled like dew on the still foliage. He dipped his fingers in the pool as he passed, little droplets scattering to the old stones of the wall.

He walked into the Inner Temple and paced without hurry to the door of the Malia Shai's room. His heart was pounding, but not with fear. If he'd met any Yamani guard he would have struck the man down, but there were no priests in evidence. Perhaps the gods were favouring him. Perhaps this was destiny, or the force of his own will that, hardened by bitterness and brandy, was capable of reordering the world. No light shone from her door. There was only a moment's hesitation before he lifted the curtain and went in.

She was asleep on the pallet, he saw at once, and his jaw tightened in parody of a smile. He recognised the shape of her back and hip in the moonlight as she lay turned away on her side, though the shadow of the window sill lay across her head like a veil. He stalked noiselessly to the bedside, looked down at her for a long moment and then squatted on his heels. A thin sheet covered her to the armpits, but beneath that she slept naked. In the moon's glow it was easy to make out the sheen on her skin, the curve of shoulder and spine, the swell of her hip.

He placed the cup on the floor. The emptying of his bladder had emptied all the warmth from him, too, and now all that was left in his guts was a great cold hard knot like a nest of snakes. Though he had crouched down and his hand was only inches from her warmth, he seemed to be looking down on her from an infinite height, a frozen bitter mountain top. He wanted to hurt her. He wanted the Malia Shai to feel the pain that she had caused him.

The only part of him that was not cold was the pulse hammering in his groin.

Suddenly she rolled over onto her back and his breath shuddered in his throat in anticipation of her waking. But she did not open her eyes; through the shadow over her face he could just make out the delicate strokes of her closed lashes. And her breathing flattened at once, slowing to a calm sigh. She did not know he was there. The sheet still covered her breasts demurely, though the cotton did little to hide the curves beneath. She was completely vulnerable to his touch, and it made the snakes in his belly spasm.

Wake up, he commanded her silently. Wake up and see me crouched over you, hands about to grab you. See the intent in my eyes, so that I can see the fear in yours. Try to scream; see how far it gets you. I'd like that.

With infinite care he took hold of the edge of the sheet and folded it back, slowly exposing her breasts and her narrow waist, dark nipples that looked up at him like eyes, the tiny pursed mouth of her navel. Now his hands were clenched into fists. Still she did not wake. He swallowed despite the dryness of his throat.

She did not look like a goddess, or a monster; she looked like the wanton he had dreamed of on the first night in Mulhanabin. She looked like everything he had ever imagined of her. She was slender and soul-tearingly beautiful and he wanted to possess her more than anything he could name. Her soft, rounded breasts, flattened by gravity, made the palms of his hands burn. Moonlight silvered her flat belly. He could smell the warm scent of her skin and that scent nearly drove him mad. It would be so easy, he thought, to cover her mouth, to pin her beneath his weight, to force his way into her tight sex with a few hard thrusts. She was far too slight to fight him.

He would make her pay. He would teach her what it meant to mock and shame and hurt him. There was nothing the priests could do to stop it, and nothing that they would be able to do the next day. Who would believe her? Who would defy the might of the Irolian army?

He could feel the snakes within him coiling and twisting, the terrible lust that was making his hands and legs tremble. He wanted to feel those slim wrists straining under his hands, wanted to bite those tawny breasts, wanted to rip her thighs apart with his hard legs and his cruel cock and feel the slap of his balls that were so full to bursting against her sex. He wanted to break her and impale her and empty the weeks of frustration into the raw wound. He wanted to feel her convulse beneath him.

He shut his eyes and stood up and walked out of the room.

Only when back in the garden courtyard did he dare to breathe again. The night spun around him. Now he wanted to howl at the moon like a chained dog.

There was nothing he could do but start walking, and once he had started nothing he could do but keep going. He walked back through the maze of corridors and right out of the temple, out into the Citadel, following instinct, almost blind. He only stopped when he reached the sacred pool, the great tank where the pilgrims bathed. Even at this time of night there were a few people gathered around it, and lamps dancing on the ripples of the water. Veraine stared at the flames. His head felt like it was going to burst. He wanted to splash the cool water over his face and arms, so he started down the steps, but an accidental glance at one of the pilgrims made him pause. A middle-aged woman was standing in the pool washing sheets. Presumably the sacred waters would cleanse not just laundry but also the souls of those who slept under them. But those cloths were streaked with dirt, and even from the edge of the pool Veraine could tell it was shit and blood he was looking at. He grimaced and jerked away from the water.

In another part of the tank, oblivious to the filth contaminating the liquid, a knot of aged Yamani men were bathing and drinking from their cupped hands. Veraine felt the brandy aftertaste in his mouth sour. He shook his head and was about to leave when his glance happened to fall upon a lone woman at the far edge, and at once his overheated mind saw with perfectly clarity what he had to do.

She was dressed in white and her long braided hair was uncovered, though she had obviously left childhood behind her. She kneeled near the edge of the pool, letting the water run through her fingers as she prayed inaudibly. Veraine clenched his fists. There was only one class of Yamani who wore bleached cloth, and that was the Sajaal sect. They were a community who believed that illumination and salvation came through restraint, through avoiding contamination. They ate no meat or animal product, refused to own slaves and scorned alcohol. They married late in life and only within their own sect. Introverted and notorious for a careful business sense, they were despised and distrusted by the larger society around them.

But this one did not look rich. As Veraine circled the pool and walked past her, he noted how ragged her scrupulously clean dress looked, how thin her wrists were. He went and stood in the shadows a little way away. As yet unmarried, this one was certain to be a virgin. He waited until she had finished her prayers, gathered her damp skirts about her and climbed up the pool steps. She set off down the hill. Then he followed.

'Wait,' he said, as they passed under the shadow of a colonnade. It was a mark of the trust the sect had in the gods that she did not flee at the sound of a masculine voice coming from the dark, but turned and looked at him.

'I saw you praying,' he said, keeping his voice gentle. 'Are you troubled?' He noted her round face and the youthful fullness of her lips with predatory approval. He also saw the desperation in her eyes.

'Everyone has troubles,' she replied, those eyes wide as she watched him close in on her. 'My father's ill with the Kiss of Malia. I was praying for him.'

'I'm so sorry. Will he die, do you think?'

She shrank from him a little, but he had circled her by now, cutting off her exit. 'If the gods will it,' she replied.

'What will you do then, without him to support you? You don't look well off.'

She flinched. 'We'll go to our relatives.'

'We? You have a mother? Younger brothers and sisters?'

She nodded.

'That's a lot of people to support. A terrible burden to inflict on your relatives. Who are not so wealthy themselves in these hard times, I would guess.' He smiled. 'I could give you money.'

She opened her mouth and shook her head suddenly. Now she looked nervous.

'Here.' He took out his coin-pouch from the purse sewn into his belt and held it out to her. 'Take a look.'

When she shook her head again he quickly and efficiently snatched up her hand, closed it around the pouch and then released both. She was left holding the small but heavy bag in her palm.

'Count it,' he suggested. 'There's enough there to buy you many acres of good land. Herds of cattle. Or for a dowry.' He smiled again as she stared down at her hand. 'For a good, kind husband who will look after your family.'

'We don't do this,' she whispered weakly.

'You could buy medicine, tonight, for your father. You asked the gods for help. This is it.'

She hesitated then, tempted by a wealth she could never have imagined. And in that moment she was lost.

'All I want is a few minutes of your time,' Veraine said, the epitome of reasonableness. 'It really won't take long at all. You'll hardly notice a thing.'

The Sajaal maiden seemed to have gone into some sort of shock. She could neither let go of the purse nor reply to him. He took a step closer.

'Do you want it?'

She nodded, barely; the twitch of a chin.

He placed his hands round her waist and put her back against a stone pillar. 'Clever girl,' he said.

She shut her eyes as he pressed up against her. He didn't mind that. She felt tiny and delicate against his body, and he had to stoop to lift up her skirt and get his hand on her bare skin. He ran it roughly up between her thighs and located the join at the top, the hair and the faint dampness of her slit. She was going to be painfully dry and tight. Suddenly he had a raging, uncontrollable erection. He removed his hand from her groin to loosen his own clothes, then took her hand – the one without the money in it – and wrapped her cold fingers around his hard, hot flesh.

'Never held one of these before?' he breathed. 'Like it?'

Her face was all screwed up. He rubbed her unresisting hand up and down his cock and it was wonderful and obscene and wonderful because it was obscene. He was going to come very quickly, he knew; the pressure wave of lust and frustration and vile anger was too powerful to hold back for long. He pulled her hand off his cock and spat into her palm, then used it to smear the saliva over his swollen glans, lubricating the thick plug of flesh. Then he lifted her against the pillar.

'Shh. It's not going to hurt,' he lied.

He lowered her onto his hips and shoved himself hard and deep into her. She tried to cry out, but he already had one hand clapped over her mouth, while the other supported her weight, and only a muffled noise leaked through.

'Shut up,' he whispered, as he thrust over and over into her flesh. 'I'm paying for this.'

He spent in a wave of loathing darker than any Yamani demon-god. Then he released the girl and stepped away. She held herself up against the pillar, skirt rumpled and eyes closed, but she did not make any noise and she did not move. One would, indeed, hardly notice a thing had changed, except for the scalding tears that coated her cheeks.

'Just don't expect your next trick to pay so well,' Veraine told her. He walked away, back towards the Outer Temple.

Halfway across the open space the nausea hit him. It washed over in wave after wave, until by the time he reached the front steps his self-disgust was a physical thing that doubled him over and hammered blow upon blow into his stomach. He caught desperately at the stones as he began to vomit. He couldn't stop. Acid bitterness erupted from him and even when his belly was empty he kept heaving, as if he were trying to eject his entire body.

Dimly he heard the sound of someone calling his name. He looked up at last, half-blind with tears, and saw an Irolian scout staring down at him, his hands still tangled in the reins of a sweat-soaked pony.

'General Veraine!' the man cried. 'You must close the gates! Prepare the men! The Horse-eaters are less than a day's ride from here!'

7 I Saw Smoke and Gold

There were men up on the Citadel wall already as the Malia Shai ascended the new mud-brick steps by the gate; priests in yellow, workers in drab homespun and, she saw, Irolian soldiers who had to a man wrapped their white army tunics about with Yamani cloaks. Rasa Belit was not there, otherwise there would have been an ostentatious welcome; instead the priests in their gossiping huddle did not notice her, and the workers drafted in from the lower city did not recognise her without her ritual regalia. That did not matter to her. What did matter was that Veraine was there, his smoky hair visible among a knot of his officers, so she made sure that she walked away from them along the battlements.

She leaned against the wall and stared out over the roofs of Mulhanabin, into the desert beyond. There a second city had sprung up; a sprawling suburb of tents that surrounded three sides of the hill: the Horse-eater army. This morning it was still, the bustle of pitching camp over and done with, the first probing assault upon the city gate thrown back. The standard ultimatum had been issued – surrender at once, or every inhabitant would be butchered when the city fell – and duly ignored. Siege had been laid, and now the waiting had begun. The twisted bodies of prisoners staked out by the Horse-eaters for the education of the besieged had long ceased to twitch. Only lone figures and the thin smoke of dung fires moved among the tents. The Malia Shai could see many horses tethered between the felt walls, and a few dogs nosing about. The Horse-eaters had brought everything they possessed with them, including their families and livestock, and their sheer numbers put the annual pilgrim influx to shame. She had not imagined that there were so many people in the world.

The morning sun caught on bright gold discs raised high over the tents. Standards of some kind, she guessed. The Horse-eaters were supposed to worship the sun.

She turned her head as a man approached her, then realised it was General Veraine. She had deliberately avoided going near him, but now he came up to her and nodded. She noted the shadows blotched under his eyes, the stubble on his chin starting to resemble a beard.

'Malia Shai.'

'General Veraine.' She looked at the brown cloak wrapped around his shoulders. 'Has army uniform changed then?' she asked, after waiting for him to break the skin of silence between them.

He smiled awkwardly and jerked his head towards the besieging army. 'A precaution. If we're lucky, priestess, the Horse-eaters don't know anything about an Irolian presence here. I would like to keep them in ignorance as long as possible. They can't shoot us from there, but they can see us.' He glanced about them. 'I came over to apologise.'

'For what?' She watched as he leaned back against the wall, thinking that he did not even move or stand in the same way as a priest, that there was a litheness and a power in his unconscious motions that confounded her experience. He was alien to her closed temple world.

'I was rude to you. I was at fault. I'm most sincerely sorry.' He kept his voice low; workmen were passing frequently.

'You were perturbed by the Drought Ceremony,' she

said. 'I knew it would happen. You weren't adequately warned.'

He looked away from her, obviously uneasy. 'Well, maybe. I'd made some rather foolish assumptions about you, priestess. I was wrong, and I don't think any warning would have made a difference. I learned a hard lesson.'

'Oh. What did you learn?'

She thought she saw him flinch almost imperceptibly. 'That I'm not in any position to expect perfection of others.'

She mulled this over. 'Well, it's my purpose to strive for perfection,' she said slowly. 'But not by Irolian standards.'

'We all have faults and failings, priestess. We're human.'

'No,' she said gently. 'I am not.'

He frowned at her, but did not answer. She was not used to being looked at as she was by him. Most people who encountered her saw the mask, the robes, the title, or never raised their eyes above their own feet, and there was a glazed look to their expressions as if she were not really there. With Veraine, almost uniquely, she felt that he really saw her.

'You don't believe in me, do you?' she asked. It was a hard question to shape. 'My divinity, I mean. You think that when I take a man's life it's because I'm an evil Yamani woman.'

'I think that you do it because that's what you've been taught to do.'

'Then that must make me a stupid Yamani woman instead.'

'No,' he answered, 'you're not stupid.'

She shook her head, bemused and a little disturbed. She had never encountered disbelief before. 'I wish I could show you, so you'd understand. I am the goddess Malia. I was there at the creation of the universe. I remember it! Can you understand that? I remember the first human beings, and the great Flood, and the Battle of the Sky-Mountain. I remember the hero Gidindhi, and his quest against the tiger-lords. I was there to help him.'

'I suspect,' Veraine said, very slowly, 'that what you remember are the stories you've been told since you were a baby.'

She recognised the sour taste in her mouth as frustration. 'In Mulhanabin there are thousands and thousands of people who believe in me. They are praying to me right now to save them from – that.' She indicated the Horse-eater army below.

'Can you hear them?'

'They whisper at the back of my head, without cease.'

'Hmm. Will you answer them?'

'Maybe. I cannot act from fear, or pity. I must act out of my own nature.'

He snorted. 'Well, you certainly are just as useful to your worshippers as any other god.'

'So, are you trying to be apologetic or rude right now?'

'No.' He looked away again. 'I didn't mean to be rude.' There was an ant crawling on the wall. 'See that insect?' Veraine asked. 'Suppose it was to worship me. How would I know? How would I hear its prayers? Why would I care what it wanted?' He stubbed out the small life with the tip of one finger, then looked her in the eye. 'I think the gods must be like that to us; they have no interest in our life or our death. The gods are high up in heaven and they can't hear us.'

She was dismayed. 'How can you pray to them, then?'

'I don't, I'm afraid. So we do have one thing in common, priestess.'

There was a pause before she concluded, 'I think you must be very lonely.'

Some expression flickered across his face, but she had no chance to recognise it. Suddenly everything changed. The Yamani workman shuffling past at that moment had shrugged off his basket of clay and lurched in towards them. There was a flailing of limbs and a dull flash of light. The Malia Shai did not have time to react, but Veraine did; throwing up his arm and twisting to the side. The two men met. The Malia Shai just made out Veraine trying to seize the workman, then the skirmish bundled into her and she was knocked to the floor. By the time she got to her feet the Irolian was leaning out over the wall, staring down onto the roofscape below.

'Shit!' he said.

There was blood running down his left arm. She stepped to his side. A crumpled figure lay forty feet below them, unmoving.

'Now the bastard can't talk,' Veraine snarled. 'Shit!'

'Your arm,' she said. He did not seem to have noticed that he was wounded, but at her words he looked round and clapped his hand over his shoulder with a grunt of dismay. The bright blood pulsed up between his fingers.

'Sit down,' she ordered and pushed him to the floor.

'He had a knife,' Veraine said.

She tore off her headcloth, wadded one end into a pad and forced it under his fingers, against the wound. As quickly and tightly as she could she bound the loose end over the top. There was another cut across his chest, but it seemed to be bleeding a lot less.

'You all right?' she asked, her fingers dragging at the knot.

'Wonderful,' he replied. There was something strange about his voice. She looked up into his face and found he was staring at her, eyes burning.

Pounding feet broke their solitude. Suddenly there were Irolian soldiers everywhere, and priests reaching in to drag her away.

'Get the surgeon,' Veraine grunted to his men. Her last glimpse of his face before she was hustled away to safety told her that his lips were going blue with shock.

Veraine lay in his bed, propped up by a mound of cushions and with one leg drawn up, and tried to ignore the discomfort. He was not in a good mood: angry with himself for allowing the assassin to get past his guard and angry that he should be incapacitated just when the Horse-eaters had arrived, when he had to be seen to be in command of the situation. And the wound had got to the stage that with every beat of his heart a pulse of pain would run down all the way to his fingertips and up the side of his skull, so that he sat with jaw clenched. But the army surgeon, after flushing the cuts out with brandy and stitching them with horsehair, had warned him that his best chance for a speedy recovery lay in resting as much as possible right now.

His tunic had been cut away and pulled down, baring him to the waist. The bandages shone against his skin.

He dozed off for a while, wallowing through an uncomfortable sleep in pursuit of an old memory; riding the horses on his father's estate at dawn, before the grooms came out to chase him off.

He woke suddenly, and saw the Malia Shai was sitting on the edge of the bed next to him. For a moment he was confused; this was the second time she had managed to sneak into his room without him hearing – how did she manage it? Then he remembered: no, the first time had only been a dream.

'I didn't mean to startle you,' she said.

She sat so close he might have swept his good arm

around her. He could smell the incense on her clothes. His stomach tightened with dismay. 'What are you doing here?' he said roughly.

'I came to bring you this salve.' She lifted up a small pot with a wax seal. 'It's made from a desert plant; I thought your doctors might not have any. The priests use it to cleanse and heal their wounds after they are emasculated. It works well.' She paused. Her hair was wrapped away from sight again, her eyes calm. He might almost have imagined that fire in them as she had kneeled over him on the Citadel wall. 'Next time your cuts are dressed, get them to put this on too.'

'Were there guards on the door?' he demanded, but he kept his voice as low as possible.

'Yes. Two. They're protecting you now.'

'Oh shit.'

'They let me in. They must think I'm an unlikely assassin.'

There was a hint of humour in her voice, but he shook his head, not listening, and told her, 'Get out of here.'

She stared at him and put the pot down on the floor. 'What's wrong?'

'What's wrong?' he repeated. 'You're here alone with me in my bedroom. And you walked past two witnesses to get here!'

'So?'

He hissed with exasperation. 'Well, I don't know what it means among the Yamani when a woman goes into a man's chamber, but to an Irolian that has only one interpretation.'

She blinked slowly. 'What does it matter what your guards think?'

Somewhere deep inside he was disappointed. He might have been hoping for a blush or a smile or a flash of alarm – anything that acknowledged the possibility of sexual contact between them. It made him brutal. 'What about Rasa Belit?' he asked. 'How long will it take for him to hear? Get out of this room!'

She wasn't impressed. 'Don't be foolish. You're hurt. And I'm the Malia Shai – I don't indulge in carnal lusts.'

If he had not been so angry and frustrated he might have shrugged off the unintended slight. Instead he growled, 'Well that must be very nice for you, priestess. Congratulations. Unfortunately I'm made of weaker flesh and for my comfort you really should leave.'

Her mouth sagged a little. 'What do you mean?' Her breath was sweet; warm and close enough to drive him mad.

He fixed her gaze with his own. The last shreds of discretion were falling from him like leaves scorched by the desert sun.

'Do you really want to know? I'll explain exactly what I mean, Malia Shai, if you like.' He kept his voice low, but he spoke with punishing precision. 'I mean that your presence here now is giving me a most painful hard-on. My cock is up so rigid right now that you could use it as a battering ram. I mean that I can't think of you without wanting you, and I can't go a single hour without thinking of you.'

His voice was tight.

'I look at your lips and I want to see them wrapped around my prick. I want your breasts in my hands and I want your nipples between my teeth. I want to feel you move beneath me as I fuck you slowly from one end of the night to the other. I want to cover you like a stallion covers a mare. I want to hear the noises you make as you come.'

He tried to swallow, but his throat was dry.

'When you walk towards me I'm obsessed with your mouth and your breasts; when you walk away from me

I'm overwhelmed with thoughts of your arse. The turn of your head makes me sweat. I want you to sit on my face and drown me. I want to fill every hole you have, I want to fill you so full of my spend that it runs out of you in rivers, and I want to make you scream and weep and beg me never to stop.'

He shuddered to a halt, every muscle clenched, and concluded bitterly, 'Does that clear up any misunderstanding between us?'

She stared, her face as blank as her goddess mask. 'That's . . . nonsense,' she whispered.

He grabbed her hand and forced his fingers between hers, spreading the palm. 'You don't believe me?' he grinned, his lips stretched with pain. He laid her small, cool palm on the centre of his chest, feeling his heartbeat hammer up into her bones. He was feverish. He dragged that hand slowly down his naked skin, over the hard breastbone, over the burning slab of his belly, through the first flecks of hair beneath his navel. The pain of his wound was throbbing through his veins, and every pulse was making his cock jump and thicken. She was not fighting him, but he could feel the tension in her arm. He forced her hand over the top of his belt, through the folds of linen, round the wall of his upraised thigh and finally, firmly, pressed it onto the thick curve of his cock. Hidden as it was under the tatters of his tunic, to her touch as to his it was undeniably erect and struggling for freedom. It heaved under her hand, pressing the cloth against her bare skin.

And all the time he stared into her eyes, searching for any response in those brown depths. She stared back with the fathomless unreadable regard of the desert.

'Believe me now?'

Then he released her, letting his hand rest heavy upon hers. She did not pull away. He felt her fingers beneath his, lying on his prick. He could have cried out for the torment and the pleasure of that touch.

And finally something broke in her gaze, and he watched her face stir and twist with emotion, her lips shuddering with words that could not be sounded. Her gaze flinched from his and she pulled her hand away and, standing, backed off across his chamber.

He watched her go in despair. He had unburdened himself of the words imprisoned within him, words he knew he should never have spoken. They had swollen inside him for weeks, and now they had fallen. When the door smacked to he was left with an emptiness in his chest and the feeling that he had broken irrevocably something precious.

Cursing, he loosened his clothes and freed his cock, unable to resist its demands any more than he had been able to hold back the acid torrent of words. His balls were clenched with their burden. The hot skin under his grip felt like satin sliding over the wood-hard length beneath. He pulled back the foreskin, saw the angry purple of the glans and the moisture gathering at the slit. Two firm strokes and his scrotum was knotting like a fist. Pain stabbed his shoulder. He closed his eyes, picturing the Malia Shai's full lips, the soft ripe curve of them descending towards his swollen prick, the hint of moisture within, the little pink tip of her tongue preparing to lap at his burning cockhead, and with that the cauldron seething within him boiled over, the contents spouting and frothing like scalded cream over his fingers, his thigh, his twitching belly. He plunged headlong into the agony and the delight with a moan of despair.

She sat in the shrine of Lappa Han with a scroll of ancient poetry stretched between her hands. She liked the shrine because she liked Lappa Han, finding the Sun

Lord's warmth a comfort to the dark spaces within her even when it hurt her flesh. She liked the way this room had windows on all but one of the eight sides, so that it was continually filled with the golden glory of the sunlight. Often she sat and read here, when there were no rituals to perform.

But this particular parchment was a scroll she couldn't decipher, written in a language so old and obscure that only two of the most ancient priests in the temple could remember it in any depth. Upon the occasion of her first menstruation they had read the text aloud to her, one declaiming, one translating. She had never heard it since. The elaborate letters of the ancient tongue seemed to flicker in front of her eyes, and the painted pictures looked faded and dusty. A fly walked across the scroll, and she watched it as if it were pointing out the significant passages of the text.

I am looking for something hidden, she thought.

The fly washed its head with crooked forelimbs.

I am looking at a black insect on a fawn page. There are darker brown marks on the page. The fly walks across the little patterns. The patterns are words, I know that. The words are a poem. The poem is a hymn of praise to the power of the universe written one thousand years ago by a man who is remembered now only for this poem. I know this. But when I look, there are only brown marks on a brown page. What gives those marks meaning?

The fly paraded fussily across the parchment and up onto her thumb. She did not move.

I feel the fly tickling across my thumb onto the back of my hand. The sensation is like a line of light drawn across a dark place; I can't ignore it. The feeling is there. It is an insect, so I should be irritated and flick it away.

But if it were not an insect, if that same sensation were a fingertip drawn across my skin by a man, would it be pleasure I felt instead of irritation? It depends which man. The meaning is not in the feeling, it is in my response.

The fly circled her wrist.

Sometimes a look is a look. He looks at me. I look at him. What we see are only bodies. They have no meaning until we bring it to being in our minds. Then a glance is not just a glance: it is a plea, a demand, a theft, an attack. Sometimes a feeling is only a feeling. I feel warmth, and solidity, and pressure. For him it is desire in all its agony. What is it for me?

The fly tickled its way up the tender skin of her inside arm.

He is not the master of his flesh. He has not learned that significance is a habit of mind. I was taught long ago that it is not necessary to give meaning to sensation. Pain does not matter any more than pleasure. Lust is not more significant than an insect itch. The marks on the scroll do not have to be words. If you look at them, they are just marks.

But, she thought, the poem was beautiful.

I do not want it to be lost when the priests die.

I want to read it.

The door creaked open and the fly shot off her wrist, vanishing into the interlaced sunbeams. Rasa Belit was framed in the doorway.

She eased herself down from her familiar perch on the plinth of Lappa Han's statue and let the scroll roll closed.

'Malia Shai,' he said, pacing slowly into the room. She stepped forward to meet him, tilting her chin so that she could look him in the face. He bulked over her.

'Has something happened?' She took in the pouches under his eyes, the deep-carved grooves down to the corners of his mouth, the wide nostrils.

'I wanted to speak to you in private, my Malia Shai. It's my privilege as your high priest, and though your temple is full of people praying, I hoped . . .' He was staring at her, and there was moisture at the corners of his lips. 'I hoped that you would hear me. Honour me with your attention, my mistress.'

'Go on.'

'People are dying in the city, Malia Shai. The sickness runs through them like fire through dry grass.'

'I know that.'

His black nostrils flared as if he were inhaling her incense. 'The thunderous weather makes them worse, my goddess. People pray for the Rains. The wells are running dry. The Horse-eaters wait outside to butcher us all and the fear is driving men mad. The suffering in your city grows day by day.'

'What do you expect from me, Rasa Belit?' she asked. 'Mercy?'

He licked his lips.

'What has mercy to do with me?'

'Ah, no.' He drew in his breath over bared teeth. 'You are a cruel and bitter goddess. There's no kindliness in you.' He began to circle her slowly.

She was aware that she had a familiar physical reaction to his presence, a tightening of the skin across the mouth and nose and fingers. She was taken aback to identify it for the first time as revulsion.

'You are a dark and bloody mistress,' he murmured at her shoulder, very close to her. 'Men cry out to you, but they might as well be dashing themselves upon the rock face. Your heart isn't softened. You feed upon their pain. I don't ask for mercy.' He was behind her now, his words whispered over her crawling nape. 'I ask only to worship you.'

He slid his hand upon her waist.

This was not the first time. She knew what he wanted.

She pulled away, turning upon him. 'Don't touch me!' she told him.

He fell flat on his face, his yellow bulk plastered to the flagstones. 'Mistress of lamentation! Mother of suffering!' He grasped her bare ankle and she could feel the dampness of his palms. 'I'm not worthy to stand before you, but let me worship, let me crawl as a snake at your feet.'

She wanted to flinch away from him, but she did not. She felt distaste creeping over every inch of her skin, but she was not the slave of her skin. She was the goddess Malia, and she was not subject to fear or disgust, not to any emotion. She was a goddess, and it was her divine place to be worshipped.

Trembling, Rasa Belit hunched forward and lowered his hot lips over her big toe. She stared down at the back of his head, feeling the power knot in her belly. It was not often that she remembered her power, but at moments like these she felt it stirring within.

'Queen of torments,' he huffed, showering her toes with eager kisses, 'I lie before you suppliant, as one of your million victims.' His lips were wet and tickling. He smeared them up over the arch of her foot, then licked hungrily at her instep.

With a slow indrawing of breath, she shifted her weight to the other leg and allowed him to raise her foot from the floor. He moaned, 'Blessings, blessing, my goddess,' and sent his tongue darting into the little crevices between her toes. The sensation teased. When he swallowed those digits into his mouth and began to suckle loudly upon them, she felt a wet shiver crawl up her spine. There was an unsettling intimacy in the way his wet mouth caressed her unwashed feet, in unseemly disregard for dirt or humiliation or propriety, for anything but the presence of her flesh. He tasted the dust of the floor as eagerly as he tasted her skin. His tongue was everywhere on the sensitive pads of her foot. The ragged hem of her dress flapped in his eyes.

His own feet were clawing at the flagstones, his calves knotting as he pawed the ground. She stared down at the heaving of his broad back and buttocks.

'My queen, my life,' he murmured indistinctly. 'You are beauty itself. You hold the world between your breasts.' This last word came out as a groan. He released her foot slowly and pressed his lips to her inner ankle instead. His tongue began to scour at her shin and lower calf.

She stared at the filigree screen of a window. If this tickling were flies, it would be disgusting. If it were a puppy licking her it would be amusing. If it were Veraine it would be devastating. But it was none of these; it was Rasa Belit, and if she listened to her flesh it would be telling her that it felt like power flowing into her marrow with every stroke of his tongue. She despised him, and that made her feel as strong as mountains.

'Get behind me,' she told him. 'You are not fit for my gaze.'

Floundering, he hastened to obey her decree, whispering, 'Mistress, mistress,' as he shuffled round on his belly to the back of her calves. She spread her legs a little further. He lavished long strokes of the tongue and brief, sucking kisses on the smooth muscles of her braced calves. He nuzzled up under the hem of her skirt, not daring to lift it with his hands, and his lips mumbled on the sensitive flesh behind her knees.

She approved of his obedience. She gathered her skirt

at either side and pulled it slowly up so that the whole of her thighs was exposed up to the round curve of her arse. This wrenched a cry of numinous awe from her priest: 'Goddess!' and he pressed his face into one soft globe, cupping the other and kneading it fiercely with his large hand. She leaned into his pressure, feeling his nose jabbing into the mass of her arse-cheek.

'You are the divine light,' he gasped, pulling back to breathe at last. 'You are the face of heaven.' He parted her cheeks reverently with his palms and slipped between them. She felt his tongue rasp, wet and slippery, down the crack of her behind from the small of her back, down over the tender skin hidden beneath, to lap and wriggle at her tight and quivering anus. A shudder rippled out to her hips. A heavy wetness was swelling in her sex.

'Blessed are your victims,' the priest breathed as he surfaced. 'Blessed are those whose torment delights you, my Malia Shai.' His hand, invisible to her, suddenly cupped the fuzzy mound of her mons from below. A little moisture leaked onto his palm. He pressed the heel of that hand into the yielding wetness of her yoni. 'You are beautiful beyond mortal flesh. Trample me beneath your bloodied feet, my cruel mistress. I would die for you.' He withdrew his palm, and she heard the slobbering as he licked her juices from his palm.

'Oh, I would have you eat my soul. I have offered you my life, my goddess. My manhood was laid upon your altar. I want to taste your blessing.'

'You serve me only as you should,' she replied huskily. 'What priest does less?'

He hunched onto one side, his head between her legs, and began to kiss the inside of her thighs from the knee up. 'I offer you the lives of men,' he murmured. 'Even the worst of men. Even the Irolian bastard. No man loves you so much as I do. Bless me with your outpoured essence, Malia.'

'What do you mean?' she asked, easing her thighs apart so that he might fit between them. With her skirts bunched in her hands she could see the dome of his close-cropped head jutting into view beneath her tousled mound. His scalp shone through the fuzz of hair. 'The Irolian?'

'I tried to offer him up. He thinks he can bend you to his purposes, my goddess. He thinks he can ally you to his filthy empire. He blasphemes. I sent a man to spill his life on the stones.' His lips were grazing on the tufts of her pubic hair.

'You failed.' Her loins were wet with his kisses.

'I am mortal, mother of pestilence. I am weak. Do not have mercy upon me. Strike me down.'

'I will,' she promised.

His face was parting her labia now, his whole torso straining with the effort of lifting him into position and holding him there. His mouth and nose were thrust into her wetness, her juices smeared on his face. She sank a little on her hips to allow his tongue to probe deeper into her yoni, into the slippery hole that thirsted to be filled yet that his touch was so inadequate to satisfy.

The men of a thousand nations could not satisfy her. Their carcasses were flung into the soil, yet the earth was forever hungry, never satiated.

He had ceased to articulate anything more than gasps and groans. His tongue flailed and whipped like a dying snake. By chance he rubbed the sweaty, cunt-juice-smeared ridges of his face against the feverish knot of her clit, and as this made her wetter he gobbled ever more fiercely.

She was going to drown him. She grabbed his prickly scalp in her hands and held him up against her, grinding her sopping cleft down on his mouth. She would like to sink to her knees. She would like to pin him beneath her and wriggle till he choked. But instead her legs had locked and she was straining upwards, and the degraded mass of grunting priest gobbling at her muff was enough to ignite her mortal flesh into the tumbling fireball of orgasm.

Once the explosion had started she lost all her senses, and only came back from the flames when Rasa Belit slipped from her hands and crashed to the floor. She heard the sound of his head as it bounced off the stones and she stared down at him between her feet. The priest's face, slippery with her juices, was screwed into a red knot, his whole frame shaking. She saw foam beginning to work its way out at the edges of his mouth.

She stepped away from him. His hands were dug into his groin, his legs juddering on the floor. She could not tell if it was ecstasy or agony that was wracking him, but the fit was more violent and prolonged than any orgasm. She watched for a while then, as the spasms seemed to slow, she turned and walked out of the shrine of Lappa Han.

8 Spoils of War

Veraine nodded one last time to his officers, then lifted the heavy bronze helmet up over his head and settled its weight upon him. Through the eye-slits he saw the foot soldiers begin to shuffle slowly forward, though it was only their white tunics that made them visible. Little moonlight shone through the massing clouds, and no one carried a torch.

He felt his horse shift restlessly beneath him, but the beast's hooves were muffled in rags and made little noise on the stones. Even the scrape of the feet of the Eighth Host was no more than a whisper. No man spoke out loud; they knew too well how their future depended on stealth now. This manoeuvre had been practised over and over since their arrival in Mulhanabin. Now it had to be perfect.

The horses had been fretting all day; it was as if they knew of the impending battle just as well as their riders.

The city gate was narrow for the number of men who were trying to exit through it, so deployment was slow. Veraine stifled his impatience and kept his senses alert. There were lookouts based on the rooftops higher up the city; a horn note from them would signal that the Horse-eaters had woken and were aware of the attack about to take place. But so far the messages had been reassuring: the barbarian camp slept peacefully, Irolian preparation had apparently gone unnoticed and to plan.

He remembered the faces of his officers when he had announced the attack the previous morning; the satisfaction and relief mixed with the anticipation in their eyes.

'We attack two hours before dawn,' he had told them. 'We aim for the tent with the biggest golden sun-standard; a quick strike right into the heart of their army. If it's not their king then it is certainly one of their princes. The tents don't have external guy-ropes so we can get horses between them.

'I'll lead the cavalry. The rest of the men will be under Loy's command; they hit the main face of the enemy in two wedges that will form a defensive block around the cavalry when it has to withdraw. If they manage to mobilise their men, we pull back inside the city as rehearsed. But in the dark, without horses or bows, the Horse-eaters will be at their weakest. They like to fight in open country, not skirmishing on foot. We should be able to tear a hole in their throat.'

The officers had to a man nodded eagerly. Only Rumayn had voiced any protest.

'General,' he had stammered, 'You haven't a hope of destroying the Horse-eaters! They outnumber you like a wolf pack around a guard dog. And you were sent here to hold the city, not engage the enemy in open battle, surely? Can't you just sit tight in Mulhanabin? The Rains will break any day now.'

'Tell him what you told me an hour ago, Chath,' Veraine had instructed, ignoring the grim looks directed at his adviser by the other soldiers.

The chief of surgeons, a grizzled, hard-faced man, had said, 'As you wish, General. I have eight soldiers in my hospital suffering from the plague. As I told him, two died last night. The others are likely to die within days.'

'There you are, Rumayn,' Veraine had explained. 'We have run out of time. The choice is reduced to breaking the siege or sitting here while we shit ourselves to death. Believe me, there isn't a man in the Host who wouldn't prefer to fight.'

'But there aren't enough of you. You can't break the siege.'

Veraine had grinned humourlessly. 'There are enough of us to try.'

Rumayn had thrown his hands up. 'Then why in the name of the gods are you putting yourself in the vanguard, General? You can't direct the battle from there, you'll get yourself killed.'

Veraine hadn't answered, only picked up his sword from the table and sheathed it. The other officers had looked contemptuously at the civilian.

'It's the General's first command,' Arioc had explained through tight lips. 'He leads from the front.'

'The time for advice is over,' Veraine had said. 'Now we act. Get to your stations.'

The other officers had filed out of the room then to prepare their men, but Rumayn had lingered for one last attempt at protest. 'You really haven't a chance, have you, General?'

Veraine had looked at him distantly, wondering how he could make a civilian understand.

'My men are warriors, Rumayn. Battle is what they're bred for and trained for, not sitting on our arses in some Yamani flea-pit. Do you think we'd want to go back to Antoth having held this place but never raised a hand against the Horse-eaters? Do you think there would be any honour or pride in that? Do you think the Eighth Host would be the envy of the Empire for creeping back intact and unbloodied? My men would spit on my name. We're going to fight, Rumayn. The risk is irrelevant, we have to do it.'

Now the General waited on horseback just inside the

city gates, and all the words and all the reasons were like dust under the feet of his army, marching out to meet the enemy. It did not matter any more why they were going into battle, only that they fought well. The air felt thick in his lungs, heavy with the moisture of the coming rains. His left arm ached, although the wound was healing fast under the Yamani salve. His stomach was tight and queasy, his muscles taut and singing with the anticipation. He felt the familiar strength of the horse under his thighs, the weight of shield and sword in either hand, and his heart seemed to expand with joy.

The last of the foot soldiers was filing out of the gate. Veraine dropped the loosely knotted reins on his horse's neck and guided the animal into position with nudges of his calves. The other mounted warriors took up their places behind him; they were a pitifully small group for Irolian cavalry but they were expert horsemen, every one. Arioc was at his left, leading a spare mount by the reins in case the General's own should be cut from under him.

Somewhere up ahead in the darkness was Loy. Veraine awaited his signal, and eventually it came back down the line; a barely audible clicking of fingers that meant the soldiers were in position, their first defensive front split into two wedges like the claws of some giant scorpion, with a hollow between up which the horsemen could ride.

Veraine urged his horse forward, under the lintel and out of Mulhanabin. On either side the infantry were poised. In front were the tents of the Horse-eaters. The infantry broke into a trot; the cavalry followed their lead but outpaced them at once. Veraine found himself cantering between the first ranks of foot soldiers almost before he realised it, the flat sands thrumming beneath his horse's hooves, the wall of tents rising up before him.

In the gloom he only had moments to judge what was solid felt wall and what was gap, but he steered his mount adroitly between the obstacles, down the maze of alleys that led into the heart of the enemy camp.

As the tents closed in he heard shouting behind him; some sentry must have been awake. But it was too late now – the twin jaws of Irolian infantry were across the arrow-gap and punching into the Horse-eater host. And in moments all Veraine could hear was the thunder of hooves beneath him and his own breath magnified by the walls of the helmet. He rounded the flank of a tent and saw an open space before him. In the centre was a fire pit still glowing and beyond it the bulk of the greater tent, large as a house and grand with spires and carved frame, where the golden disc glimmered high over the doorway even in the darkness.

The Irolians were over the fire pit before the men sleeping around it had begun to rise groggily to their feet. Veraine stooped from the saddle to slash straight through flesh and bone, barely glimpsing the scarred faces before they fell away before him. The open area rapidly turned into a maelstrom of circling horses and hacking men. They tried to work silently but all around the gasps and cries of battle were going up; further back the first screams were shrilling out into the uncomprehending night.

Veraine jerked a cloth-and-feather standard from a pole and thrust it into the fire, hurling it as soon as it was alight onto the roof of the great tent. Flames began to lick at the structure. He was not rash enough to enter the building, ordering his men to surround it instead in case anyone tried to cut their way out of the back. Even as his soldiers moved into position the doorway filled with the shapes of men, their features indistinct but their curved swords glinting as they raised them against their attackers. Veraine threw himself forward into the struggle, shearing bone from bone with every blow that hit its target. One of his men hacked away at the far doorpost and it tumbled in, forcing the defenders to stumble out from under the weight of the felt doubled over and presenting an easy target for Irolian blows.

Flames were running along the eaves of the cloth palace now.

Suddenly his horse screamed and folded beneath him. He rolled away from it and as he rose buried his sword to the hilt in the belly of the squat figure that loomed over him, stinking of animal fat. A blow hammered into the top of his helmet but rebounded without biting. Hot blood gushed over his arms as he kicked the body free and whirled around.

'General!' Arioc shouted from nearby. He lunged towards the voice, slashing down in passing at a wounded Horse-eater struggling to rise from the ground, and grabbed the mane of the horse waiting for him. Throwing himself into the saddle, he cast around quickly, getting his bearings. There were horsemen everywhere, but they all seemed to be clad in the white blur of an imperial tunic. The figures on foot were suffering badly, getting hacked to pieces even as they lurched into the fray.

'Drop the tent!' he ordered. The designated men unslung bronze axes from their saddles at his command and began to hack at the slender supporting frame of the tent. It sagged under their blows, felt and horsehair and oxskins slumping to the ground in great heavy folds. The smell of burning hair was disgusting. The screams from inside were louder now. Women's voices were audible among them but Veraine swallowed his compunction. He held his ground until the tent was irretrievably alight and no more warriors seemed able to emerge, then he rallied his men with a yell.

More Horse-eaters were running into the fight from all around, but they seemed to have little organisation and came in knots of two or three men, not warbands. It was steady work to beat them off. The sound of metal on bronze armour rang through the smoke amidst the cries of dying men.

Between Veraine's men and the city, the noise was growing to a great hubbub. The glow of several fires dyed the air. The whole Horse-eater encampment, Veraine judged, must be startled awake by now, though most would have no idea what was happening to them.

'Fall back!' he yelled. 'Rejoin the ranks!'

He had barely been in time. As they wheeled and began to ride back through the seething camp a band of riders came charging at them from a flank. The fighting on horseback was brutal and far more dangerous; horse slammed against horse, men were shoved against tents and thrown from the saddle to be trampled underfoot. The Horse-eaters screamed as they attacked, far more confident once their feet were off the floor, and Veraine found himself fending off blow after blow. He felt one land upon his hip, but such was the aggression and the ferocity of the fight that there was no pain and it did not check him for a moment as his own blow sliced vertically down though his opponent's collarbone and ribs, toppling him from the saddle.

Everyone in the Irolian group was by now smeared dark with blood and flecked white with great gouts of foam from the labouring horses. Sweat was pouring down Veraine's face and stinging his eyes, but he did not dare lift the helm to wipe it off. The grip on his sword was slippery with gore. Still the Horse-eaters kept coming, appearing round every twist in the pathway. Their way back seemed inordinately long and Veraine almost suspected that they had lost their way in the confusion and were heading off at a tangent to the main army. That would be fatal.

'Form up,' he snapped, wheeling his horse to survey their surroundings.

'General?' Arioc said. His voice was pleading. Veraine turned to him and saw with shock the spearhead jutting out of his belly just below his breastplate. Slowly the young man folded forward over his horse's neck, masking the wound and the sheet of blood spreading down his abdomen from it.

The Horse-eater poised behind him howled. Then Veraine's sword took his throat out.

Other Irolians close by tried to aid the chariot-driver, but the spear had come in at an angle down through his lungs and he was already dead.

They let him tumble from the saddle. It was impossible to stop or for the healthy to carry the fallen; Horse-eaters were pressing in at every side, never in numbers sufficient to overwhelm them, but allowing no rest. The sound of fighting was very close by, but Veraine could not see the rest of his forces. He sought out the glimmering bulk of Mulhanabin beyond the tent-tops.

'That way!' he yelled.

There was a shudder in the wall of the tents hemming them in. The shudder went up through the hooves of the horses and sent them stumbling, then screaming mad with fright. All around, on both sides of the battle, they bucked and reared and fell. Veraine felt his beast stagger beneath him, but at first he had no idea what was happening. Then as he jumped from its back and his feet hit the ground, he felt the earth ripple and heave beneath his soles and he saw the tents start to collapse in on themselves.

The Horse-eaters were howling with fear.

A thick dark crack snaked through the pale sands not a body-length from Veraine. He saw a barbarian stagger, his feet slipping into the crevasse.

'Earthquake!' someone was yelling close by.

The barbarian clawed his way to safety and began to crawl away, but a horse dashed over him and split his skull wide. It was almost impossible to stand on the fluid sand, even without the panicked horses that were bolting everywhere. Veraine grabbed the shoulder of the Irolian nearest to him and they staggered like sailors on a rough sea. A bass vibration too low to hear was pounding up through his diaphragm, threatening to burst his heart out through his ribcage. He saw the same strain and horror on the faces of his soldiers as was carved, he knew, on his own.

When it stopped, they stood for a moment stunned. Then they heard the noise. The quake itself had been almost silent, but this was a great roaring grinding noise, as of earth masticating earth. It seemed to go on for ever.

'What in hell was that?' Veraine asked as the last echoes died.

Then the dust hit them. It came on a wind that hit like an open hand, lashing them with grit. Everyone threw their arms over their faces. Even when the unnatural gust dropped, as abruptly as it had started, it left the air full of choking dirt.

'Regroup,' Veraine coughed when he could finally speak. 'Fall back to the ranks!' They did not try to collect their horses but simply shouldered their way through the pall of dust, climbing over the collapsed tents. No

Horse-eater opposed them. The barbarians were running, those that were still on their feet. From every direction came the flat wailing of wordless terror, and in every direction the dull glow of flames was springing up. Veraine guessed that many of the tents had collapsed onto the embers of cooking fires.

They found the Irolian ranks, but there was no battle going on now. The men stood with bloodied weapons, staring about them as if they had woken from a dream and did not know where they were. Their enemies had melted away before them, fleeing into the brown darkness. Those few Horse-eaters that were braver or had no route of escape were being cut down with a mechanical efficiency that belied the confusion on the faces of the soldiers.

Veraine found an *optio* and demanded, 'What happened?'

The man shook his head, scattering droplets of blood clotted with dust. 'I don't know, sir.' He stared behind him. The men were shouting, a boiling wave of words rippling through the ranks from east to west.

'The city, sir!' the soldier repeated, as if Veraine couldn't hear for himself. 'They're saying that Mulhanabin has fallen on the enemy camp!'

An hour later he stood among the ruins of the Horse-eater horde and stared up at Mulhanabin, the dust still plastered over his skin and cold horror in his belly. In the grey light just before dawn, even through the pall of dirt and smoke and the gloom of the lowering storm clouds, the city seemed to slouch in a misshapen heap. A great slice had been cut from its eastern flank; a scoop taken out of the rock by some invisible hand. The Citadel wall ended in mid air. Half the Outer

Temple had disappeared, though the smaller and older Inner Temple beyond seemed to be missing only part of its walls.

Some unseen weakness in the rock had, when wrenched by the earthquake, caused the cliff to fall away into space, and those thousands of tons of rubble had plummeted to the desert floor below and exploded across the flat plain; straight through one half of the Horse-eater encampment.

Veraine felt as if a freezing hand were clawing his guts. He lifted off his helmet and stuck it under his arm. The horsehair plume was matted with dried blood.

'Sir,' said Loy, coming up beside him.

Veraine dragged his gaze away from the city. Its shattered elevation was like an open wound. Simply staring at it did no good at all.

'Your report, Commander,' he said.

'No more resistance encountered, sir. They've bolted, the ones that could. We hold the camp.'

'Good.' Veraine did not feel like expressing more enthusiasm. He swung round to survey the scene of devastation and chaos that stretched to the horizon, and thought that it was as if some god had eaten the entire Horse-eater nation and them vomited it out in a vast slick of ash and corpses and smashed tents. Where human beings remained, they huddled together in shock and terror. The sound of weeping drifted on the wind, over the triumphant shouts of the Irolian soldiers who strutted through the detritus.

'Set sentries to watch the perimeter. Then detail men to collect our wounded and get them in to the surgeons. Find the fallen. I want Arioc's body to be recovered, and a full funeral arranged.'

'Very good, sir.' Loy cleared his throat. 'He died well,

I hear. He wasn't that popular, but he was a brave man.'

'You have no idea,' Veraine agreed bleakly. He sighed, mostly with regret at the young man's death, partly because he suspected that Arioc's family were going to nail him to a wall for the loss. 'He deserves full army honours.'

'Of course, sir.'

Veraine's gaze strayed back to the city. 'Have the locals shown their faces yet?'

'We have a detail on the city gate, sir, holding them off until you give the word.'

'Right. I want every man that hasn't another duty to take charge of a group of civilians and sweep the camp. Sort the spoils and get the *tesserius* and his staff to make a full count. Prisoners, weapons and valuables we keep. The Yamani can have whatever they find of Horse-eater food, tents and clothing. The horses are to be put aside so they can be sorted in due course. Keep the men busy. They can celebrate later.'

'Sir.'

Veraine's voice remained flat and businesslike. 'Bind the male prisoners and kill any that show fight.'

Loy nodded.

'And find me a rider on a strong horse. I'll be sending a message to the Emperor.' He allowed himself to smile as he said that, though he still hardly believed in his own triumph.

Loy grinned. 'Congratulations, General – it's an honour to serve with you! The gods are with you.'

Veraine nodded slightly. 'Well, we have work to do. Get the men together; I'll address them before we get started. Then I suppose I'll have to find Rasa Belit.'

* * *

There was dust on her lips, dust in her mouth, dust gluing her eyes shut. The Malia Shai could not see or think for the dust. It had crawled in under her skin and soaked through to her bones, as cold as spring water. It clogged her throat. It left her too numb to feel and too weak to move, the ache in her cheek and the fire in her skull dowsed by its chill, soft, smothering touch. She had grown used to the pain a long time ago, but now she could not feel it.

Noises echoed in her head, but they were muffled by the dust and she could not identify them. She did not move. Only when hands gripped her shoulders did she realise that the noise was a voice; only when her torso was raised from the floor did she realise that she had been lying down.

The hands slipped her mask off and dropped it to the floor. She saw the stone staring up at her through the empty eyeholes. The Earthquake Mask was cracked red enamel.

'What happened?' the voice demanded. 'Can you hear me?' She tried to focus on the face connected with the voice. It was General Veraine. His hands were so hot they seemed to burn her skin.

'The earthquake,' she tried to say. Her tongue was dry like a wad of felt. She shook her head and then winced as pain lanced across the top of her skull.

'Shit,' he muttered. 'Hold still.' His fingers slid deftly across her scalp, through the tangle of her hair, probing for wounds. She sagged against his forearms.

'You've got a lump like a duck egg at the back here,' he informed her, then glanced around them at the floor. 'It looks like plaster's fallen from the roof.'

She remembered a blow that went through her bones in a great jarring wave right to her fingertips. 'The earthquake,' she repeated, with more success.

'Yes. There was an earthquake. The cliff fell.' His voice was harsh. 'I thought you were dead. Your temple took dozens of priests with it when it went down the cliff; I thought you'd gone with them. No one knew where you were. The city's in chaos.'

'I called the earthquake,' she mumbled. Only his hands were holding her upright. She felt as weak as water.

'No you didn't. There was a landslide. The Horse-eater camp was hit and they fled. The siege is over!'

'I did it,' she said.

He laughed, shaking his head. 'No . . . you were hit by plaster. How long have you been on the floor? You're as cold as the stone!'

She couldn't answer. She was barely able to recognise the altar stone they were kneeling behind. They must be in the *Garbhagria*. Why was the Irolian in here?

'Shuga's fire. You're like ice.' He scooped her up in his arms with no apparent effort and carried her through the lurching shadows. Where his body touched hers, it felt as if he was branding her. She realised she must be regaining her senses because she could smell him now; he reeked of smoke and fresh sweat and blood. She recognised the coppery smell of blood without difficulty.

The room was spinning and it only stopped when he lowered her onto a soft surface. She felt the cloth beneath her folded legs and realised it was her throne at the top of the dais. As he released her she stared at his tunic, which was rusty red and stiff.

'It is not my blood,' he reassured her and she realised she had put out numb fingers to touch his arm. He was not telling the whole truth, because he was covered in little cuts. He was kneeling over her on the bed of the vast throne, bronze greaves biting into the sanctified fabric, boots scuffing the cloth-of-gold.

'You won,' she said.

'I came to find you,' he answered. 'I thought you'd fallen with the temple. No one knew where you were, that's why I came in here.' His hands had not relinquished their grip on her shoulders and she was glad of that because otherwise she would have fallen over. His hair was plastered to his skull and his eyes were burning in his filthy face. His muscles were sharply defined and hard as wood under the stained linen of his uniform. He looked as if he had come straight from the middle of battle.

She had started to tremble.

'You're frozen,' he muttered. He ran his hands up and down her arms, chafing the bare skin. She shut her eyes and felt the shuddering take hold of her whole frame. She heard the slow intake of his breath. 'It's a good thing I found you.'

She nodded dully and watched as he took her right leg in one hand and tucked her bare foot into the warm cave between his thighs. His hand carefully massaged the locked muscles of her calf; it felt as hot as embers. His other hand was on her shoulder, his calloused thumb resting on the soft curve of her throat. Perhaps he could feel her pulse.

From her calf his touch moved slowly up beneath her skirts, testing the crease at the back of her knee, the smooth muscle of her upper leg. She did not protest; she didn't feel she had the strength to. The shivering was making her teeth chatter softly. His fingers kneaded her outer thigh, his touch strong and sure.

The breath hummed in her throat, issuing as a soft noise she had never intended to make.

Veraine's gaze, which had been avoiding hers, locked searchingly on her face at this. Whatever it was that he found, it was not rejection. He slipped both arms round her waist and folded her in closer to him, so that his arms could reach right round her, his fingers search the knotted braid of her spine. She rested her forehead on his shoulder, feeling the warmth beating out of his body like a caress. She was trembling uncontrollably.

'Shush,' he whispered, as if gentling a mare. One palm was firm on the small of her back, the other between her shoulder blades. He lowered his face to her hair, breathing in her scent until his chest swelled against her. Gentle pressure tilted her head to one side. She felt his cheek on her bare neck, the rasp of his stubble, the softer touch of lips drawn across her skin. His breath was suddenly hot and moist in her ear. He was barely breathing, but she could sense every flutter.

Very gently he tilted her head back, cradling it on his arm, exposing the long line of her throat. She closed her eyes. His lips floated down over the edge of her jaw, down to the vulnerable skin of her neck; those lips parted and hungry and scalding. He ran the very tip of his tongue up the length of her throat, and as he did so a groan escaped between his searching lips.

The door of the *Garbhagria* groaned too.

Veraine snatched himself away to arm's length and for a moment the Malia Shai dangled in his grasp like a doll. She felt pain knot inside her.

'What are you doing?' the voice of Rasa Belit boomed.

'Me? What have you been doing?' Veraine yelled back. 'You haven't been looking after your Malia Shai for certain! She could've been dead by now!'

Rasa Belit, flanked by four lesser priests, came running up the length of the hall faster than she had ever seen him move before. 'What?' he demanded.

Veraine swung his feet off the throne and stood up, still supporting her with one arm. 'She was injured in the earthquake.' He paused until Rasa Belit had galloped up the steps to just beneath him and then snarled, 'She's been struck on the head and been lying on the floor all night with the strength ebbing out of her and not one of you yellow shit-maggots thought to check on her. I found her.'

The priest opened his mouth but so great was his fury that no words came out. His chest was heaving.

'Now,' said Veraine, 'you look after her. Do your job for a change!'

'And what,' Rasa Belit, asked, 'are you doing in here at all, you Irolian bastard?' His voice was shrill with anger.

'Oh, don't worry. I'm out of here right now. And we'll be away from Mulhanabin just as soon as my men are packed up. Not a day longer.' He grabbed the priest's hand and shoved it onto the Malia Shai's shoulder, forcing him to prop her up. Then he strode away down the steps.

'General Veraine!'

The soldier ignored him.

'General Veraine, I want you to confine your men to their barracks until you leave!'

This did cause him to stop and turn, halfway down to the *Garbhagria* floor.

'Your men are drunk, General! They're roaming the streets of Mulhanabin looting buildings and assaulting the people.' He sneered. 'You do your job. Get them under control.'

Veraine's face grew very hard. 'Those men just saved all your lives, priest,' he said. 'And your temple, and your Malia Shai. They risked their lives for you. Some died in the attempt.' He shook his head. 'That doesn't come for free. You pay. But you live.' He clenched his jaw. 'I will not lock my men in their rooms like naughty children. But,' he added, 'I will post a guard on the Citadel gate, with instructions that no Irolian except myself comes in.

And if the people of Mulhanabin wish to find sanctuary up here then they can.'

He turned on his heel and walked away. The Malia Shai was the only one who did not watch him go. She had her eyes closed. Her muscles were still mostly clenched with cold, yet inside she nursed, like meltwater under a mountain glacier, a wet and swelling heat.

Veraine stood in his room, one hand on the stone lattice-work of his window, and stared at the darkness beyond the *jali* screen. It was after midnight, but how long after he did not know. The city was still loud with celebrating soldiers, but Veraine had left them to it. He had praised them, walked among them, accepted drinks and listened to both sober reports and outrageous boasts. He had also instructed Sron to quash any burning or wholesale looting of property. Then, when the men were so deep in their cups that they would hardly recognise him, he had left. They no longer needed his presence, and he gained nothing from theirs.

Although he had changed his tunic and made a hurried attempt at washing hours ago, when he looked at the back of his arm he could still see the green stain left by his bronze vambrace.

He wanted solitude. He had retired to his room because it was the only place where he was not going to be disturbed in the whole of Mulhanabin, and he had filled the room with the light of glimmering lamps. The light made the night beyond the window more opaque, but there was nothing to see out there anyway. Roiling clouds masked the moon and the night was gravid with rain that would not fall. Veraine stared at the blackness outside and within.

He had triumphed. Against every expectation, by his

own efforts and by good fortune – never despised by any soldier – he had pulled off a military victory and broken the back of an invasion that had threatened the Eternal Empire. An earthquake had come to his aid; that only proved he was favoured by heaven, everyone would say. The gods themselves fought on his side.

During the battle, he had felt like that himself. While on horseback among enemies he had known that he was born to ride with a bloody sword in his hand. Among his men, for the first few hours of celebration, he had felt that. He had gloried in their victory and delighted in the life that was his.

He knew now what his future held. He would march the Eighth Host back to Antoth with prisoners and spoils in their train. He would be fêted in an official triumphal march through the streets of the capital, and be honoured by the Emperor himself. He would be gifted with an estate, with slaves, and with a fifth part of the spoils of his victory. He would be permitted to marry a wife from among the nobility. He would become a man of influence and some power, with a glorious career laid open before him. Perhaps by the time he died he would be mentioned with the same reverence as his father.

He had been born a slave, and now he stood on the threshold of greatness.

It meant nothing to him.

Over the last few hours, the joy singing in his blood had leached slowly away. He had slipped away from the Eighth Host when he realised he no longer shared their delight, and he had come to a quiet place to face the truth alone.

The truth was, he now knew, that there was only one thing he wanted in life. It was not power or wealth, freedom or praise. It was the one thing he could not have: a slip of a Yamani girl blessed with neither breathtaking beauty nor obvious sexual allure. A madwoman who thought she was divine.

It was incomprehensible.

And yet she was the one thing that filled his mind, that haunted his nights, that made his blood run like fire through his veins. He had never desired anything or anyone the way he desired the Malia Shai. It made him sick with longing. It made his triumph taste like ashes. It made him feel as if his entrails had been torn out and that the hollow within him could never be filled. He would have sold every achievement of his life for her.

He held on to the carved stone screen and told himself that at least he had discovered what it was he desired from life. Most men do not even know that.

Then he heard the door creak.

He turned and saw her standing there in the doorway.

'There were no guards,' the Malia Shai said.

He did not reply. Words had failed him. She took a few steps forward into the room. He had never seen her look so hesitant. Slowly she reached up to her headcloth and pulled it free, letting the burden of her thick hair fall loose upon her shoulders.

'I dreamed this,' he said.

She was biting her lower lip. 'This isn't a dream,' she whispered.

He crossed the space separating them between one breath and the next.

When Veraine pulled her against him it snatched the air from her body; she opened her lips in a gasp and he smothered them with his own, so that their exhalations mingled and it was his breath, the taste of him and of rough red wine, that she drew into her throat. His hand was on her jaw, her cheek, pulling her in closer, the callused thumb smearing the dew of perspiration across her skin. His mouth was on hers, taking possession with a soldier's brutal efficiency.

She could not respond. She didn't know how. She simply gave way before the strength of his lust. His body was hard, harder than she could believe, seeming composed entirely of muscle and bone. His other arm was around her waist, jamming her against the unyielding wall of his torso. The scent of him, as sweet as baked bread, filled her head. She felt her spine loosen in his grasp, her belly moulding itself to his, the bulge at the meeting of his thighs crushing into her soft body. Surely his lingam must be bone, too, she thought – mere flesh could never be that hard.

He pulled away just as brutally. 'This time,' he whispered.

Then he took her lower lip between his teeth, as if the only way he could express the urgency of his desire was in mimicked violence. His bites printed their way up the line of her jaw to the sensitive lobe of her ear; all hot, promising lips and threatening teeth. But it was when he used his tongue on her neck that she felt a great shudder of weakness run up through her spine and the warmth explode in her belly. It was like being on fire and drowning in deep water, both at the same time, and for a long moment it threatened to overwhelm her, but she dragged herself back from the brink and slid her hands up over his chest. She could feel his heartbeat against her right palm. She braced her shoulders and pushed him away.

He released her at once, his hands groping to the back of his head, his face twisted with confusion. She ignored his expression and glanced anxiously down at his body where equally obvious evidence of his frustration confronted her, the great knot of his erection marring the smooth front of his tunic. She put one hand out, but not on his cock; gripping his belt instead, holding him tightly like a dog on a leash. She lifted the other hand to his face and laid her fingers on his lips. She needed to possess this moment, though it meant ignoring the agony in his eyes. She felt his breath on her skin, the scab and the swollen patch at the corner of his mouth where he had taken some minor knock in the battle. He quivered at her touch.

She was used to the inexorable, infallible passion of the gods. But this man was no deity; he was flesh and blood, strong and frightening and yet so vulnerable at the same time. Their connection seemed too fragile, her understanding of him too uncertain.

Their union was baulked by stupid obstacles like clothes. How did human lovers manage?

She needed to use both hands to undo the knot at his belt. She bent her head over the task, working at it as seriously as a child. For a moment he let her, then he took her face in his hands and raised it again, forcing her to look into his eyes. She saw the skin crease around them as he smiled.

'My goddess,' he murmured.

He ran one hand through her hair, his fingers pulling gently at the curls, and that made shivers crawl up her spine. She pressed her cheek to his palm. Even his hand felt strange on her face, the scent alien, the fingertips callused. She licked at it, exploring with her tongue while her hands, distracted, worked at his clothes. Veraine gave a shuddering groan as she sucked each of his fingers in turn, tasting leather and metal, the ingrained dirt of a lifetime spent training for battle. Her tongue traced the creases in his palm, the lines of his life. He bit his lip, breath rumbling in his chest, and his other hand tightened in her hair.

The belt was gone. She released his finger slowly as

she moved to concentrate on her next task; the exploration of what lay beneath his tunic. Gathering the fabric to his hips she slid her hand up beneath the cloth, discovering with the lightest touch of her fingers the rough texture of his thighs and the coarse curls of hair peeking from beneath the edge of his loincloth, then the sudden smoothness of the skin around his waist and the broadening expanse of his ribs. There didn't seem to be an inch of him that was not flat, hard muscle. Nevertheless, he did not have the endurance to stand still beneath her questing hands; without warning he snatched up his tunic, pulled it swiftly over his shoulders and threw it to the floor. She looked at his naked torso for the second time, and only the straining pouch of his loincloth concealed him from her eyes now.

For a moment all she could think was how much smaller she was than him. Veraine was not particularly tall or broad for an Irolian warrior, but her lips were almost on a level with his nipples, which stood proud at this moment like brown lentils despite the warmth of the night. Tufts of black hair, soft as carded cotton, peeked from under his armpits. She tried to assimilate the strangeness of his body. Yamani men were as smooth and brown as polished wood, but Veraine's chest was stippled with dark hairs that overlaid the swell of his pectorals like the shadow of a bird in flight. She licked one nipple curiously and then stood back, seeing the lamplight glisten on his moist skin. He shivered visibly and gripped her shoulders.

She touched his scars; some old and white, some bloody scabs from earlier in the day. There was a bruised encrustation on his left hip, which she skirted carefully with her fingertips. He submitted to her exploring fingers, watching her, the breath hard and shallow in his throat.

There was more hair below his navel; a line like a seam bisecting his belly leading down into the hidden places under the loincloth. She traced its path, as straight as an Irolian road across a hard plain, from well to jungle. But where that road plunged into the forest her journeying fingers hesitated. With every step the territory was becoming more unfamiliar. Her fingers were trembling.

Veraine covered her hands with his own and guided them firmly down over his crotch, so that their anxiety was crushed against the hot and rugged contours beneath the linen. She felt the swollen length of his penis kick under her palms. For a moment he held them there, then he brushed her hands aside entirely, their work done, so that he could pull her whole body against him. He stooped and lifted her, wrapping her thighs around his hips, and she clung to his chest, shocked by his strength. He held her up with one forearm, the hand tight under her splayed arse, as he carried her swiftly to the plinth in the centre of the room. With the other arm he swept it clear, armour and weapons clattering to the floor carelessly, so that he could lay her down on the stone.

He stood firmly between her parted thighs, her own legs trailing helplessly over the edge of the dais to the floor; and when he leaned forward his crotch ground into hers.

Braced on the length of his arms, he stared down at her. There was no trace of a smile around his eyes now; she thought it was more like the look of an executioner. She looked up into his eyes and it was like staring into the darkness of the night sky. His sallow face was outlined by the black ink-strokes of beard and brows and lashes and by his cobweb-hued hair that was starting to come loose from its thong.

Shifting his weight to one arm, he tugged loose the drawstring knot of her dress and pulled the neck wide.

But he could not reveal her breasts; they were still swathed in the spiral of her sash. He slipped the end of that cloth free and jerked the first loop from under her supine weight. She arched her back to aid the unwinding, but it made little difference; the homespun sheath was incapable of resisting. She watched the play of muscles in his forearm as he stripped her of the outer garment twist by twist until her crumpled under-dress was fully exposed. Then he stretched the neckline wide and pulled that down over her shoulders and arms, down to her hips. Her nipples, dark as honeybees, tightened as they met the lamplight.

Veraine was not in the mood to waste time; he cupped her breasts in his hands and bent over them like a tiger to the kill. For the attention she had offered him moments before he repaid her a thousand times over, lips and tongue and teeth combining in an impassioned assault on the most sensitive skin of her body. Where his mouth could not be, there his hands caressed, rolling each nipple in turn between his fingers until it was as hard as a pebble, and then he turned the ministrations of his mouth upon it, tugging and suckling at it until each breast felt as if it were incandescent.

Then he withdrew and worked his way down the length of her body to belly and pubis, yanking her dress violently to her ankles when he found it was in the way. Thus he ended up kneeling between her parted thighs, his face hovering over the mahogany fleece of her sex, and with his thumbs he smoothed and parted that unruly nest to reveal the pearly egg within.

His kiss was, to the Malia Shai's utter confusion, as tender as the breast of a brooding bird, settling on her with a warmth that suffused her veins. And his tongue was slow, winding through the labyrinthine folds of her labia with none of the urgent teasing with which he had provoked her breasts. Here he lavished his kisses with the numinous awe of a mystic in communion with the divine. That softness, the liquid caress of his mouth, nearly drove the senses from her. She could tell she was wet, and getting wetter. She pressed her palms against the stone beneath her and arched her back, pressing her aching clit into his mouth. But he seemed unwilling to satisfy her straight away. With tiny kisses and little licks he pulled free, rising to his feet again and stretching full length over her body once more.

She felt as if she must be pulsating beneath him.

This time she could see the glisten of her own juices on his chin and lips, smell the sweet-sharp musk of her own eagerness as he stooped over her. His mouth covered hers. She could taste her own sex. His tongue slipped between her swollen lips, easing them gently apart. It caressed her lips and teeth and tangled with her own tongue, stroking the soft and sensitive tissues, the wetness of their mouths intermingling, the taste of her musk burning in her throat. Without deliberation or knowing how it was happening, she found she had opened herself to him, fully and without reservation. And though Veraine was not thrusting into or upon her sex, merely resting the weight of his body upon hers, his still-clothed erection was pressed hard against the mound of her yoni and she was so aroused that that was enough to send her. Orgasm blossomed like a flower, unfurling petal after petal of crimson sensation. She did not cry out, or writhe. She felt her flesh invert silently, secretly.

But when Veraine lifted his lips from hers, somehow the light of recognition was in his eyes already.

'What happened there?' he asked in wonder. 'You came?'

She nodded. She could feel the flush starting to mount in her cheeks.

'You're very quiet.'

She nodded again.

He touched his lips to hers. 'I would like to hear you.' His voice was the huskiest of whispers.

'I . . . I don't cry out,' she replied.

'Oh,' he murmured, his mouth to her ear this time, his voice buzzing down her spine, 'you will.'

She felt him reach down to his hip with one hand and fumble there, while his mouth concentrated on the slow and moth-soft teasing of her lips and cheeks and eyelids. In a few moments he managed to drag free the last remaining rag of cloth that separated them, and then she felt the rough linen give way to hot flesh. He rested his cock there, coiled at the gateway of her sex, and he stared into her eyes.

'Tell me what you want,' he demanded.

She quailed before that question. The goddess in her acted according to her nature, without contemplation or introspection, while as a mortal woman she had never listened to the voice of desire. She had no vocabulary for it. 'I don't know,' she said weakly.

Veraine raised his eyebrows. 'Ah.' He took one of her nipples between thumb and forefinger and pinched it softly. 'Do you feel this?' he asked, the slightest nudge of his hips sending the hard neck of his cock pressing into the wet furrow of her sex.

She felt as if she were melting. She managed to nod.

'Do you want it?'

She tried to smile but her lips were trembling. 'Yes.'

'Tell me –' he planted soft kisses on her chin, her throat '– what you want.'

'I want you,' she gasped.

'Yes. How?' His tenderness was torture.

'I want – oh! – you to do those things. That you said, here, when I came into your room. All of them.'

'Ah. You remember.'

'Yes.'

His voice was as gentle and cruel and deadly as the stirring of a cobra against her cheek. 'Do you want me to fill you with my prick? Do you want it inside you, splitting you wide? Do you want my cream in your cunt, and your mouth, and your arse?'

'Yes.'

'So you want me to fuck you,' he concluded, his murmur thick with unspilled desire.

'I want you to fuck me,' she groaned in surrender.

He bit her earlobe softly. 'I'm glad you said that,' he whispered. 'Because I have to warn you: your tight little quim is so hot. And wet. And sweet. That when I get my length inside it, I won't be able to hold back. I will not be able to wait for you. I'm going to come inside you. It may be . . . rough.'

Her reply was to reach up and lick his throat, a response that made him groan and judder against her. 'Fuck me,' she ordered desperately.

It took only a rock of his hips to align himself. She felt the hard fist of his cock slide down the slippery, swollen folds of her sex and press into its hidden mouth. And she felt herself open up around him as more and more of his thick member entered her, stretching her wider than she could imagine, feeding into her without pause or mercy until he was rooted full length in her soil. Her body yielded – not just the shocked muscles of her yoni but the whole aching length of her, bone and flesh and skin, enfolding him in her arms and her thighs.

'Sweet gods!' Veraine said with feeling, his eyes fluttering shut. Then, despite all his threats, he lay still, buried to the hilt in her, savouring the moment. The

Malia Shai fought to get her breath back. When he did move, it was to raise himself on his arms and then pull her up against him, arm round her waist and then under her arse, keeping her straddling his hips, his member rigid inside her, as he carried her over to his bed. He kneeled on it, lowering her down upon the cover, their hips still locked. Once his hands were free he ran them over her, caressing breasts and belly and flanks, his palm as heavy upon her flat stomach as if he could feel his own cock beneath it.

She writhed beneath his touch, afire with sensations that had never before been aroused in her by mortal flesh. She reached up to him, caught his face in both hands, held him tenderly for a moment and then knotted her fist in his loose hair and pulled him down prone upon her. He came down hard, with a low cry, and the thrust that accompanied it repaid her impatient cruelty tenfold. She arched under him. He grabbed her wrists, pinned them wide and continued to thrust into her slender body. Their skins, slick with the perspiration of the warm night, seemed to melt into one another, their heaving torsos fused. His hips pushed her thighs wide, his face was buried in her tumbled hair. And every blow of his pelvis against her stoked the flames higher, like a man pumping a furnace bellows who does not dare stop until the metal turns to liquid fire.

Pinned beneath him, wrapped around him, the breath trapped in her chest, she felt the flame begin to run through every channel of her body from the white-hot crucible of her molten cunt, up her belly, filling her spine and lungs until she whiplashed under him in the inferno of orgasm and the fire ran up into her throat and came spilling out as a wailing sob of helpless abandon. She had never uttered a sound like that in her life. And Veraine caught it, smothering her mouth with his, swallowing her cry. Then the fire boiled through him, igniting his flesh, and he came in her with a violent shuddering thrust of his muscular arse that sent new flames washing through her twisting frame.

She thought it would never end, that they would burn like that for ever, that she would die there wrapped in fire.

She only knew that the conflagration was over when Veraine raised himself up onto his elbows and wiped the tears from her cheeks. She opened her eyes onto his gaze, still as intent as the glare of stars in the midnight sky, but softened now by a smile.

'You outran me, then,' he said.

She did not reply. The breath was heaving in her throat. He eased himself from within her and rolled off onto his back, but he caught her up as he went and tumbled her up against him, half-sprawled across his chest. They lay and let their panting slow. His left hand was tight on her back and she could hear his heartbeat thumping up from under his ribs. He ran his spare hand through his hair and over his scalp.

The Malia Shai twisted herself against him slightly so that she could look down the length of his torso, burning to see for the first time his cock, the pestle that had ground within her mortar. It lay against his belly, flushed dark with blood but quiescent now. It was glazed with her juices and to her eyes it looked improbably large; she could not believe she had managed to engulf such a thickness within her. She reached down to stroke it and felt it throb against her palm. It was not as smooth as she had expected, gnarled instead with thick veins.

'Ah,' said Veraine with satisfaction.

She pushed herself up on one elbow in order to reach further, down to his bollocks. She cupped them in her hand, feeling the weight of the velvety purse, the soft-ness of the hairless skin.

'Gently,' he cautioned as she found the firm stones within, and then whimpered helplessly, his lip caught between his teeth, as she rolled them slowly together. His penis jumped. She was pleased and intrigued and she sat up so as to better examine these new toys. But as she kneeled on the bed there was an unfamiliar rush of moisture between her legs.

'What's that?' she asked, frowning at the wet that had leaked out upon her inner thigh.

'Me, mostly,' Veraine said. He reached in and cupped her fur, his fingers delving in the sopping folds of flesh and teasing the hot embers of her pleasure into new flames. 'Us.' He withdrew his hand again and showed her the pearlescent slipperiness painted upon it. She sniffed cautiously at it, scenting an entirely unfamiliar musk.

'Taste it,' he suggested as her parted lips hovered an inch from his palm. His voice was husky again.

She lapped at the slippery dew, kissing the moisture eagerly from his splayed fingers. And under her own palm she felt a wave of tumescence surge up his mem-ber, stiffening its turgid length to utter rigidity.

'Oh sweet Shuga,' blasphemed Veraine, bundling her over onto the sheets and covering her with his weight.

'I thought we'd finished,' she gasped, and then gasped again as the thick length of his cock penetrated her swollen sex.

'Oh no,' he told her. 'We've hardly started.'

9 Desecration

He has fallen asleep at last. He lies against me, the weight of his head pinning my right arm to the bed, his lips pressed softly to the side of my breast. I can feel the warmth of his slow breathing. His arm is wrapped around me, long fingers framing my bruised and tender left nipple. His skin looks pale against my own.

My arm has gone numb, but I wouldn't dream of shaking him off.

What do I see, looking down the length of my body as I lie beside him? I see the muscular peak of his shoulder, the thickness of his upper arm and the long hard wedge of his forearm draped across my ribs. I see the smooth curves of his back receding to an arse as solid as the clay mound of a potter's kiln. I see the hopeless tangle of his strange, strange hair that escaped from its tie during our sweaty rutting and has fallen everywhere like a pool of wood-ash, black and grey.

When we fucked...

Under his hair I can make out part of his face. The angular black arch of a single brow, the sharp curve of nose and cheekbone. The dark lashes sweeping from eye-lids blue with exhaustion. The stubble creeping up from his jawline where he has neglected to shave for a day. I could never get tired of looking at that face.

The sweat has dried upon my skin now and the pulse has stopped rippling across my belly like an earthquake. My thighs have relaxed and ceased to shake. The strain of *our coupling took me to the edge of my strength, but I survived.*

When we fucked it was like we were trying to kill each other. Or kill ourselves. Like a man running into the heart of desert. Like a woman throwing herself under a landslide. A blur of grasping hands and thrusting limbs and choking breath. Teeth biting into tender flesh, nails raking vivid lines across tortured skin.

I am swollen and bruised in places I never imagined could be battered. And to the multiple cuts and bruises of battle I have added my own marks, across the length and breadth of his wonderful body.

He's got long legs; his feet seem to be miles away at the bottom of the bed. The legs are flecked with dark hair, like his chest. But his arse and back are as smooth as a Yamani's. He's strange. His body is a foreign land. I can't understand it, though I try and try to find out what makes him gasp, what makes him flinch, what makes him laugh, and I've learned so many of these things in just hours. What makes him harden like a tent-stake, instantaneously.

He is beautiful.

When we fucked it was like the monsoon rains, it was like heaven and earth colliding and mingling, it was like the elements fusing in chaos at the end of the world. It was like the apotheosis I shall achieve when three hundred and thirty-three lifetimes on earth have been completed, and I am able to return to the godhead.

This is not desire. I was taught to reject desire. This is not lust. Lust is an itch, an appetite, a selfish yearning for something that will satisfy the flesh. Scratch an itch and it will fade, feed a hunger and it will be sated. But what I feel now is not of the order of things that are satisfied by the material world.

It took me a long time to recognise that. At first I

thought only, he is a man and my female flesh desires him. It is of no importance. But there were other men he brought with him, and for them I didn't feel the same. Veraine only has to look at me and I know that I am being torn apart. He smiles that crooked smile of his and I feel the skies peel back and the stars shake in their spheres. If this is lust, then it is a lust that consumes the soul.

Every time I thought of him – his glance, his hands, the way he moved and turned and walked – then something would knot in my belly beneath my navel, something as sharp as the stab of a knife. Even now, with my flesh so wracked by pleasure that I would hardly have the strength to stand, there is a white-hot fire in me that is not quenched.

I could fuck Veraine from now until the end of time and it would not take away this need.

They never told me about this. I have no memory of it happening before, not in all my lives. What am I to do? I don't even have a name for this thing. In the arch of his eyebrow I see the vault of heaven, in the curve of his fingers I recognise the swell of the ocean, in the shadow of his throat I apprehend the depths of the underworld. He has become the universe itself to me.

I am earth, and he is water. I am darkness and he is light. I am the goddess – I am all goddesses – and he is the god. We consume each other. We make each other whole, and in doing so we become nothing. Sunyata. For the briefest moment when we meet in that holy place outside of time which is orgasm, then there is nothing, perfect and indivisible. The world is annihilated. We are not individuals, not matter, not existent. That indescribable union of all creation which thus becomes the Uncreated – that is the godhead. That is the state to which Malia has striven across the vain lifetimes.

I do not understand why we come back. Why does the universe return to existence?

He is beautiful. I want to bite his arse-cheeks and kiss the small of his back where the satin skin meets the cleft between them. I want to lick his nipples. He likes that. It makes him squirm.

My own nipples are tightening at the thought, firming like dried peas. If he stirred in his sleep and closed finger and thumb, he would have hold of the left one now. He would have hold of my soul by a golden chain. Oh. When his lips close over my erect nipples I feel as if I'm melting with pleasure. When he buries his face between my legs it is as if I'm a flower opening to the morning sun. He fills me with light. He puts his hand on my yoni and I'm wet for him. But a hand on my waist would do as well.

My right arm has gone to sleep. Otherwise I would reach up and brush the tangled locks back from his face as gently as he does for me. Oh, the tenderness in his fingertips when he strokes my mouth and my hair and my cheeks. It makes my eyes fill with tears that I don't understand but he seems to, kissing them away with lips as soft as feathers. He is most possessive when he is being most gentle. When he pins me down and we fuck hard, then I feel like a tigress, but when he touches me with the tiniest, most delicate of caresses, then I shake in his arms helplessly, like a fawn in a tiger's jaws, like a sacrifice on the altar.

I think he could do anything with me.

It is late. Most of the lamps have guttered out. I need to feel him inside me one more time before dawn.

She shifted beneath the Irolian General, trying to wriggle from beneath his weight, but he murmured in his sleep and tightened his arm about her.

'Roll over,' she whispered, as if she could avoid waking him. She pushed gently at his shoulder and watched as he tumbled slowly over onto his back, rucking the already rumpled sheets as he turned. She sat up so as to be able to see him, the whole supine length from head to feet. His amber skin looked golden in the lamplight and his hair was spread wildly about his head like a nimbus. She had never seen a man sleeping and she marvelled at his utter relaxation, at the graceful lines his body had fallen into, as if it were a small miracle.

She put her hand as softly as she could upon his breastbone to feel the rise and fall of his chest and he half-opened his eyes. He smiled at her, a slow, sleepy smile.

'Shh,' she breathed and bent forward to lick softly at his nipple. She felt the long indrawn breath pushing his ribcage up. Then she traced each ridge and furrow with her tongue all the way down the length of his chest, down to the warm plain of his stomach, down to the thicket of hair at his groin. She found cock and balls with her hands and separated them gently. Veraine made a small noise of resignation and spread his thighs a little further to assist her endeavours.

His prick was thick and heavy but soft with exhaustion, warm even in her warm palm, and bruise-dark. The scrotum beneath was almost as hairless and as velvety and the plums nestled within were firm under her fingers, as ripe as the damsons that yielded the fiery Yamani brandy. She kneeled over him, testing the full pouch with her lips and tongue, faintly aware of his sigh of pleasure. She ran her fingertips through the glossy thatch of hair that framed these treasures, teasing out the curls stiffened by her own sex juices. The hair was very dark, almost black, but she was intrigued this time to notice a couple of silver strands glinting among the jet ones. She kissed his cock warmly and felt it stir beneath her lips.

'You're insatiable,' mumbled Veraine with a tired grin.

Gently she took it in her mouth, nursing on it, letting the full, limp length settle on her tongue and in her throat. But it did not remain manageable for long, swelling instead to the rhythm of her suckling and filling the wet cavern of her mouth until she could no longer contain it and still breathe. She relinquished her hold on him and pulled away far enough that she could use her tongue to tease him into even greater rigidity, testing and probing the little wrinkles, the smooth glans, the moist eye of his cock. She was in no hurry. She made him wait patiently for each frisson of pleasure, building up the multi-layered edifice of arousal slowly stage by stage like the immense wedge of the towering temple *goparum*, until his member stood engorged and proud once more, slippery with her saliva and twitching at each caress of her lips. So engrossed was she in the manipulation of that length of masculine flesh, in the exploration of its moods and preferences, that she almost forgot the end to which she was aiming and only Veraine's hand descending to rest heavily on the back of her head roused her from her reverie. He tried to push her down further on his prick. Shaking free of his grip she rose and straddled him, trying not to brush against the ugly contusion on his left hip, pressing down on his chest through her splayed hands. His rigid member sought and easily entered her puffy sex-lips, still slippery with previous pleasures. She ignored the stinging of her abraded flesh and bore down on him, taking him as far as she could.

The smile had gone from Veraine's eyes now, to be replaced by the look of concentration she was learning so well. She shook out her hair and wriggled on him, which made her breasts jiggle. This did not escape his attention; he pushed into her further than was comfortable, and she felt the strange kick of pain that was also arousal deep inside her. His hands moved to grip her hips, his strong thumbs sliding up and down her skin, into her pubic hair and back again. The muscles in his arms flexed as he urged her to rise and fall on the thick stake of his member. She rolled her hips, frustrated by the way he was not quite touching her clitoris, biting her lip.

Veraine dug his heels into the bed and pushed up shudderingly beneath her and inside her, stretching her wet hole wide and digging it deep. His thumbs moved in a merciless circular caress on the skin above her pubic mound, and to her amazement she felt the fire from the ember of her clit begin to creep up her belly, as if the whole of her pubis was becoming sensitised beyond endurance, as if he could turn her body into one pulsing star of arousal. New moisture was brimming from her yoni, slathering him in juices that lubricated each thrust and twist of their coupling. Her breasts slapped together with the rhythm of her thrusts. She knew her end was within reach, that she only had to ride a little further, a little faster, that she could whip him to the finish in moments, and she watched dazedly as her fingers bit into his pectorals.

'She's there,' said Rasa Belit from the doorway. 'Get them.'

The Malia Shai pulled herself off his prick and was out of the bed by the time the priests reached her, but it was too late to get any further. She felt her arms grabbed in hands of iron and she was dragged into the middle of the room, thrown into Rasa Belit's grasp as the priests reached past her for the man on the bed. Half-blinded by her own loose hair she was flung aside roughly, tumbled across the stone floor while one arm was held captive in a biting grip. She looked up, gasping, in time to see the men in saffron robes seize a Veraine paralysed by his own arousal and jerk him from the sheets. His knee cracked upon the stone.

Veraine was yelling something in Irolian, his face twisted in rage. The priests had hold of his wrists. They held him on his knees, arms twisted and locked out behind him like the wings of a swooping hawk.

'Go on!' Rasa Belit yelled. 'Shout as much as you like! None of your men are within the Citadel, remember!'

Veraine fell silent and glared up at him. Rasa Belit kicked him in the head and the Irolian snapped to the side, trapped on the frame of his own sinews. Blood ran from his mouth when he turned his face back into view. His eyes were black pits of hate to match Rasa Belit's. The Malia Shai felt her heart freeze.

'You piece of shit,' the high priest pronounced, his voice thick and low. 'You stupid piece of shit. Did you think we wouldn't find you here?' He turned his glare on her. 'She didn't attend the Waning Moon Ceremony. We went looking for her. She wasn't in her room, but this was hidden under the bedding.' He held up a small bronze cup of Irolian design.

She saw recognition in Veraine's face, and something that might have been shame as he dropped his gaze.

'Let me go,' she whispered.

Rasa Belit's grip tightened so far that her blood began to well up under his nails. She felt the pain, but it was a distant distraction. 'You. I don't believe you've been so stupid,' he told her. 'You've thrown away your chance at ascension this lifetime.' The lines around his mouth were like scars. 'All my work. Everything I've given you. You're finished.' Further words were unable to escape his tightly twisted mouth and he released her suddenly, pushing her away.

She was dimly aware that the lesser priests were staring at her nakedness furtively, with horror and fascination.

'I'm the Malia Shai,' she said numbly. She didn't know where to start.

'Put your dress on,' he ordered. 'You are disgusting.' He turned away from her. 'And you,' he said, 'I will enjoy killing you.' He kicked Veraine again, hard, straight in the groin with his sandaled foot. His prisoner spasmed and folded, retching with pain, and the Malia Shai felt a white explosion of fury flare in her chest and burst out through her throat.

'Don't touch him!' she shrieked, throwing herself at the high priest with hands stiffened to claws. She raked at his face and saw the shock blooming there before he turned, threw up his arm and knocked her across the room. She hit the floor and sprawled, speechless, feeling the pain swell in her cheekbone. Everyone was staring at her now, Rasa Belit not seeming to believe what he had just done, the priests registering fear and doubt, and Veraine from under the tumbled rags of his hair meeting her eyes with a flash of heartbreaking warmth.

She found she was shaking uncontrollably.

'Look what you've done,' Rasa Belit said at last, when the silence had swollen to a monstrous thing. 'Look at you. What a waste.' His mouth worked. 'I said get your dress on.'

Two of the priests came forward at the savage gesture of his hand, though they looked uneasy. They found her dress lying crumpled on the floor and began to stuff her into it as if she were a stubborn child. She didn't fight them.

'Belit,' croaked Veraine, 'if you don't release me now

then I swear the Imperial Army will reduce your fucking temple to sand. Let us go.'

The priest made a choking sound as if about to cough. 'But you've already gone, General,' he protested. 'Drunk, in the dark, you must have fallen over the cliff-edge, forgetting that the walls were torn away in the earthquake. We will regretfully find your body in the morning, mangled beyond recognition by the plunge but –' he glanced around the room at Veraine's possessions '– identifiable by its accoutrements. Distinctive armour or something. And while your men mourn you I shall be making sure that your funeral is, although premature, fully justified.' He bent, as hunched and foul as a carrion crow, over Veraine's kneeling figure and dropped his voice to a whisper as he concluded, 'I shall conscientiously search through every steaming, glistening inch of your entrails until I find whatever sorcery it was you used on her.'

'Maybe you should just ask her,' Veraine said, attempting a sneer through the blood. It was dripping on the high priest's toes.

'Rasa Belit, let him go,' she said. 'It's my command. Listen to me.'

The priest closed his eyes slowly, as if in pain. 'Be quiet. You've lost touch with your divinity, and you have nothing to say. When you have been released from this incarnation you will see it all clearly. You'll be grateful to me.'

Disbelief pinned her.

'What are you going to do to her?' Veraine demanded.

'Don't worry, General, you will die first. I lack the . . . restraint to prolong your punishment beyond a couple of days. The Malia Shai will be confined to await her next life.'

Veraine said nothing, but he looked over at her. She

saw a terrible hopeless regret in his eyes and that hurt her more than anything the priest had done.

'Take the Malia Shai to her room. And you – get this Irolian offal covered up.' Once more he kicked Veraine brutally in the crotch.

As the priests pulled her to her feet, she found her own voice again. 'I curse you, Rasa Belit.' Her voice sounded old and weary even to herself. 'I set the curse of the goddess on you. You will not lay eyes upon me for a thousand lifetimes.'

His mouth twisted, but she knew he did not believe her. 'Take her away,' he repeated.

She was pushed into her room just as the grey of dawn was starting to show through its open windows. The two priests released her arms but they made no move to leave, taking up positions at either side of the door instead. The Malia Shai turned to look at their faces, but realised there was no point speaking to them. Hamin and Pajlet were two of Rasa Belit's closest acolytes and she could not imagine them disobeying him. She glanced around her room hopelessly, seeing the mattress of her bed lying askew and disordered. She went and kneeled upon it, having nowhere else to go.

Her dress was hanging off her shoulder. She reached up to gather in the drawstring collar, and caught a waft of musky scent from her hands. She raised them to her face, breathing in deeply. It was Veraine, the smell of him, the aroma of his body and his sweat and his sex, trapped on her skin. Even now that scent, that ephemeral yet intimate reminder of his body, made the warm ache surge inside her.

She did not want to imagine him broken by torture and her mind shied away from the picture. Once she was stripped of her own mortal flesh, she told herself, she would intercede with the divine powers so that Veraine, heathen barbarian or not, would be reborn into a noble and dignified life. She would –

The entry of Rasa Belit into the chamber broke her reverie. She looked once at him and then away, suddenly finding his features repulsive beyond words. His colour was high and he was breathing with effort. A few whispered words were exchanged with the priests and then, as they left the room, he advanced upon her. He was carrying the short ebony staff of the high priest, the badge of office he wielded on formal or solemn occasions.

She did not look up or acknowledge him in any way, even when he walked over her bedding, circling her. There were still little spots of blood on his toes, she noticed.

He put a heavy hand upon the crown of her head and dragged his fingers slowly through the length of her damp, tangled hair. Then he took hold of it at the nape of her neck, twisting it into a rope around the ebony rod, and used it to pull her to her feet. She didn't resist, rather she hung weakly from his grip, her legs taking her weight reluctantly.

'Look at you,' he murmured into her ear. His voice was heavy and thick with disgust. 'You are a mess. You're filthy. You stink.' He crushed her scalp to his face, inhaling the scent of her hair. 'Do you know what you smell of?'

She knew.

Rasa Belit wiped his nostrils across her cheek. His lips felt hot.

'You smell remarkably like a whore,' he said, each word as slow and considered as a blow. 'Your mother was a whore; a snatch-peddler from the lowest cat cage in the city. God knows what your father was. Well, you look like her.' He put his hand on her bare shoulder. 'Why did you let him do it?'

She shut her eyes. She could feel his words crawling over her skin.

'That's what I can't understand. His kind have conquered us, sacked our palaces, desecrated our temples. They've made us into a slave nation. Butchered our children. Raped and burned and starved and humiliated us. Haven't there been enough of our women forced to spread their legs for his kind, without you doing it willingly? I don't understand how you can touch him without choking on your own vomit.'

His open palm slid down over her breast and settled over her sore nipple. His moist hand seemed to burn through the thin cotton.

'I know, this isn't the first time you have failed in your mission. You've taken on frail mortal flesh, after all. You are subject to temptation. All the weakness of your woman's body, craving carnal knowledge of a man. The Malia Shai has stumbled before, and been cleansed, and begun her journey anew.' He squeezed her breast slowly, kneading it between hard fingers. 'I know what you want,' he whispered. His tongue brushed her earlobe. 'You burn for a man's weight pinning you down and a good, thick bone banging into your wet hole.'

She could not help thinking of Veraine and the hot dew moistened her clenched thighs.

'But,' he murmured, 'you have never been so debased in all the centuries as to offer your cunt to an Irolian. You might as well have been discovered in a sty being fucked by the boar. You're truly defiled this time.'

His hand slid down over the length of her belly and settled on her pubic mound, taking a good firm handful of the soft flesh. She felt her treacherous body, so recently aroused to the brink and still not sated, respond to his touch. Inadvertently she whimpered.

'Too late for regret, my Malia Shai. Perhaps in your next life you will remember this shame.'

He licked her exposed throat. His fingertips were digging into her labia and the pressure on her clitoris was making her burn.

'I can taste him on you,' he whispered. 'Quite an unmistakable stink. Corruption. Degradation. I bet he did things to you that would make whores blush.'

Her legs felt too weak to hold her up. She could feel the moisture gathering in her sex, despite her desperate need to ignore his thick, probing fingers. When the door-curtain was suddenly lifted and the two acolytes re-entered the chamber she did not know whether it was relief or frustration that stung the most as Rasa Belit released her crotch and gestured the two priests over.

Hamin was carrying a bronze laving bowl, and as he came closer she saw that inside it nested a jar of soap and a silk cloth. Pajlet heaved the weight of a copper vessel full of water. She stared at the water, aware of how dry her throat was, how her thirsty body craved to gulp it down. What has happened to me? she thought.

'Fill the bowl,' instructed her captor and the two priests hurriedly obeyed. He forced her back to her knees in front of the dish and unwound the rod from her hair. 'You must be washed before you proceed to your next incarnation.'

With that he pushed her shoulders forward and down, forcing her head into the water, and his other hand shoved down on the back of her head. She opened her mouth in a silent cry, her eyes seeing only the metallic sheen of the bronze through a swirl of her own floating hair. She thought for a moment that he intended to drown her, but just as the pressure in her lungs became pain he yanked her back up into the air. She gasped and blew out water from her throat. The weight of her wet hair slopped down on her breasts. Water ran down through her clothes onto the floor, cool on her sweat-slicked body; a brief and tantalising delight. The cotton clung to her wherever the water went.

Rasa Belit slapped the silk cloth into the water, then tilted her face up and struck her stingingly across the cheeks with it. Then he roughly scrubbed her face and throat.

'Remember how it is to be clean,' he sneered.

The wet cotton she wore was all but transparent, her nipples jutting up against the cloth. Rasa Belit's breathing was harsh.

'We must wash off his taint.' He sloshed more water over her head and ran his fingers cruelly across her scalp, ignoring the tangles that he tore through. Tears sprang unasked-for to her eyes. 'He's been in your mouth, hasn't he?' he sneered, and forced the wodge of silk between her lips. It clogged her throat as he scrubbed mercilessly at every inner surface, the sodden cloth making her gag. Eventually he whipped the rag out again and stared at her with malicious satisfaction.

She could no longer look him in the eye.

'Get the dress off,' he ordered. When she didn't obey the two lesser priests, who had struggled so assiduously to dress her just before, came forward to strip her naked. They hauled her to her feet and held her up for Rasa Belit's inspection. He looked down at her breasts with an expression of loathing. Her nipples were like small pebbles after their dousing. He took up the jar of soap and scooped out handfuls, splattering them on her soft orbs. She thought that the pale slop looked like semen gleaming on his fingers and on her skin. It dribbled down across her belly.

'You need a thorough scrubbing,' he told her. Beads of sweat glistened over his shaven scalp. He set to work with hands and cloth, smearing the soap over every inch, kneading and mauling her breasts. She was bruised and he was rough. It hurt. She clenched her teeth against the stabs of pain and the deep, throbbing ache of her abused flesh. He squeezed and pinched her breasts, the slippery globes sliding under his palms, the nipples perversely hardening as if offering themselves for torture. She arched her back and shuddered, helpless in the grip of the two eunuchs, jerking under the extremities of sensation inflicted by the third.

His soap-slathered hand finally slid down between her thighs and thrust into the space between them. There he finally discovered, to her shame, quite how wet she was; slick with neither water nor soap but with her own hot juices. Her labia were swollen and unfurled around the open well of her sex.

He stared into her face. 'Whore,' he breathed, so softly the other priests probably never heard.

He withdrew his hand. Over two out-thrust fingers he draped the wet silk cloth, and then he dipped his gloved hand deep into the soap. Slowly, watching her every nuance of expression, he sought out the unguarded gate between her thighs and thrust those rigid fingers deep inside her. She took him easily. He twisted his wrist, scrubbing her cunt as he'd scrubbed her mouth, his breath coming hard as he worked his fingers round and up. The lubricated silk was slippery over stiff, splayed digits and he forced her inexorably wider, while at the same time his thumb pounded on her clitoris.

She came on his hand, unable to resist. Heat flared through her pinned body. She held her face immobile and she let no breath of a whimper escape her lips, desperate not to let the priests realise, but she could not disguise the clenching spasm of her inner muscles, and Rasa Belit knew. She saw it in the narrowing of his eyes, the twitch of his sweat-beaded lip. Her sex mouthed and clenched his hand.

When she ceased to spasm, he withdrew. She expected him to say something, to spew further abuse, but he only stepped aside and told the priests, 'Let her down.' They dropped her and she fell to hands and knees. The stone was awash with milky water beneath her palms. She heard him swirl the rag in the bowl, then he slapped a great gob of soap onto her bare back and followed it up with the wet silk. Water dribbled down her ribs and off the tips of her dangling breasts. He scoured her unmercifully, then put his hand on the small of her back and forced it down, arching the spine, the tilt of her pelvis throwing her arse up and open. Suddenly her wet and gaping pussy, still throbbing with the pulse of orgasm, was displayed to the priests standing behind her.

Then Rasa Belit raised the silken cloth and slapped it stingingly straight between her thighs, striking her cleft with an audible smack. Shock waves ran up her backbone and across her buttocks, followed by the slower, hotter wash of pain that was somehow arousal too. She bit down on a cry. Her thighs were trembling visibly, her arse aquiver. She felt the soapy water sliding down the burning valley between her splayed cheeks.

Rasa Belit put one wet finger on her pursed hole.

'He's had his prod in there, too, hasn't he? Sodomite. I knew it. I bet that was his favourite position.'

Veraine hadn't, in fact, having exhausted his strength before his invention. But she remembered with terrible clarity his strong, clever fingers easing into her, the way they had coaxed her to total surrender. And the memory made her tight muscles dilate to this new touch.

She heard the stertorous intake of his breath. Then her consternation turned to horror as, after a moment's muffled preparation, something cold and hard was placed against the offending orifice. Her aroused senses identified the wet slickness of soap and the smoothness of silk but the underlying mass did not make sense to her – too unyielding and cool to be any part of human anatomy – until she remembered the high priest's staff of office.

'Don't,' she said, her first word since entering the room. She knew as she uttered it that it was a mistake, and she bit her lip.

'Open for him and you'll open for this. You will.' And to make his point, Rasa Belit grabbed hold of her hair and reined her head up tight, so that she was unable to pull away from the invasion about to take place.

Her muscles clenched against the intruder, but the rigid tip bored into the tight circle with insistent pressure. She tried to swing her hips around out of the way, but he followed her as she circled and she could not escape. Her knees scraped on the rough floor. Then the unseen rod rotated slightly, and with that movement all her body's resistance collapsed. She felt her arse yield to the staff, and it yielded willingly, admitting the rounded tip and the succeeding slippery inches.

'Shit. You love this, don't you,' groaned her violator. He twisted the stick, pushing it from side to side in the tight grip of her orifice, spreading her wider open, but for her all the initial discomfort and the instinctive fear were drowned in a rush of physical pleasure so vast that she couldn't cope any longer. Thrusting herself back, further on to the ebony staff, she opened her mouth and let the scream of orgasm come tearing from her throat, uncaring of her witnesses, of her dignity, of her spiritual well-being, her whole frame shuddering like an earthquake. She gave vent to every pent-up and disregarded emotion that had ever haunted her body in a howl of bestial abandon, and she finished in helpless sobs.

Rasa Belit, frozen with shock, held on tight until her crisis was over and then let her head fall limply forward. He pulled out the stave without a word, but he left the silken sheath inside her, the wet fringes dangling down against her sex.

Then he walked away, out of the room. But she heard his last instruction to the acolytes as he left.

'Wall up the doorway.'

10 **The Mask**

Veraine opened his eyes to absolute blackness and wondered how long it was since he had last opened them. He had not been asleep, he was sure, but the darkness was so complete and his mind had been in such turmoil that it was impossible to tell how much time had elapsed since he'd last been lucid and watchful. He could smell damp stone and feel the cool, still air against his skin, but apart from his own breathing there was no sound. It was as if he'd been buried alive.

He'd been imprisoned in a chamber beneath the Outer Temple, part of a complex of tunnels and rooms that he and the Irolian engineers had never guessed about. How many other secrets had Mulhanabin kept from them? he wondered groggily. The priests had dragged him here, his arms twisted to breaking point, his mouth stuffed with a rag to prevent any noise. He had a jumbled recollection, painted in lurid colours by anger and desperation, of the route taken behind some insignificant-looking carved screen, down winding stairs into the bowels of the mountainside.

He cursed himself again for his own overconfidence.

Before the journey they'd hastily shoved him into a pair of trousers to cover the nakedness which Rasa Belit seemed to find offensive, but his torso was bare and, for the first time that he could remember since getting to the city, he felt cold. And sore: his body ached like one great bruise. But at least they hadn't managed to knock out any of his teeth or break any bones. The priests of the Malia Shai, in his estimation, were not experts at inflicting damage.

That would all change, he suspected, when Rasa Belit arrived.

They had strung him up here in this tiny room, his arms roped to beams over his head, his feet tethered apart to rings set in the floor. The beams and rings had been carved all of a piece from the living rock. There were no windows. He hadn't seen much else of the room; the priests had lingered only moments to secure him before they had departed with every source of light.

He was desperately thirsty. The damp smell of the stones made the craving worse.

He could bring his hands to within a span of each other but no closer. They were tied up high over his head and at the moment most of his weight hung off them. No chance to pick the knots. He couldn't move his feet at all. At least he had managed to work the cloth out from behind his teeth and spit the gag from him before he choked on it. But it gave him little hope. He was helpless.

Alone in the darkness he had chased the same thoughts over and over again; how stupid he'd been to return to the Citadel alone, how reckless to assume that Rasa Belit would never move against him; how idiotic to bed the Malia Shai in his own chamber, where they could be easily discovered, where there was no back-up to call upon. If he'd had the sense to stay near his men, to let the Host loose through the city, if he'd had his sword nearer to hand, if he'd jumped up faster, if he'd anticipated what would happen if they were found, if he'd thought of anything at all except the intoxicating warmth of her body against his ... Gods, if he'd thought with his wits instead of his balls then he'd never have ended up here waiting for torture and a slow death.

He would never have lain with her at all, if he'd been smart.

The cold was seeping into his flesh, and at last he managed to damp down his fury and his fear in order to think more clearly. He rested his head against his right biceps, feeling the firmness of the muscle, the smoothness of the skin against his cheek, the warmth under that skin. He was painfully aware that he was about to die. He had no control over his situation and he could see no way out of it; the moment he had taken her in his arms he had signed both their death warrants.

He thought of her being walled up in some room or corner in the complex and guilt stabbed him again. But not fear, and not pity. He had infinite faith in her strength and he knew she could never be broken by mere fear or pain. She would face her fate calmly, with detachment and confidence, as she faced everything else.

Well, not quite everything. In the fragile moments of their time together he had unlocked a secret place in her soul that he had never seen before, and perhaps had never been discovered by anyone. He remembered her breathless, trembling kisses, the wide-eyed wonder with which she had bestowed her caresses, the heat of her yielding; and at the memory he closed his eyes. It made no difference to the blackness, nor to the dancing pictures that his imagination painted on that backdrop. Her full lips. Her breasts soft beneath his hands. The firmness of her backside as he pulled her into him. The sweet wet cleft between those thighs that parted to his touch so trustingly. The honeyed scent of her skin.

If he had been sensible, he would never have known those things.

And now they were gone. They were part of the past, lost for ever. He found it hard to believe that it was only a few hours ago – perhaps less; he had lost all track of time down here – that he had been immersed in a physical pleasure close to rapture. Now he was about to pay for it.

Under his cheek the blood ran warm, his pulse beat, his aching muscles flexed. He was tired beyond words, but he was still young and strong. He was alive, not dying. And yet, though his body worked as it had always worked, though his lungs still swelled to draw each breath into his body, though the scab on his hip was hardening – and itching while it did so – yet in a few hours he would be dead. The body shattered, the blood cold, all these breaths and heartbeats wasted. It seemed to make no sense, and he felt protest coiling in his guts, an aching denial that said that fate was wrong, the gods were wrong, that he was not ready. He clenched his teeth. Didn't every person that faced execution feel that way? It was infinitely unfair, the childish part of him cried. Yet it happened.

He wished that he had the Malia Shai's detachment. He didn't.

What he had instead was courage. He was a soldier, and since he was fourteen he had known that it would end this way, or worse. Face down in a pool of his own blood, that was how he had imagined his last moments, when he was being optimistic. He had never had any prospect of dying in his bed, peaceful and happy. How many people did? Civilians got to fool themselves that death was not inevitable, that it wouldn't hurt, that it would wait until you were ready. But soldiers knew the reality. In his career he'd seen every kind of death in all its rainbow variety of repulsiveness, humiliation and agony. Death was not an option; it was an inevitable encounter. What you had on your side was not hope or defiance but courage. Simply the courage to face it.

I shall die silent, Veraine told himself. He will not make me scream.

And after that? He had shone brightly enough in life; perhaps the priests were right and there would soon be a new star in the shimmering heavens. But somehow he doubted it.

There was one shred of comfort and he wrapped his heart around that thought as round an ember. Every man died, and few in the cause of anything of worth. They lost their lives for trivial reasons; for standing in the wrong place at the wrong time, for turning their head to the right instead of the left, or the left instead of the right. For a misinterpreted glance, for an incautious remark, for being too cowardly to act or too brave to run. For lack of money, or for an excess that brought deadly attention. They died by mischance, by bad luck, by stupidity, by ignorance, by the casual malevolence or the cool indifference of others more powerful than themselves. But he, Veraine, was going to die because he had made a choice. He had let the gods know that there was something he wanted more than fame or riches, more than anything else in the world. Something he would sell everything in his life for. His soul's desire. And for once the gods had listened, and he had been granted that desire – and if now he died for it, what was that in comparison to such an achievement?

He'd had her. For only a few hours, but with such intense passion that even before the priests had discovered them, he had known that he would not emerge unscathed or unchanged.

In the darkness, invisible, his dry lips tightened in a fearful smile.

The ghostly lights that drift behind the eyelids flared and bloomed, then, as if he were pressing his eyeballs. It took him a moment to realise that his lids were in fact open, and that what he was seeing was no illusion, but real light. A warm glow was creeping into the room from where the stairs descended from the ceiling, revealing the hidden details of that ancient chamber, the carved tables and benches, the hooks and beams, even a slab in the far corner that looked to be some kind of trapdoor. Veraine blinked hard and steeled himself, his stomach knotting. The glow, like some holy aura, illuminated a pair of sandaled feet and the edge of a yellow robe descending into view. The figure beneath the robe was rounded and moved with a stately grace born of great girth. He recognised the priestess Muth.

She glanced at him briefly as she reached the floor, and smiled; a smile as cold and sticky as congealed fat. He looked beyond her at the stairs, but there seemed to be no sign of anyone else coming to join them. Muth carried in her hand a lantern and as soon as she had put this upon the table she used it to kindle other lamps which she set about the room. Only then did she give him her full attention.

'I thought I'd come and take a look, General, before Rasa Belit made too much of a mess of you,' she said conversationally.

Veraine hung from his fetters and declined to answer.

'He'll be on his way shortly, but you must understand he's had a number of things to deal with. Irritating but inescapable details, mostly, to do with the mourning of the Malia Shai.' She sniggered. 'Oh. You hadn't heard, of course. He announced her death to the temple and the people today; it emerges that she gave up all her mortal strength to the earthquake that defeated the Horse-eaters and has departed this fleshly existence for her next incarnation. A sacrificial miracle. I'm sure you'll join in offering your respects.'

She paused, but Veraine kept his face blank, only his

eyes moving to follow her as she strolled. She halted in front of him, hands on her broad hips. He hung before her like a carcass on a butcher's hook; meat on display for her perusal.

'I knew you were trouble the moment I set eyes on you,' she said in a low voice. She looked him up and down with lascivious care. 'Too pretty by half for a soldier.'

Veraine only blinked. He could feel the cold beads of sweat tickling down his spine.

She licked one fingertip and drew a line from the hollow of his throat, across to his left nipple, then down the old scar over his ribs, to the pit of his navel.

'Rasa Belit didn't see it coming. He might not have a prick, but he still thinks like a man.' She showed her teeth. 'He still doesn't know what happened, what hit him. Years of the most stringent care and vigorous training, and then the silly bitch opens her legs to the first set of moving parts that come her way. That's how he sees it.' She quirked one eyebrow. 'Might as well have a look at what all the fuss is about.'

The trousers were held at the front by a cross-threaded linen cord. She slipped the thong unhurriedly, pulled the cloth wide and dragged the garment low down over his hips. He couldn't move to resist. She reached in and pulled out his sex organs into the light. Veraine stared darkly past her as if she didn't exist.

'Well, General, no need to be shy,' Muth breathed. 'Quite a pretty piece.' She hefted his balls, cupping their soft weight in her hand, squeezing his prick confidently between her fingers. 'And a fair size, too, even for a goddess to cope with. I hope she appreciated such a fine set of tackle.'

He said nothing. In fact, overused and bruised by several blows, his genitals were all but numb.

'These will be the first to go,' Muth said, staring up into his face. 'Rasa Belit will never forgive you for these. For what he hasn't got. He will take this –' she rolled his cock lovingly in her palm '– and cut it off slice by paper-thin slice, I imagine. Or perhaps he will flay it raw first and rub it with salt.'

Veraine closed his eyes, mostly so that he wouldn't have to see her.

'Was she good, soldier?' Muth asked, stroking his satiny length with one finger. 'I hope she was, for your sake. Because you are going to pay a very high price indeed for balling her. Rasa Belit is going to carve you into gobbets so small even you won't be able to recognise your own bits. You have destroyed him, soldier; he's a broken man. And he's going to break you in return.'

She put her face to his armpit and inhaled deeply. 'You know, I suspect she wasn't even that good. Just another Yamani snatch. What a pity. You must have had a hundred like her.' She pawed at his arse, sighing with pleasure to find the hard muscles there clenched. 'But I knew when I first saw you that you had the horn for her, because we get men like you every day in the temple. They have a thing inside them which goes for anything they can't have. Anything forbidden. They sniff around us priestesses like dogs just because they can't get one up us. It drives them to a froth.' She drew one hand over his chest, caressing the muscle like it was horseflesh. 'You're like that. I saw it in the way you looked at her. You just have more ambition than average, soldier. You had to go after the Malia Shai herself.'

Veraine set his jaw as her wet tongue ripped briefly at his nipple.

'So when Rasa Belit is cutting into you here ... and here ... and here ... soldier, I hope you understand just why he's so upset. You've been places he could never go.

You see? He's looked after her all her life. He held her in his arms the day she was first brought into the temple as a baby. He deflowered her when she came of age – did you know that? He has known her as a child and as a woman and as the living goddess. He's obsessed with her. She was his life. He loved her, soldier – but you got to fuck her.

'You can understand,' she whispered, nipping each nipple in turn between her incisors, 'that he's just a little jealous.'

The lamp-wicks shuddered as tears of pain started to fill his eyes.

'And,' she sighed, pausing for breath, 'he still has no idea what she saw in you. All he sees is some Irolian grunt. It's funny, isn't it?' She stroked his face tenderly and wrapped her fingers in the tumbled length of his hair. 'Look at you. I could have told him. She's a young woman, after all. Young women are vulnerable to these things. And you are such a pretty, dangerous boy.'

She shifted her stance so that she could straddle his right thigh, her large breasts flattening on his naked chest. 'And I'm going to enjoy you,' she informed him, lingering over the words. 'Right now.'

One of her arms snaked round his waist to grip him, while her right hand delved deep between his thighs to take possession of his bollocks and his prick. Veraine realised with a peculiar horror that he was completely helpless in the face of this invasion, that he couldn't pull away or thrust her off, that there was nothing he could do to stop her rubbing slowly and rhythmically up against him, her pubis grinding into the hard muscle of his thigh. Her fingertips, thrusting past the pathetic barrier of his trousers, scrabbled at his perineum. Normally stimulation there would have been pleasurable; in these circumstances it was almost unbearable.

'I hope,' she grunted, raising her face to his, 'that you appreciate the irony of the situation.' She rubbed her bulk up and down on him, rolling her hips. 'Makes a change for one of you to be used by a Yamani woman. D'you like being fucked, soldier?'

He could only stare at the ceiling and clench his teeth as she made use of his body, humping his leg and mauling his crotch with a brutal hand. But he didn't cry out, even when her nails dug into the tenderest flesh of his groin, even when she lowered her ravening mouth to his chest and fastened it over his nipple, tongue stabbing and teeth grinding into the pectoral muscle. She bit until the blood ran. He shut his eyes tight against the lights exploding in his skull. And her rhythm changed from a regular thrusting beat to a broken staccato heave, her vast curves wobbling as she slapped against him, her gasps a slobbering snorting counterpoint to the jerking of her body against his tight frame. When she came, he thought she was going to crush his cock to pulp.

But she stilled at last and pulled away, leaving him in a wringing sweat of fear and violation but still silent. His right nipple was framed by the crescent imprints of her upper and lower teeth, and blood was trickling down his ribs. And his eyes spoke his loathing, even though no sound was permitted to escape his throat.

Muth lifted her gory lips and tried to kiss his mouth, but he jerked his face away, too tall for her to reach. She laughed, long and derisively.

'Naughty boy,' she sneered.

She licked her lips then wiped them on the back of her forearm. Her face was flushed and her robes clung to her with the lingering heat of her pleasure.

'Rasa Belit has given me dispensation to watch your punishment,' she said, still breathing heavily. 'I'm looking forward to it.'

She had quick ears. Some noise must have warned her; she glanced once behind her and then reached to stuff his battered genitalia back inside his trousers, hitching the garment up to a more proper angle on his hips. She had stepped smoothly to the side before the new feet came into view down the stairs.

It was Rasa Belit, accompanied by three priests. Despite his resolve, Veraine's heart lurched. Then he took up his soldier's stoicism like a shield and met his torturer's gaze squarely.

Rasa Belit looked awful. His face was the wet grey of a drowned man, except for two hectic spots high on his cheeks like a whore's rouge, and he moved across the room with a hobbling gait. Dark sweat stains painted his robes in patches. He clutched in his hand a roll of leather. He leaned against a stone table as the others took up their positions around the periphery.

'It's done,' he said, his voice tight and cold. 'She's dying at this very moment, General Veraine –' he gave the title bitter emphasis '– and I do trust you're proud of your work. You've killed her. She is starting again upon the long ladder of reincarnation, from the very bottom. Three hundred and thirty-three lifetimes to go. And in all those generations millions of innocent people must suffer from famine and sickness and drought, their redemption snatched a little further away from them once more. And as for you; you are going to suffer torments you can't even begin to imagine.'

He paused, looking with unalloyed distaste at his victim.

'Was it really worth it, General?'

And without warning Veraine felt something move within him, something warm and bright and glowing like a flame, that grew in his chest and up his throat and filled his mouth so that his cheeks were stretched helplessly wide into the sweetest smile. 'Yes,' he said, eyes alight. 'Yes, it was.'

Rasa Belit seemed to turn to stone for a moment. Then he dropped the leather pouch onto the table and swept his arm across to unroll it. It was full of knives. In his haste one of the knives slipped from the edge of the table and fell ringing to the floor.

Rasa Belit stooped to pick it up. But he never got there. Veraine, facing him, saw the spasm that crossed his face, the agony twisting his features. Everyone in the chamber saw him clutch at his belly, and heard the sound as of ripping cloth that accompanied his whole frame collapsing to a heap. In the moments that it took the priests to gather their wits and hurry to his aid, the enclosed space was filled with an unmistakable cesspit stench. The priests flinched back, and Rasa Belit let out a shriek of anguish.

Veraine knew what this was, recognising it even as he tried to stop breathing. They called it siege-fever or the bloody flux all across the Empire, though here it was the Kiss of Malia. Whatever its name, it was fatal.

Muth, to her credit, was the first to reach the stricken man, pushing a floundering priest aside so that she could grab him under the arm. 'Help me!' she ordered one of the others. 'Help me get him up, we've got to get him to his bed!'

They hauled him to his feet, though he seemed unable to take any of his weight upon his own legs. Rasa Belit's eyes rolled open briefly.

'Throw him in the pit!' he gasped.

Muth seemed as if she were going to protest, but thought better of it. She jerked her head at the two remaining priests and they hurriedly pushed the raised flagstone aside. Light, green as water, spilled up into the room. It revealed the true terrible pallor of the high priest, and the pool of foulness that was already leaking across the floor. He groaned again as the waves ripped through his entrails.

Working like men in a nightmare, the two priests cut Veraine down from the beam and dragged him across the room. He tried to fight them, but to his despair found his arms had set through lack of bloodflow and movement, and were as weak as a baby's. They hauled him over to the hole in the floor and despite all he could do to struggle, threw him down it head first.

He bounced off a sloping wall part way down; it probably saved his neck. Even so the impact with the floor knocked all the wind out of him and he lay there stunned for a long time. He heard the grinding of the trapdoor being replaced, and then only silence.

He raised his head. He could see the rock face in front of him. Slowly he rolled over, feeling the blood course back painfully into his cramped arms. Above him the roof disappeared in an inverted funnel to the flagstone door, the walls as curved as the inside of a wineskin. The light was coming from the side, not above. He turned his head and saw daylight, saw clouds, felt hope running through him like fire. He was on his knees and then his feet and three steps took him out from under the rock roof and into the open air – and the fourth nearly sent him over the edge to his death. He teetered on the brim, staring with disbelief.

There was only one exit to the tiny cell he now inhabited, and that led out into the yawning void. Hundreds of feet below him was the desert floor, a chaos of rubble and shadow. Above him the cloud cover was as heavy as another cavern roof. The cliff face was absolutely sheer. Unless he could fly, there was no way down. He looked across to the hills and saw that they were picked out in yellowy green light. Those were the hills that faced west from the Amal Bhad river; he was looking east, back towards the Empire. Even as he stared, mind working furiously, the light on the hills died and a great thick dusk settled like a veil over the whole landscape. The birds of Mulhanabin set up their sunset clamour, swirling flocks of starlings swooping out from the walls far over his head.

Sunset, he thought. I've been hanging there all day.

His legs, heavy and useless as sacks of flax, gave way beneath him and he slid to his knees. The stone was firm beneath his hands and he felt weakly grateful for it as he laid his cheek against the rock and let the darkness suck him down.

I am lying awake on my bed, just as I have done every day of my life. Strange how some things don't change. Strange how some things do. This time, for the first ever, I am not alone on my mattress. My new lover stretches out beside me, his hands gentle upon my skin. I'm waiting for the moment he rolls on top of me and splits my yoni wide.

But Death is a considerate lover, and he does not intend to force me. Instead he tries to persuade me to yield, his touch seductive, his kisses soft on my shoulders, down the length of my spine. I'm in no haste to submit, so I let his caresses smooth my skin and I watch the darkness. His hand is cool on my belly. When he touches my breasts, cupping them in his palms, my nipples stir to life.

He explores every inch of my body, languidly, using fingers and lips and tongue. Every part of me. Even between my toes and my fingers, even down the cleft of my arse; stroking, tickling, teasing. He wants me to surrender to him. Death wants me to grow wet and pliant for his cold flesh, to part my thighs for him, to guide him into my intimate and aching places with sighs and little moans of need. He wants me to want him.

He is an experienced and implacable lover. It is only a matter of time.

It was sunlight on his face that woke Veraine. He flinched from the sudden discomfort and pushed himself partially upright, trying to blink, then found that his eyes were all but gummed shut and he had to rub them clear. The interior of his lids felt like the floor of the desert, but that unpleasant sensation paled into insignificance as he became aware of his thirst. There was no moisture in his mouth; none came even when he swallowed. And the pounding in his head was dehydration too; he recognised that pain. He scraped his hair back and stared about him, remembering with mounting dread where he was and how he had got there.

It was broad daylight. He had supposed at first that it was dawn that had woken him, but the sun was high overhead. Even so, the only reason he could feel its radiance was because it had found a gap in the boiling firmament of clouds, and that gap was already diminishing. The clouds were as swollen and black as gangrene and the air was thick with the smell of rain. Veraine felt his throat spasm as he inhaled, as if he was trying to slake his thirst on the atmosphere itself.

He checked himself over for wounds, flexing every joint, and was relieved to find nothing worse than bruises and scrapes. Dirt and sweat had left a dull patina over his exposed torso, broken in places by fresh and bloody scabs, but the muscles beneath were undamaged. Then he crawled to the edge of the precipice and looked down. It was as sheer as he remembered it. He looked up and found no better vista; the cliff face even beetled outward as it approached the top, far above, where the walls and rooftops of the Citadel could just be discerned.

To his left, looking out, he could see the huge wound

made by the rockslide in the cliff face. That put him somewhere under the Outer Temple, he thought.

He climbed to his feet and walked to the back of his cave. It wasn't far: only three times his own body length lay between rock face and void, and that was the longest dimension of his prison. The walls at the back curved like the interior of a water jar, providing no surface that he could possibly climb to the trapdoor directly over his head. And anyway, that gap was blocked by a slab that he would never be able to shift. Veraine chewed his lip, tasting blood where it had cracked, as he looked slowly all around him. The floor was even, the walls smooth, and his prison was featureless except for the hole in the roof at one end and the gaping abyss at the other.

He hoped distractedly that this place had been constructed as a cell for meditation, far from the tumult of the world. But in the pit of his stomach he knew better: this cave was a chamber of torture. It simultaneously confined its victim and taunted him with freedom – more freedom than anyone could bear. The void yawned like the mouth of a beast. There was no way out, nothing to do except wait for handouts of food and drink dropped from above – if they ever came – that would only prolong the agony and the degradation until you went mad or summoned enough courage to drop to your death on the rocks below. From this height, Veraine guessed, a man would burst into pieces too small to be collected. His empty stomach contracted painfully.

He walked back to the edge and turned his gaze down again, unable to resist looking into that terrible plunge. He felt light-headed with lack of sustenance and he had to struggle to control the swaying of his frame; here, he couldn't afford to be careless. He noted that the desert floor was strewn beneath him with the debris of the landslide. Probably the Horse-eater camp was buried down there somewhere in that jagged litter of boulders. Now his triumph felt like it was a lifetime ago.

He raised the line of his sight, staring out into the desert, towards the hills, towards the home he had left for ever. He knew he would never get back to the river, or to the Empire that would give glory to his name. He had lost everything now, unless the gods in their infinite capriciousness decided to reach down and pluck him from his shelf.

He noticed a strange feature on the desert floor and he frowned. It took him a moment to recognise it for what it was, to identify shape or even movement at this distance, but when he did it felt like he had been kicked in the stomach yet again. The breath stopped in his throat and his lips peeled back in pain. It was a column of men in pale costume, heading east. Their horses were throwing up a lot of dust, but not enough to disguise from him their identity, once he knew the scale. It was the Eighth Host. They had left Mulhanabin. They were running out on him.

For a moment he didn't believe his eyes, and then hope, as cruel as any torturer, ripped through his chest and he threw out his hands and howled until it felt as if his lungs were torn. 'Loy!'

But the desert air swallowed his cries and the commander never heard him; the column of men marched on without a moment's hesitation, and Veraine sank to his knees upon the precipice edge, his face twisted. He didn't waste his breath in cursing them; it already felt like his throat was bleeding.

He felt nauseous. Frustration and despair curdled his stomach.

He was forced to watch his army as they slowly diminished into the distance, tracing the faint line of the road all the way back to the hills. He didn't understand it. Even if they believed that he was dead, there was no way they should have retreated so soon, and with so little to show for their pains. At the most, he was sure, this could only be the third day since the battle, and though they'd buried their dead the full funeral rites wouldn't yet be complete. And their column – the men had been mounted, presumably on Horse-eater steeds, but there should have been many more horses in the train, all laden down with loot, and long lines of prisoners strung out behind the rearguard. The Eighth Host he had seen there had been moving in tight battle formation without any significant baggage-train.

It was almost, he thought, as if they'd been fleeing from something. But nothing had been visible in pursuit.

When they were out of sight Veraine sat for a long time just staring into his hands. He felt as if he'd been emptied of everything: his power, his hope, his strength. When he tried to think, the only idea his fragmented mind could build was the bitter desire, as keen and stinging as a knife-edge and just as fatal, to have the Malia Shai in his arms once more, to bury his face in her breasts and taste the spice and the honey of her skin. But he thrust that image aside, knowing it was nothing but a need for sanctuary and that she couldn't grant him that now. All that he was left with was a choice. Stay; climb; jump. And it was his decision, and he had to make it soon.

He chose to climb. He made the choice without hope of success, without anything but the warrior determination to fight on until the last breath. He was not going to wait for death.

If I slip, he thought, then I fall; but whatever happens I won't surrender to this place. I'll learn to fly before I learn to crawl.

When he had made the decision he rose to his feet

and turned his face away from the drop; there was no point in contemplating that abyss any more, it was the rock of Mulhanabin that mattered to him now. He surveyed the scoop taken out by the landslide and decided that that was his only logical goal; the exposed face was less sheer and there was a chance he might be able to climb it. The real problem was getting across to that concavity. The horizontal distance was so short that he would have been able to run it in a few moments – if, that is, he'd possessed the miraculous power to stroll across vertical planes like a fly.

The only shred of hope he could grasp at was that the earthquake had changed the nature of the hillside. A few days ago the facade would have been impassable, but now even the intact and sheer parts of the mountain face were fissured by cracks. He guessed that the priests hadn't even noticed them. How stable these splits were he had no idea; they might be full of dust and edged in crumbling sand for all he could tell, or perhaps whole slabs were poised to slide down the hillside at the slightest pressure, but there was really no other option than to trust his weight to that tenuous web.

He stretched slowly, feeling the muscles bunch and clench across his back and shoulders. He just wished his legs didn't feel as though they were made of leather.

He put one palm on the rock of the cave-lip, groping up to the first tiny ledge. 'Malia,' he said as if she were some talisman.

The mountain growled.

Veraine froze. A warm gust of wind struck him between the naked shoulders. Then a dark spot opened like an eye on the rock surface just by his wrist. Something tapped at his outstretched forearm and he saw a drop of water tangled in the lines of dark hair.

At last he realised that it wasn't the earth that had

spoken but the air. Thunder crunched overhead once more. Another raindrop hit him stingingly on the cheek. He turned and faced into the wind and, as if it were a signal to the elements, the heavens at that moment opened.

It was as if an ocean was falling from the sky. Veraine screwed up his eyes and lifted his face to the rain and the rods of water fell on him in blow after blow. It stung across his raw skin and scoured over his scalp, ruthlessly stripping the grime and the sweat and the caked blood. It soaked through his single item of clothing and ran down his legs; it deafened him and it blinded him. He raised his arms wide as if to embrace it all, though the weight of the rain threatened to batter them down. In moments he was sodden in every pore, his trousers were plastered to his legs and his hair was a metallic sheet streaming over his shoulders. No dry patch even as big as a thumbnail remained on the entire surface of his body and his parched tissues gloried in the sensation as if he could soak up the moisture like a wick. His throat hurt with yearning for that rain, so he just opened his mouth and let moisture sting his parched tongue, and when he had tired of that he cupped his hands and watched them fill so that he could slake his thirst with mouthful after mouthful.

Only when his thirst was quenched did he retreat to the shelter of the overhang and sit himself in a dry spot. The water on the floor ran down the incline and spurted off the edge of his precipice like a miniature cataract. It wasn't cold, not even after hours of the pounding monsoon when the sun, somewhere behind the clouds, disappeared over the bulk of Mulhanabin and left the cliff face in shadow. Veraine stared out at the rain, as content as any condemned man given a reprieve might be.

The storm ceased around sunset, but the glowering clouds did not depart. Veraine stretched his legs, inspected what he could see of the rock above and to the side of him, but didn't start his climb. He didn't dare risk an ascent in fading light, especially now it was slippery. The sandstone was steaming.

Bats issued from the city far above and began their wheeling, flickering hunt through the humid air.

He settled down for the night as patiently as he could, though he slept only in fits and starts. When hunger and tension woke him, which they did repeatedly, he distracted himself from the discomfort by remembering in loving detail his hours of pleasure with the Malia Shai. He grew warm with the recounting, the embers of life still burning bright in his flesh, until he was impelled to loose his hardening member from the damp cloth that imprisoned it and nurse his erection. He stroked himself slowly, drawing out the act of masturbation, lost in a reverie of soft breasts and responsive little nipples, of yielding lips and slender hips that tilted towards him needfully, of stifled cries like bird calls and a tight, slippery cleft that opened to fingers and tongue and probing cock. Above all, he cherished the memory of her body, warm and alive and indescribably tempting, shuddering beneath his own.

Although his body responded urgently to all of these and clamoured for an immediate resolution he refused to give in to his own demands, instead taking measured strokes that would neither let him rest in his tumescence nor whip him towards a climax. He managed to prolong the ecstatic torture for an hour at least, until he simply dissolved into orgasm and unconsciousness, his semen spilling through his sleeping fingers onto the wet rock.

* * *

In the first light of dawn he woke and caught one of the smooth lizards that clambered over the walls of his cell. He ate as much of it as he could, knowing that he needed the strength despite his distaste for the task. This was likely to be the only chance he had to escape. The clotted sky threatened more rain, though the rising sun was still peering under that canopy; soon the preliminary storms that heralded the change of season would give way to the true Rains, which could descend for days at a time without respite. He couldn't climb in a downpour any more than in darkness; and every passing day was weakening his physical strength. He had to get going now.

It was not easy to trust his body to the rock face, but he took hold of the sandstone without hesitation and without looking down into the desert below, stretching up to grip the first meagre cracks, then pulling his torso up so that he could plant the balls of his feet against the rough sandstone. For the first few moves he could find no foothold at all, so it was the strength of his arms almost unaided that pulled him away from the false refuge of the cell and up onto the wall. After that he found a toe-grip on a tiny protrusion, and that gave him the breathing space he needed to be able to survey his next few moves.

And so it went on. The climb was agony, both physically and mentally. He was a strong man and as fit as any soldier in the prime of life, and he had the advantage of long limbs and callused fingers that allowed him to reach far and grip in places where another might have slipped. But nothing could make that journey easy; most of his mass hanging most of the time from arms and shoulders, his neck throbbing with the ache of trying to crane for a better view of the hillside to his right and above him. Breathing was difficult in that position, his inhalations shallow. His toes bit into sandstone where there was no other purchase and he simply ignored the pain. Sometimes it seemed that only the friction of the stone against his body was holding him up.

But if the physical effort was terrible, the mental one was all but insupportable. To be able to concentrate every effort on each individual move, over and over again, and yet to keep in mind the route as a whole; not to let the sharp pain of his grazed skin or the deeper protest of his muscles distract him; not to despair, not to let his mind wander, not to allow the pain to become anger and then rebellion against the task – those were far more difficult. The agony in his cramped fingers would build to a crescendo and he could force his hands still to cling to their purchase, but a moment's carelessness and those tendons would automatically slacken. His hands and wrists and ankles knew nothing of the void, they could not imagine the appalling drop below him nor the long and sickening plunge to a wet death; his body knew only the distinction between pain and rest. It took the discipline and concentration of a general to keep those limbs obedient, still functioning as a team.

Then came the moment when he realised he had failed. Somehow, he had worked himself into a position where he was spreadeagled at full stretch and he couldn't move up or down or sideways. Loosing any single limb would mean losing his grip. His head was resting against the rock face, the stone coarse on his cheek, sweat stinging in his eyes. He could feel the heat of the morning sun between his shoulder blades. His ribs were too taut to rise and fall, so he was breathing from his diaphragm, his belly fluttering against the curve of the rock. The rest of him was flattened against that gritty surface as tightly as a lover. And he knew that he didn't have the strength or the reach to make any further move.

It was like the moment before orgasm, when the abyss yawns before you, and you know all other options are lost and you are about to fall.

He squeezed his eyes shut against the bite of salt and felt the world spin around him. Gravity seemed to fade. His body was no longer locked against the sheer cliff face but lying upon it, the earth solid beneath him and thrusting back against his weight. He felt the body of the rock like a lover pressing on his own, the pain of the scrapes on his chest like the stinging of nails drawn in passion over his ribs and nipples. He could feel the earth's heartbeat thudding in his cheekbone and in the tips of his fingers. He could feel her warmth oozing up into his stomach and his pelvis. His cock, crushed between his bones and hers, was swelling and hardening, searching with the blind instinct of a beast for the yielding concavity that would allow it in.

And it found it. Not the deep wet cleft that it wanted, but a gap, a cup in the surface where some ancient rock trapped in the sandstone had fallen out. Enough to allow the thickening bulge under his trousers to expand into it. The ghostly precursor of an orgasm tingled through his veins, and at that Veraine's eyes flew open. He was clinging to a cliff face hundreds of feet above the desert floor, but at his groin, unseen but unmistakable, there was a hole in the rock big enough to provide a foothold.

He didn't have time to explore this new possibility or even to think. He released one hand and, as he started to slip downwards, rolled his body to the side so that he could hook his left leg up and into the gap. He shoved up and leaped the wall half a body length, throwing his arms high and right to find new purchase. His right hand found a jagged edge of rock and as he fell against the hillside once more, he realised that he had reached the gash left by the landslide.

That break in the cliff face was his road to freedom. The moment he was inside it he knew he was going to live, because after the vertical face of the cliff this slope, steep though it was, presented little threat. He could use his legs far more than his arms now, and that was enough. Instead of inching his way across the rock he could climb it properly, and though the breath was heaving in his lungs and the blood pounding in his head, he made it step by step up the incline to the lip of the cliff-top, and pulled himself arm over arm through the shattered wall onto the horizontal surface beyond.

He kneeled there, palms on that wonderful, flat ground, until he had got his breath back. He felt like kissing the cobbles. When, finally, he raised his head, he looked about him like a man reborn into a new world. A tired grin pulled at his mouth. He had scaled the hillside to come out into the garden courtyard between the Inner and Outer Temples. Although the enclosure had lost its eastern wall, in front of him there were green bushes and the low tank of rainwater, still intact.

There was no human being in sight.

Veraine got to his feet, trying not to stagger, and made it to the pool. Gutters were still dribbling fresh rainwater into its depths. He plunged his hands in, scooping the water over his face, gulping enough to cool his swollen tongue, to wash the bitter taste of fear from his mouth. As he raised his head he caught a brief glimpse of his reflection in the pool, his hair ragged and wild, his eyes surrounded by black hollows. I look like some wild barbarian, he thought, glancing down at a torso that was stippled with sand and webbed with uncountable scratches – not to mention the bloody and obvious imprint of teeth around his right nipple.

Then he laughed, and raised his fists to the sky. He was alive, and he had escaped the prison, and now he was going to get out of Mulhanabin even if he had to take down every inhabitant on the way.

First he needed a weapon, and he knew where to get one. Moving cautiously he entered the corridors of the Outer Temple, flitting between the shadows as best he could. He knew he was not exactly inconspicuous, and his best chance lay in keeping out of sight for as long as possible. He headed for a niche he had seen where two corridors met, in which there was a statue of Malia in one of her more martial aspects.

The passages were quiet and Veraine saw no one, reaching the statue without any problem. The idol itself, vermilion-skinned and six-armed, was made of plaster but the weapons she held in each hand were real enough. He toppled the whole structure onto the floor and picked up a sword from the wreckage, glancing quickly about him in case the noise had alerted someone. The sword was made of bronze and was longer than the iron one he was used to, but Veraine was not fussy. He grinned unpleasantly as he tested its balance, spinning it in his wrist. It was good to be armed again; he was no longer a victim and if he met Rasa Belit, he swore to himself, the priest would not escape with his life.

But it wasn't Rasa Belit he needed to find, nor was it a way out, not just yet. South lay the gate to Mulhanabin, and perhaps a horse to ride out of the city. Veraine went north, back through the courtyard and into the Inner Temple, sword in his hand, heart in his mouth. Thunder growled as he mounted the steps.

He ignored the great doors to the *Garbhagria* and went down the corridor, stepping cautiously, sword ready. He expected to meet priests or even guards, but there was no one and the passage was unlit, forcing him to feel his way in almost pitch darkness. Light spilled through a single doorway as he rounded the curve; and he saw that the doorway was that to the Malia Shai's chamber.

Puzzlement laced his trepidation. The corridor outside her room was strewn with mud bricks and patches of crumbled mortar. The mortar smelled fresh. But the doorway stood open and the chamber within was silent. He stepped cautiously inside, whirling to face anyone lurking by the door, but his caution was wasted. There was nobody in the room. Outside, rain was hammering from a leaden sky. On the floor were a mattress, a copper bowl and a wooden platter. There was still food on the plate; half a loaf of bread and some dried dates. And next to that, a small wineskin.

Veraine's guts contracted at the sight of the food. He could not confidently interpret the signs, other than to assume that she had been here and wasn't any longer. His guts growled. He ripped the bread between his teeth and devoured every last morsel of the food. He washed it down with the wine, wondering. He wasn't aware that she had been in the habit of drinking wine.

He made his way back to the *Garbhagria*, but stopped in the doorway. The chamber was all but empty, and the only inhabitant lay on the floor at his feet in a swathe of stained yellow cloth and a stinking black pool. Flies rippled all over the prone figure, rising in a cloud as he entered but settling back at once, torpid with the excess humidity and food.

Veraine stepped back from the corpse, lips tight. He had a good idea what the Eighth Host had been fleeing from, now.

'Malia Shai?' he asked the great hall. His voice echoed in the emptiness.

He was glad to get back out into the rain, feeling it on his skin like a cleansing spirit. But agitation made him impatient and careless; when he re-entered the Outer Temple he walked straight into a priestess.

She took one look at him, squealed and tried to flee, but he grabbed her and threw her against the wall, pinning her with the edge of the sword at her throat.

'Where's the Malia Shai?' he demanded.

The priestess gaped at him. With her shaven head and big Yamani eyes she looked terribly young.

'Where is she?' he repeated. 'Is she alive?'

'In the Throne Room,' she whimpered. 'Don't kill me.'

'And what about Rasa Belit?' he growled.

'Please, don't. He's dead.'

'How? The plague?'

'Uh-huh. The Kiss of Malia.'

He let her go, and she stumbled away.

He knew where the Throne Room was; here in the Outer Temple. Whereas the *Garbhagria* was used for the most sacred of ceremonies and normally only accessible to the priests of Mulhanabin, the Throne Room with its great gilded statue of the goddess was open to the populace day and night. It was the focal point of public worship. Veraine and his men had consciously avoided going near it during the occupation.

This time he walked in without hesitation, marching past the guardian statues at the door as if no one had a more natural right to be there than a half-naked Irolian with a bared sword.

The hall was full. This was where all the people were. Clusters of priests lurked by the arched colonnades on either side, tolling gongs and chanting. But nobody took any notice of him, for they were all too wrapped in their own misery. The hall stank. Even the thick pall of incense did not disguise the reek of sickness, and the murmur of prayers did not drown the muffled weeping. Most of the worshippers were in groups, many huddled around prone figures. Fathers held children and wives held husbands, all begging the goddess, he realised with dull shock, not for any mercy, not for a cessation of the plague, but for a blessing upon their dying kin as they passed into their next lives. He was appalled at the numbers. The sickness must have flared up like fire in dry straw, all in the last few days.

On her huge throne, the golden statue of the goddess watched, her face serene, her hands held up in the ancient gestures that mean 'Fear not,' and 'I will hear your prayer'. This was the greatest statue of Malia in all the Eternal Empire, and here she was beautiful. At the top of the steps to the throne sat the goddess in human form, cross-legged, her hands held in the same signs. Veraine's heart jumped painfully and the blood began to pound in his loins.

He walked the length of the hall, through the suppliants, to the bottom of the stairs. He expected resistance or at least some reaction to his presence and held his sword in readiness, but he was disconcerted to find that not even the priests seemed to recognise that he was intruding. The multitude were dull-eyed with sorrow or locked in private worlds of suffering and prayer; no one spared him more than a glance. It was as if he had somehow become invisible and he stalked among them like a ghost. At the bottom of the stairs he paused, apprehension and desire at war within him.

The Malia Shai was wearing a robe of red silk that left her arms bare. He knew those slender arms well, and the long hair that curled over her shoulders. But her face was masked. The mask was blue enamel, shaped like a skull, and pocked with red jewels for sores.

Behind the mask, he saw her eyelids flutter. Her arms fell to her sides.

He put one foot on the stairs and began to climb. The Malia Shai uncoiled herself. By the time he reached the top she was standing, waiting for him, her eyes wide behind the holes in the enamel. He could see her pointed chin and her full mouth, but the upper part of her face was made grotesque by the Plague Mask, and he couldn't look at it. When she put her hands out as if to touch him, he simply fell forward on his knees, the sword clattering to the floor.

She stepped up and put her arms around him, and he buried his face between her breasts, breathing in her scent in great gasps, his arms tight around her waist, his shoulders shaking. Relief and exhaustion and joy were tearing at his entrails, washing through him like a hot wave, stinging in his eyes. She clasped his head, raking her fingers across his scalp.

'They told me you were dead!' she moaned. 'They said you were dead!'

He shook his head, bruising her breasts through the silk with his lips. 'No,' he laughed. 'Not quite. Not yet.'

She spoke his name, several times, as if calling him back from some other world. The fact that they could be seen by everyone in the hall was not of the slightest concern to either of them. Then Veraine sat back on his heels, pulling her down on top of him so that she straddled his lap. They stared into each other's eyes.

'What happened?' he asked. Her weight on his thighs was almost nothing, he thought.

'They had me immured,' she answered. She was trembling, just as she had when he'd first held her after the earthquake, though this time it wasn't from cold. 'But then Rasa Belit died, and they came to get me out. They were so frightened of what they'd done! The priests have been struck down. And the people of the city. They're dying. The plague is everywhere.'

'I saw.' She was so slender, so fragile in his arms that he felt she might break if he held her too tightly.

'Lots of people have fled the city. Your – your soldiers. They've gone. Did you know?'

'Yes, I know.' He pulled her in close to him, so that her sex nested on his.

'They were afraid. I'm sorry.'

'What for?' he asked.

'I only cursed Rasa Belit. That was all.'

He shook his head. 'There was sickness in the city already. It wasn't you.'

For the first time, her gaze dropped from his. He reached up and touched her lips with his fingers. He wanted to see her face. 'Take the mask off,' he said gently.

'No,' she whispered.

'Take it off,' he repeated, his tone more urgent.

Her body stiffened in his hands. 'No!' she cried, though her voice was kept so low that no one else could have heard the pain in it. 'I can't. I'm the Malia Shai.'

He was shaken by her refusal. There was no room for negotiation in her tone, and though she was not pulling away from him, she held herself rigid in his arms as if her body was rejecting his touch. He felt his own throat tightening. He looked at her lips, the only part of her face he could bear to focus on. He hated the mask, its ugliness and everything it represented, but he wanted to kiss those lips. The pressure of her thighs around his and the heat of her mound upon his groin was something like torture.

He surrendered to it at last and pulled her mouth against his. The hard surface of the mask pressed on his skin but he didn't have to look at it, he simply closed his eyes and let the sweet heat of her kiss flood through his veins. He did not want the murderous goddess of pain, he wanted the passionate woman who had broken every taboo to come to his bed, driven by a carnal hunger so fierce that she had risked everything for him. He wanted her fire and her courage and her shuddering, unrelenting need. And if he had to accept her goddess in order to possess that other side of her, then he would.

She seemed to melt in his arms, her body flowing against his, her mouth moist and tender and easily teased open. Her arms tightened on his shoulders. He was peripherally aware for a moment of the hall and their audience behind him, but her lips and tongue and waist and hips at once demanded all his attention, especially as she rocked against him, and the tumescence that had stirred at his crotch the moment he laid eyes on her kicked undeniably awake.

Everyone in the hall who was conscious and not blinded by their own grief must be watching by now; the priests and the people alike. They must be watching their living deity being tightly clasped by this stranger, and yet there was no outcry or audible movement.

'Oh yes,' he whispered, his lips not leaving hers.

The silk robe she wore was gossamer-fine, allowing his hands to explore the length of her back almost as if she had been naked, from the fuzz at her nape to the splayed globes of her buttocks. As he cupped those beautiful curves he felt her jerk and tremble. His kisses possessed her mouth. He slipped one hand up between their two bodies to take a nipple captive, wishing that he had a dozen arms like a Yamani god so that he could caress every bit of her at once.

She moaned softly, the sound fluttering in her throat and buzzing against his tongue. She was so responsive that he was unable to resist – and that groan banished all caution from him. He could feel the heat and a suggestion of moisture seeping into his crotch through their clothes. He wanted to know more. He pinched her nipple until it was erect and as fat as a tree-bud between his fingers, then abandoned it in order to reach down beneath the edge of her dress, finding her bare thigh and pushing his hand up its entire length. She shuddered again as he reached the stretched skin at her taut groin and her mouth grew slack under his. He saw through the mask her eyelids flutter closed.

He knew then that he had her at his mercy. There comes a moment of arousal for every woman when she loses her hold on caution and all rational thought drowns in a tide of sensation. The ego falls away, all self-consciousness is lost, and it is as if she becomes possessed by some burning elemental spirit. Veraine felt that change wash over the Malia Shai and knew that he could do anything he wanted with her. This was a goddess he knew how to evoke, one that he was very familiar with.

His thumb brushed her fleece as his hand sought her mound, and she writhed her hips from side to side in instinctive response. From beneath his cock was pressing up, into her softness, into the hollow of her sex. He twisted his wrist and slid his fingers under her, cupping her mons, his knuckles pressing down hard on his own throbbing flesh. He found her sex-lips swollen and hot and between them a welling moisture, as slippery as melted butter, as rich as cream. The perfume of her arousal was driving him mad.

'Oh,' she breathed.

He needed to fuck her. It might have been possible to satisfy her with his hand, but his need for her was like a wound that could not be ignored. He had to plough her, he had to get inside her, he had to feel her sweet cunt wrapped around him again as he came, or the wound would kill him. And the presence of all those witnesses to their copulation only made it imperative.

He pulled out his hand just far enough to be able to pull at the cords of his trousers. The Malia Shai's eyes, wide and melting and drugged with desire, stared into his. He wanted to throw her down on her back and take her deep and hard, but some half-rational part of him warned that nothing so indecorous would be tolerated by their audience. At the moment she was on top of him and they were both all but silent, hardly moving unless you looked closely. Those observing might interpret their embrace, intense and intimate for all that it was public, as the ultimate rite of worship; and, Veraine thought, they might not be wrong.

His trousers gaped open, the cloth damp with her juices. He lifted her hips momentarily, long enough to free his prick and slip its thirsty head into the wetness promised, then pulled her weight back down on him so that the length of his meat slid into her depths. She arched and quivered in his grip, her breasts shaking under their silk, then he kissed her hard, holding her so tight that she could not struggle, pushing her hips down so that every last inch of his shaft was sheathed in her purse. She bit his bruised lips painfully, but when he finally slackened his grasp she didn't pull away. They were both gasping as their lips parted.

Veraine knew then that he was going to come very quickly. Like a boy on his first lay, he thought with disgust, but he also knew that this time he had little choice. He was so aroused, so tense, and their situation so dangerous that he was on the edge of losing control already. Now that he was in her, he didn't dare move.

Instead, the Malia Shai moved for him; not her hips or her thighs, but tightening her inner muscles, squeezing his swollen cock deep inside her. Veraine arched, fighting back the first waves of orgasm, gritting his teeth.

'Hold still!' he gasped. He slipped his hand between them and sought out the tiny pebble of her clitoris, finding it stiff and erect and slick with the wetness of her invaded sex. 'Now,' he told her, as his thumb circled the nubbin of flesh.

She whimpered. That sound, the animal helplessness of it, made him harder than he thought any man could be, and it steeled him to resist his own pleasure – long enough at any rate to play her like some sacred musical instrument until it sent her tumbling over the edge of orgasm. He watched her eyes close, her lips tremble, her throat fill with the unvoiced cry, the flush rise in her face. He loved to make her come, and he loved to watch.

She's mine, he thought.

Then her eyes, unfocused in the trance of ecstasy, met his again and her wet cleft clenched deliberately around his pole like a fist and it was enough to strip the last rags of control from him and thrust him into his own fire. Veraine lurched up, lifting her on his braced thighs, his head thrown back as he poured himself out in gouts. Only when his own merciless rip tide had ebbed did he realise that she – clinging to his shoulders with her nails, her hips twisting under his hands – was still coming.

It took a long time for the last pulses of her climax to drain from her body. She came back to herself to find her forehead resting on his shoulder, her arms slung loosely around his neck, the taste of his sweat and his skin salty in her mouth. Weakly, she raised her head. Somewhere in the depths of her last orgasm she had begun to cry, and now tears were trickling down from under her mask and wetting her cheeks. Veraine was staring at her in wonder. He caught a tear on his hand. His other arm still supported her shaking frame.

She tried to smile at him but failed, and the dark concern in his eyes was not assuaged. He looked haggard and brutal and so beautiful that her heart turned over in her breast just with looking at him. He took her face and laid it against his, their bodies so close that she could feel his heartbeat racing against hers.

'Come with me,' he whispered, his breath like feathers on her cheek. 'We can't stay in this city. Let me take you away.'

'Where to?'

'Back over the Amal Bhad,' he said. 'We might even catch the Eighth Host at the river.'

She had a sudden momentary vision of what life in the Empire would mean for her; he the exalted general, she the trophy of battle. No matter how well she was treated, that was what she would be; a trophy for the Irolians, a shame to the Yamani people.

She stroked his face and regretfully murmured, 'No.'

Veraine pulled in a deep breath then, but he didn't hesitate. 'Then we'll go somewhere else. North. Or west. We can see what the Horse-eaters have left of the Twenty Kingdoms. Anywhere. I don't care. Just...' The words were catching in his throat. 'Just please come with me,' he concluded.

The Malia Shai felt as if something thorn-sharp and infinitely sweet had been driven straight into her breast. She was astounded that Veraine would offer her this, and appalled that he could need her as badly as he did. As badly as she needed him.

She wound her fingers in his hair.

She didn't have to think about what might befall them, about what it would mean to the city she had lived in all her life, or to the temple that had raised her. She knew she had failed her great task in this incarnation, but she was still Malia, and the goddess acts according to her nature. 'If you want me, then, yes,' she told him.

He pulled back so that he could look her in the eyes, as if he did not believe her words alone, as if he had to read it in her face too. She nodded and tried again to smile, with greater success this time.

'We need to leave at once,' he said hoarsely. He looked stunned. 'We have to get to high ground before the Rains make the plain impassable. We need food, and beasts to ride –'

'I know.' She stood up, easing herself gently from him, the silk robe falling back demurely into place as she rose from his thighs. Only the way the sheer silk clung to her hot skin betrayed her recent wantonness. Then she faced the hall.

Everyone in it was turned towards them, watching, as silent as the dead lying at their feet. She cleared her throat. The hall was designed to enhance the acoustics of anyone speaking from the raised dais, so when she began to address them her words fell clear through the air.

'Listen to me, all of you; priests and pilgrims and people,' she said. 'I am the Malia Shai, the voice of the goddess! Hear what I'm telling you. Take the words and spread them among my people!

'I am leaving Mulhanabin. I will go out into the world and live there. And when I die in time and am reborn, it will not be here in the city. It will be among the people. Perhaps you will find me, and bring me to my home. Perhaps not. I will live among you as your daughter, as your sister, as your wife. And this will continue until I have completed the cycles of rebirth and am cleansed of human passion, and that will be the end of this age of woe. Because I tell you, you cannot conquer the world by hiding from it. The battle against evil is fought within the human heart.

'I still have a long way to go. A great journey. We all do.'

She swallowed despite her dry throat and turned to seek out Veraine. He had tidied himself away and now rose from his knees, retrieving his sword.

She took one step down the great flight and, at that signal, everyone still capable of movement on the floor of the Throne Room went to their knees and bowed forward, resting their heads upon the floor. She looked at the ranks of submissive shoulders and realised that it would be for the last time in this life. She reached up and slipped off the Plague Mask.

'The Rains have come; the plague is ended,' she told them. A low groan swept through the hall from every throat. She let the mask fall onto the top step.

Then she led the way down and through the prostrated ranks of her worshippers, Veraine stepping like a shadow just behind her. By the time they reached the door his hand was on her waist.

Just a few corridors down she stopped and turned to him. They were in front of a latticed window, and she could see that the rain had stopped for a moment and that the sun was shining through a gap in the clouds, striking brilliant light off the steaming puddles everywhere.

'What do we do?' she asked, putting her hand on his bare chest, suddenly lost. 'What do we do?'

He pulled her up against him. 'Anything,' he promised her, his kisses hot on her lips, on her throat. 'Anything we want.'

LOOK OUT FOR THE ALL-NEW BLACK LACE BOOKS – AVAILABLE NOW!

All books priced £6.99 in the UK. Please note publication dates apply to the UK only. For other territories, please contact your retailer.

THE BEST OF BLACK LACE 2
Edited by Kerri Sharp
ISBN O 352 33718 4

The Black Lace series has continued to be *the* market leader in erotic fiction, publishing genuine female writers of erotica from all over the English-speaking world. The series has changed and developed considerably since it was launched in 1993. The past decade has seen an explosion of interest in the subject of female sexuality, and Black Lace has always been at the forefront of debate around this issue. Editorial policy is constantly evolving to keep the writing up-to-date and fresh, and now the books have undergone a design makeover that completes the transformation, taking the series into a new era of prominence and popularity. *The Best of Black Lace 2* **will include extracts of the sexiest, most sizzling titles from the past three years.**

SHADOWPLAY
Portia Da Costa
ISBN O 352 33313 8

Photographer Christabel is drawn to psychic phenomena and dark liaisons. When she is persuaded by her husband to take a holiday at a mysterious mansion house in the country, unexpected events begin to unravel. Her husband has enlisted the help of his young male PA to ensure that Christabel's holiday is eventful and erotic. Within the web of an unusual and kinky threesome, Christabel learns some lessons the jaded city could never teach. **Full of dark, erotic games, this is a special reprint of one of our most popular titles.**

Coming in September

SATAN'S ANGEL
Melissa MacNeal
ISBN O 352 33726 5

Feisty young Miss Rosie is lured north during the first wave of the
Klondike gold rush. Ending up in a town called Satan, she auditions for
the position of the town's most illustrious madam. Her creative ways
with chocolate win her a place as the mysterious Devlin's mistress. As his
favourite, she becomes the queen of a town where the wildest fantasies
become everyday life, but where her devious rival, Venus, rules an
underworld of sexual slavery. Caught in this dark vixen's web of deceit,
Rosie is then kidnapped by the pistol-packing all-female gang, the
KlonDykes and ultimately played as a pawn in a dangerous game of
revenge. **Another whip-cracking historical adventure from Ms MacNeal.**

I KNOW YOU, JOANNA
Ruth Fox
ISBN O 352 33727 3

Joanna writes stories for a top-shelf magazine. When her dominant and
attractive boss Adam wants her to meet and 'play' with the readers she
finds out just how many strange sexual deviations there are. However
many kinky playmates she encounters, nothing prepares her for what
Adam has in mind. Complicating her progress, also, are the insistent
anonymous invitations from someone who professes to know her
innermost fantasies. **Based on the real experiences of scene players, this
is shockingly adult material!**

THE INTIMATE EYE
Georgia Angelis
ISBN 0 352 33004 X

In eighteenth-century Gloucestershire, Lady Catherine Balfour is struggling to quell the passions that are surfacing in her at the sight of so many handsome labourers working her land. Then, aspiring artist, Joshua Fox, arrives to paint a portrait of the Balfour family. Fox is about to turn her world upside down. This man, whom she assumes is a mincing fop, is about to seduce every woman in the village – Catherine included. But she has a rival: her wilful daughter Sophie is determined to claim Fox as her own. **This earthy story of rustic passion is a Black Lace special reprint of one of our bestselling historical titles.**

Coming in October

SNOW BLONDE
Astrid Fox
ISBN 0 352 33732 X

Lilli Sandström is an archaeologist in her mid-thirties; cool blond fisherman Arvak Berg is her good-looking lover. But Lilli has had enough of their tempestuous relationship for the time being so she retreats to the northern forests of her childhood. There, in the beauty of the wilderness, she explores and is seduced by a fellow archaeologist, a pair of bizarre twins, woodcutter Henrik and the glacial but bewitching Malin. And when she comes across old rune carvings she also begins to discover evidence of an old, familiar story. **Snow Blonde is also an unusual, sexy and romantic novel of fierce northern delights.**

QUEEN OF THE ROAD
Lois Phoenix
ISBN O 352 33131 1

Private detective Toni Marconi has one golden rule: always mix business with pleasure. Provided, that is, she can be in charge. When she sets out on the trail of a missing heiress her friends worry she may have bitten off more than she can chew. Toni's leads take her to a nightclub on the edge of the Arizona desert where she meets characters with even stranger sexual appetites than her own. And then there is 'Red' – the enigmatic biker who holds a volatile sexual attraction for her. One thing's for sure, Toni will not give in until she's satisfied, whatever the consequences. **Macho bikers and horny cops get sleazy with a sassy heroine who likes to be in charge.**

THE HOUSE IN NEW ORLEANS
Fleur Reynolds
ISBN O 352 32951 3

When Ottilie Duvier inherits the family home in the fashionable Garden district of New Orleans, it's the ideal opportunity to set her life on a different course and flee from her demanding aristocratic English boyfriend. However, Ottilie arrives in New Orleans to find that her inheritance has been leased to one Helmut von Straffen – a decadent German count, known for his notorious Mardi Gras parties. Determined to claim what is rightfully hers, Ottilie challenges von Straffen – but ends up being lured into strange games in steamy locations. **Sultry passions explode in New Orleans' underworld of debauchery.**

Black Lace Booklist

Information is correct at time of printing. To avoid disappointment check availability before ordering. Go to www.blacklace-books.co.uk. All books are priced £6.99 unless another price is given.

BLACK LACE BOOKS WITH A CONTEMPORARY SETTING

☐ THE TOP OF HER GAME Emma Holly	ISBN 0 352 33337 5	£5.99
☐ IN THE FLESH Emma Holly	ISBN 0 352 33498 3	£5.99
☐ A PRIVATE VIEW Crystalle Valentino	ISBN 0 352 33308 1	£5.99
☐ SHAMELESS Stella Black	ISBN 0 352 33485 1	£5.99
☐ INTENSE BLUE Lyn Wood	ISBN 0 352 33496 7	£5.99
☐ THE NAKED TRUTH Natasha Rostova	ISBN 0 352 33497 5	£5.99
☐ ANIMAL PASSIONS Martine Marquand	ISBN 0 352 33499 1	£5.99
☐ A SPORTING CHANCE Susie Raymond	ISBN 0 352 33501 7	£5.99
☐ TAKING LIBERTIES Susie Raymond	ISBN 0 352 33357 X	£5.99
☐ A SCANDALOUS AFFAIR Holly Graham	ISBN 0 352 33523 8	£5.99
☐ THE NAKED FLAME Crystalle Valentino	ISBN 0 352 33528 9	£5.99
☐ CRASH COURSE Juliet Hastings	ISBN 0 352 33018 X	£5.99
☐ ON THE EDGE Laura Hamilton	ISBN 0 352 33534 3	£5.99
☐ LURED BY LUST Tania Picarda	ISBN 0 352 33533 5	£5.99
☐ THE HOTTEST PLACE Tabitha Flyte	ISBN 0 352 33536 X	£5.99
☐ THE NINETY DAYS OF GENEVIEVE Lucinda Carrington	ISBN 0 352 33070 8	£5.99
☐ EARTHY DELIGHTS Tesni Morgan	ISBN 0 352 33548 3	£5.99
☐ MAN HUNT Cathleen Ross	ISBN 0 352 33583 1	
☐ MÉNAGE Emma Holly	ISBN 0 352 33231 X	
☐ DREAMING SPIRES Juliet Hastings	ISBN 0 352 33584 X	
☐ THE TRANSFORMATION Natasha Rostova	ISBN 0 352 33311 1	
☐ STELLA DOES HOLLYWOOD Stella Black	ISBN 0 352 33588 2	
☐ SIN.NET Helena Ravenscroft	ISBN 0 352 33598 X	
☐ HOTBED Portia Da Costa	ISBN 0 352 33614 5	
☐ TWO WEEKS IN TANGIER Annabel Lee	ISBN 0 352 33599 8	
☐ HIGHLAND FLING Jane Justine	ISBN 0 352 33616 1	

☐ PLAYING HARD Tina Troy	ISBN 0 352 33617 X
☐ SYMPHONY X Jasmine Stone	ISBN 0 352 33629 3
☐ STRICTLY CONFIDENTIAL Alison Tyler	ISBN 0 352 33624 2
☐ SUMMER FEVER Anna Ricci	ISBN 0 352 33625 0
☐ CONTINUUM Portia Da Costa	ISBN 0 352 33120 8
☐ OPENING ACTS Suki Cunningham	ISBN 0 352 33630 7
☐ FULL STEAM AHEAD Tabitha Flyte	ISBN 0 352 33637 4
☐ A SECRET PLACE Ella Broussard	ISBN 0 352 33307 3
☐ GAME FOR ANYTHING Lyn Wood	ISBN 0 352 33639 0
☐ FORBIDDEN FRUIT Susie Raymond	ISBN 0 352 33306 5
☐ CHEAP TRICK Astrid Fox	ISBN 0 352 33640 4
☐ THE ORDER Dee Kelly	ISBN 0 352 33652 8
☐ ALL THE TRIMMINGS Tesni Morgan	ISBN 0 352 33641 3
☐ PLAYING WITH STARS Jan Hunter	ISBN 0 352 33653 6
☐ THE GIFT OF SHAME Sara Hope-Walker	ISBN 0 352 32935 1
☐ COMING UP ROSES Crystalle Valentino	ISBN 0 352 33658 7
☐ GOING TOO FAR Laura Hamilton	ISBN 0 352 33657 9
☐ THE STALLION Georgina Brown	ISBN 0 352 33005 8
☐ DOWN UNDER Juliet Hastings	ISBN 0 352 33663 3
☐ THE BITCH AND THE BASTARD Wendy Harris	ISBN 0 352 33664 1
☐ ODALISQUE Fleur Reynolds	ISBN 0 352 32887 8
☐ GONE WILD Maria Eppie	ISBN 0 352 33670 6
☐ SWEET THING Alison Tyler	ISBN 0 352 33682 X
☐ TIGER LILY Kimberley Dean	ISBN 0 352 33685 4
☐ COOKING UP A STORM Emma Holly	ISBN 0 352 33686 2
☐ RELEASE ME Suki Cunningham	ISBN 0 352 33671 4
☐ KING'S PAWN Ruth Fox	ISBN 0 352 33684 6
☐ FULL EXPOSURE Robyn Russell	ISBN 0 352 33688 9
☐ SLAVE TO SUCCESS Kimberley Raines	ISBN 0 352 33687 0
☐ STRIPPED TO THE BONE Jasmine Stone	ISBN 0 352 33463 0
☐ HARD CORPS Claire Thompson	ISBN 0 352 33491 6
☐ MANHATTAN PASSION Antoinette Powell	ISBN 0 352 33691 9
☐ CABIN FEVER Emma Donaldson	ISBN 0 352 33692 7
☐ WOLF AT THE DOOR Savannah Smythe	ISBN 0 352 33693 5
☐ SHADOWPLAY Portia Da Costa	ISBN 0 352 33313 8

BLACK LACE BOOKS WITH AN HISTORICAL SETTING

☐ PRIMAL SKIN Leona Benkt Rhys   ISBN 0 352 33500 9 £5.99
☐ DEVIL'S FIRE Melissa MacNeal   ISBN 0 352 33527 0 £5.99
☐ WILD KINGDOM Deanna Ashford   ISBN 0 352 33549 1 £5.99
☐ DARKER THAN LOVE Kristina Lloyd   ISBN 0 352 33279 4
☐ STAND AND DELIVER Helena Ravenscroft   ISBN 0 352 33340 5 £5.99
☐ THE CAPTIVATION Natasha Rostova   ISBN 0 352 33234 4
☐ CIRCO EROTICA Mercedes Kelley   ISBN 0 352 33257 3
☐ MINX Megan Blythe   ISBN 0 352 33638 2
☐ PLEASURE'S DAUGHTER Sedalia Johnson   ISBN 0 352 33237 9
☐ JULIET RISING Cleo Cordell   ISBN 0 352 32938 6
☐ DEMON'S DARE Melissa MacNeal   ISBN 0 352 33683 8
☐ ELENA'S CONQUEST Lisette Allen   ISBN 0 352 32950 5
☐ DIVINE TORMENT Janine Ashbless   ISBN 0 352 33719 2
☐ THE CAPTIVE FLESH Cleo Cordell   ISBN 0 352 32872 X

BLACK LACE ANTHOLOGIES

☐ CRUEL ENCHANTMENT Erotic Fairy Stories   ISBN 0 352 33483 5 £5.99
    Janine Ashbless
☐ MORE WICKED WORDS Various   ISBN 0 352 33487 8 £5.99
☐ WICKED WORDS 4 Various   ISBN 0 352 33603 X
☐ WICKED WORDS 5 Various   ISBN 0 352 33642 0
☐ WICKED WORDS 6 Various   ISBN 0 352 33590 0
☐ THE BEST OF BLACK LACE 2 Various   ISBN 0 352 33718 4

BLACK LACE NON-FICTION

☐ THE BLACK LACE BOOK OF WOMEN'S SEXUAL   ISBN 0 352 33346 4 £5.99
    FANTASIES Ed. Kerri Sharp

To find out the latest information about Black Lace titles, check out the website: www.blacklace-books.co.uk or send for a booklist with complete synopses by writing to:

Black Lace Booklist, Virgin Books Ltd
Thames Wharf Studios
Rainville Road
London W6 9HA

Please include an SAE of decent size. Please note only British stamps are valid.

Our privacy policy
We will not disclose information you supply us to any other parties.
We will not disclose any information which identifies you personally to any person without your express consent.

From time to time we may send out information about Black Lace books and special offers. Please tick here if you do not wish to receive Black Lace information. ❑

Please send me the books I have ticked above.

Name ....

Address ....

....

....

....

Post Code ....

Send to: Cash Sales, Black Lace Books, Thames Wharf Studios, Rainville Road, London W6 9HA.

US customers: for prices and details of how to order books for delivery by mail, call 1-800-343-4499.

Please enclose a cheque or postal order, made payable to Virgin Books Ltd, to the value of the books you have ordered plus postage and packing costs as follows:

UK and BFPO – £1.00 for the first book, 50p for each subsequent book.

Overseas (including Republic of Ireland) – £2.00 for the first book, £1.00 for each subsequent book.

If you would prefer to pay by VISA, ACCESS/MASTERCARD, DINERS CLUB, AMEX or SWITCH, please write your card number and expiry date here:

....

Signature ....

Please allow up to 28 days for delivery.